THE ELIXIR

A PARANORMAL ADVENTURE OF COURAGE, FRIENDSHIP, AND THE WISDOM OF BLOOD

JENNIFER DANIELS NEAL

SemiTone
BOOKS & MUSIC

For Kate and Colin

who astound me every day
and make me certain of divine appointments.

May Creator guard your ground and sky.

CONTENTS

1

THE COFFEEHOUSE CHAUS

BEAM'S POINT OF VIEW

I haven't been allowed to see my uncle since I was five, and my dad found him catching my blood in a jar. Every year, though, on my birthday, Uncle finds a way to smuggle his contact information to me, just in case.

This year, it showed up in my locker tied to a shock of long, prairie wildflowers—causing students up and down the hall to speculate upon my nonexistent love life for the better part of a week.

Some girls enjoy that sort of thing. I do not. (The public scrutiny. Not the wildflowers. Those were nice.)

Anyway, I've never called. I'm not allowed to.

I trace the handwritten phone number now, while I hunker down at the table furthest from the coffeehouse action. There's a note too.

Dear Beam, Please consider spending some time with me after graduation to find out who you really are.

At first, I just thought it meant like—*take a gap year*—as if that would ever happen—but in light of recent events, I think it may mean something more...existential.

On the flip side of the card, watercolor wildflowers sway in the wind, the same kind that Uncle left for me, only these beauties are still joyfully rooted in the grasslands of South Dakota. It is not lost on me that I was once rooted there too, but I'm not supposed to talk about that. We left the reservation when I was three.

The chimes on the coffeehouse door make me jump. They're immediately swallowed by the stark laughter of the girls who've caused them, and three pairs of platform heels clomp to the counter to order the kind of sugary drinks that make me gag.

I'm grimacing, aren't I? I am.

Those boisterous girls are going to make it hard for me to concentrate, and there is *a lot* upon which I need to concentrate. If I call my uncle, I defy my father. He absolutely forbids it. But if I don't, my mom could lose her life. Or worse.

CHAUSIE—PRONOUNCE IT CHOW-SEE—CHAUSIE'S POINT OF VIEW

In forty-two minutes, I get to rejoin my unit and copter out of here. I've been grounded for months, but in forty-two minutes I get to take part in something *real*. Something where life and death decisions require immaculate focus. Until then, I have to wait for my mom in this coffeehouse and act like a nice civilian. And I have to finish my homework, or the whole op gets canned.

I *can't* finish my homework, though, because three jabbering bird-girls have occupied the table next to me, each one poised—impossibly—upon the very edge of her stool with perfect legs extending from a short skirt, and crossed so hard that the top of one foot wraps around the back of the other.

They inspect every poor guy who walks through the door, and every girl too for that matter, raking them over the coals of their imperial judgment. It occurs to me that they've stationed themselves here, at this high table, for that very purpose.

I can feel the tether of my patience fraying, and I beg them, in my mind, to just shut up. The last thing I need is to make another scene.

A loud quandary surfaces between the girls about what to wear, the blue-green blouse or the green-blue blouse. I glance at the magazine. They're the same blouse. They move on to pages about hair. There can't possibly be that many pages about hair.

"But I mean, should I braid it or use a bun foundation?" Even the girl's complexion is perfect like she's been airbrushed.

What the hell is a bun foundation?

"It depends on *which* bun foundation," is the sage advice. "They are not equal. The larger one is better. No. You know what? Braid it first. That is best. It is so unique."

The roar of the cappuccino machine is loud. It's *really* loud. Even so, the girls' voices slice through the din. Much like the bullets I'll be firing in—check the clock—thirty-nine minutes.

You may not consider covert military operations—online in a game—to be real, or important, or even worthwhile, but you must surely admit that they rank higher up than this ridiculous conversation. Anyway, they're all I have left.

"It *is* so unique," the third girl agrees. "But then should you move it forward like a unicorn? Would that be *more* unique?" The hair in question gets pushed all around.

There is zero percent chance I am getting this essay done. My fingers wait on the keyboard for me to assign them letters. I imagine them with retractable claws.

"Or maybe I should just make a tiny bump-bun on top, and let the rest of my hair—"

"Oh my gosh!" I snipe out loud. "Nobody gives a damn. Just stick a hat on top and move on!"

I'm standing up. I'm not acting civilly. The girls are gaping at me. Several of the tables are gaping at me, actually. And the folks at the counter. "I'm sorry," I rush to say—not because I'm sorry, but because

I can't afford any more trouble. I cram my laptop into my bag and haul it to a table near the door.

BEAM

I nearly choke in an effort to keep from laughing out loud. If that guy hadn't gone off on those girls, I swear I would have. He journeys to the table next to me with a leg that's too stiff to bend, and he previews me, his new neighbor, with a scowl. I don't think the scowl's for me. I don't mind either way. I find bad attitudes interesting.

He's tall. I think he plays basketball for us, though he must have been injured. He removes things from his bag. A notebook. A laptop.

The leg that *isn't* stiff bobs incessantly. His tawny hair falls forward as he digs out a pen.

It's not until his leg *stops* bobbing and he slowly raises his eyes to me, that I realize I'm staring. I *do* think the scowl's for me this time. I think it's because he's worried about his outburst.

"Something's either unique or it's not," I offer. "It doesn't get an intensifier. You've done us all a service." He doesn't reply, but his scowl does ease a bit.

I return to my crisis.

CHAUSIE

Half of my mouth reaches for her. It takes me a second to remember what it's trying to do. It's impossible that it's trying to smile because my life sucks, and I'm miserable. For another...thirty-six minutes. And then I'll be flying with my unit over enemy territory.

She's pretty, though, and it's hard to remain completely miserable when she's just made us allies. It's funny—because she's not pretty in a perfect-legs-out-of-a-short-skirt sort of way. It's her confidence. She's smart. She'd make a good cat.

Thirty-four minutes.

No, it's more than her confidence—yeah, I'm still analyzing this.

She is actually pretty. She just doesn't flaunt it. She's got a big, woven hat pulled over straight black hair and a college sweatshirt that reads, "Northwestern." That's in Chicago, right? Only this one says, "Qatar." She wears sneakers without socks and sits on one foot, taking up the whole seat, not perched upon the edge like some awkward bird. Why is she so pretty?

Why are you still thinking about it? Do your homework.

Right.

I've written three whole sentences—not good ones, but they take up space—when the pretty girl drops her forehead into her hands and heaves a magnificent sigh. Then she rolls her face to the ceiling like she's praying for something—and catches me watching.

"Sorry," she mutters and drags her elbows off the table to refocus on her screen.

Now I'm curious. I consult the clock again and heave a sigh of my own.

"I have twenty-two minutes," I inform her. "If you can tell me what's wrong in that amount of time, then fine."

She doesn't acknowledge me with anything but her eyes—doesn't even move her head. I guess she doesn't want to talk. It's also possible that I've forgotten how to be anything but rude. Being dragged back and forth across the country has had that effect on me. I hate my life here, but Mom decided to get a divorce, so there you go.

BEAM

I stare at my screen without seeing it. *Breathe, Beam. Do not puke.*

Why should this random guy's lean offer make me want to throw up? Because I really do need help. More than twenty-two minutes of it. Who offers to help somebody for twenty-two minutes? *Minute Miser,* I think at him.

I type in another search to take my mind off being sick. In truth, it's the same search I've typed about a hundred times already. "How to report an abduction to The Lakota Council of Tribes." It's so backward. Parents don't get kidnapped. Kids do. It's actually part of the word.

Did you know that when people *do* get kidnapped, it's ten times more likely that they look like me—Indigenous—rather than white, like my mom? My mom's the one who told me that. She's a civil rights attorney. After she and Daddy got married, they lived and worked on the reservation. She flew back there last week to offer legal aid to an old friend, but we haven't heard from her in days.

My dad's an attorney too. International law. He knows more than he's letting on, but he assures me everything's fine. He went to bring her back. Not before instructing me to carry on as usual and forbidding me, under any circumstance—he likes to use that phrase—to follow him to South Dakota.

His last words to me? "Wear your catcher."

It's the one thing he and my uncle can agree upon. The one Lakota item he encourages. Uncle sent it to make up for the whole blood-letting thing. A leather necklace with a hoop hanging from it, woven to resemble a spider web. In the middle, perches a small stone dove, and there's a smattering of iridescent beads. It's supposed to keep Evil from finding you. Evil that my dad says doesn't exist.

Anyway, my dad was wrong that everything is fine. I know, because I received an anonymous text, along with a disturbing video of my mom. Now I can't reach my dad. Last night I fell asleep in the living room, worried sick and scared to death. Then this morning I got up, got dressed, and went to school like I was supposed to. I just carried it inside me all day. I didn't tell a soul.

The text requires me to present myself at a set of coordinates in seven days' time. Coordinates. Like I'm a Navy pilot. If I've entered them correctly, the location is in Badlands National Park. The same park pictured on my uncle's birthday card. The same park that encompasses Pine Ridge Reservation. *My* reservation. My birthplace, I mean. Am I just supposed to hike in and hope that the ability to globally position myself suddenly lands upon me? This is all assuming I can get to the park in the first place. I live in Atlanta. I don't even have a car.

"You gonna be out for Spring conditioning?" I hear.

I recognize the speaker from AP Lit, though he's not speaking to me. When I catch his eye, he nods hello past a fist bump with the minute miser. They must be teammates. I'd probably know if I ever stepped foot in the gym.

"Yeah," Minute Miser replies. "And every season after that."

I forget to be irritated with him because voices don't come much flatter sounding than that.

Minute Miser sits back to chat, his long torso leaning to one side as he applies pressure to the top of his femur. He can't get comfortable. I wonder if it hurts all the time.

AP Lit Guy tosses a basketball to himself which, given the apparent subject matter, seems insensitive to me. "What's it mean for your scholarship?" he asks.

Minute Miser silently conveys that the scholarship is no longer an option.

I'm gonna stop calling him Minute Miser. If I lost my scholarship, I'd die. I've already got a bag packed. I really do. But I don't have time to eavesdrop because turns out, I've got even bigger problems.

I play the video of my mom again. She's sitting cross-legged on a braided rug beside a camp bed. Her eyes are a bit unfocused like she's bored, and her leather satchel sits behind her on the floor. So far so good, except that my mom never just sits around. And her face is always animated. The truly disturbing part, though, is that standing next to my mom is...my mom. And I only have one mom. They're wearing the same thing, but it's not a reflection. The standing version is observing the seated one. *This* mom's expression I know very well. It's the one she wears when she has a problem to solve. Like when she was trying to figure out how I could accept my award from Tomorrow's Mathematician and compete in the state finals for Mock Trial in two different cities on the same day.

There's nothing for it. I have to call. My uncle's the only person in my life who's connected to the rez.

When AP Lit leaves, I eye the guy formerly known as Minute Miser. "Hey, can I use your phone?" I venture. I can't help adding, "As long as it doesn't take over twenty-two minutes?"

He eyes me right back. His eyes, by the way, are this distracting shade of amber. Really they're *yellow*, and I think they'd be quite round if they weren't always peering out from beneath their lids.

"Only sixteen now," he says, but I can tell he's making fun of himself. The stubble around his slice of a grin is thicker than I think he has the years for. He takes a breath and says, "I didn't mean it the way it sounded. I just have someplace to be." Digging for his phone, he hands it over, ready to use.

"Thanks."

He's pretty cute when he's not acting surly. Who am I kidding? He's downright hot when he is.

"Yours dead?" he asks.

"What?!" I feel slightly hysterical until I realize he's asking about my phone and not about my parents. "Oh." How should I answer that? I hate to lie. He won't believe the truth anyway. "No, I just don't want anyone to be able to trace it back to me."

He doesn't dismiss this the way I mean for him to, as a flippant remark.

"Who should I look for then, when they come for me instead?"

I hadn't considered that. But—"They won't. It's me they want." *For some reason.*

He nods like he understands better than I do. Which wouldn't be too hard.

I steel myself and dial the one person on this whole Earth I'm forbidden to. "Uncle Joel? It's Beam."

CHAUSIE

It's a funny name. It suits her. She has an elf-like quality under that big hat. Sharp cheekbones. Vibrant, brown skin. Surprisingly blue eyes rimmed in black lashes. She's an interesting mix of ethnicities. There are fourteen minutes left, and suddenly I'm not as eager to leave. She's not doing much of the talking. I guess her uncle has a lot to say.

But then she exclaims, "They can't just detain my dad indefinitely. Can they?" Followed by, "What does *technically* mean? Why would the Council of Tribes be interested in my mom's work?" After her uncle responds to that, Beam ramps up further. "Why would the Council of Tribes be interested in *me?!*" I don't think she gets her answer, but I'd like to hear it too. There's only one Council of Tribes with which I'm familiar, and it's back home in South Dakota. What are the odds?

Beam consults her own phone while speaking into mine. "I can be there," she says. "Uncle Joel?" She lowers her voice and turns her head toward the window. "I'm scared," she says—like a little girl who's doing her best to stay tough. It wakes something up inside me.

Twelve minutes. I pinch the bridge of my nose. I can't believe I have to rely on my mother to pick me up. Moving to the chair next to Beam, though still at my own table, I sit with my back to her, like I'm now her bodyguard or something. She ends the call with a sniff and smooths the worry from her face, but not in time to keep me from seeing it.

There's a card lying in front of her with a picture of the national park. "I'm from there," I chance. She's not listening. I try again. "What kind of a name is Beam?" She's standing now, collecting her things.

"It's, um...it's short for Elizabeth somehow." She places my phone in front of me. "You'll have to ask"—she takes an untimely breath—"my dad."

"I'm Chausie." I stand to face her. "Are you going to school in Chicago?" I indicate her sweatshirt.

"That's the plan," she says. She's all but out the door.

"Only, it says Qatar," I point out.

It's clearly not the first thing on her mind. She waves it away saying, "They have a campus there. I just thought it was funny."

I regret my next words already, but here they go. "My mom confiscated my motorcycle, pending further review, so she has to pick me up, but if you come home with me, I'll help you—whatever is wrong." Finally, I have her full attention, so I push for a smile. "Even if, you know, it takes hours. Or days."

I get the smile, but it's sad. "I thought you had someplace to be," she says.

"Oh. I'm supposed to play war games online, but...it's not important."

Obviously. I can feel the wrinkle my nose is performing. I must seem to her as petty as those squawking bird-girls. "I don't have to do it," I add. And then, in a *brilliant* surge of genius, I come up with, "Or you could play too!" Wow. I don't know whether or not to be ashamed of how truly exciting that prospect is to me.

"Thanks," she says, and I think she means it, but I still feel like an idiot, and I still hear the emotion in her voice when she turns me down. "*I* have someplace to be." She doesn't add, "someplace *real*." She doesn't have to.

2

KANJI BRINGS JUSTICE

BEAM

When I get home, there's an unfamiliar car parked across the street. I tell my Uber driver to keep going and direct him down the next road instead. It leads to the neighborhood behind ours. I'm supposed to meet Uncle Joel at his apartment because he needs a few minutes to set the plan into motion—his words. Apparently, he's had some kind of getaway set up for ages. Will my dad be mad at me? Probably. But I don't know what else to do. I had hoped to grab some things for the trip, like the roll of cash my mom keeps on hand for emergencies, but with that strange car out front, I may be too scared to try.

Uber agrees to wait while I trespass through the Jacksons' backyard to get to my own. There's a row of trees where the properties meet, and since I am so stealthy (sarcasm) and also trained as a spy (more sarcasm), I peek out to perform a cursory scan. My arrival is immediately announced from the treetops with a series of obnoxious barks. *Shut up, stupid crow! Honestly.* I glare up at him while he studies me with one beady eye.

Beyond him, my whole house is lit up like a shopping mall, as if a scared little girl spent the night there all by herself. Which *is* what happened. (What? It's not *my* job to turn off the lights.)

I don't see anything out of the ordinary. Nothing to suggest that anyone is waiting to nab me. So, that's good. I sneak to the back door and let myself in, pausing at the threshold to listen. My heart is pounding in my ears, making it hard for me to hear anything above its own noise, but I can't stay here like this forever. I decide the coast is clear and slink through the hall.

Back at the coffeehouse, when I'd talked to Uncle Joel, he had accepted my news right away. Had seemed to think it well overdue. "They don't want any*thing*, Beam. They want *you*. But you must *not* go to them. I can't even begin to tell you how catastrophic that could be."

I've always had the sense that an unrestrained me would have lasting consequences. I half-think it's why my dad has such strict rules. What I'd *wanted* to ask my uncle was, "What about me is so dangerous?" But what I ended up asking was, "Who are *they*, and why don't they just come to get me if they want me? Why take my parents and play this game of cat-and-mouse?"

There'd been a split-second too long between my question and Uncle Joel's scarce reply. "I'm not sure." The way his voice went dark made me think he *was* sure or at least had a pretty good guess. "Let's get you safe and go from there."

It has never occurred to me not to trust Uncle Joel, even after the weird incident that caused my father to be angry with him. I'm walking through the foyer now, where they'd argued. "We need to know for sure," Uncle Joel had said. "Or we'll always be looking over our shoulders."

"If nobody knows," my dad had replied, "then we won't *have* to."

"Do you have any idea how much she'd be worth?"

That's when Daddy punched him in the face. Hard enough to break his nose. I still cringe to recall the sound of it, not a crack so much as a thunk. Like when you split a ripe melon. I cried out for my uncle, but my mother scooped me from the room while I reached back for him over her shoulder.

"Not for *my* gain," Uncle groused, though his words were muffled by the hand he was using to staunch the flow of blood. "How could you think that? There are *visions*, Hawk. 'Blood for body. Light for soul.' Someone's going to put it all together, and when they do, there'll be a price on her head."

"Why do you think we moved here?!" Dad said. "Our whole existence has been dedicated to keeping her secret—to giving her her best life."

"And you think moving a few states away and calling her *Elizabeth* is going to keep her a secret? Her best life is to fulfill her calling. To save her people."

"Yeah. Well, your idea of saving them and mine have always been different."

"I'm not a vengeful child, Hawk. At least, not anymore. But I do still love my people, and I want them to have all they're entitled to." The rest of what he said, he spoke in the Lakota language which I was never taught.

Then Daddy ordered Uncle Joel out of our house. Told him never to return. Mom caged me in so that I couldn't run back down to him, and I tracked his progress through my upstairs window with tears flowing down my cheeks. He must have felt me watching. He stopped halfway up the front path, took a swig from a little jar, and turned to look up at me. The tissue he put to his face came away fresh and white. He gave his nose a vigorous nudge, mouthed the words, "Good as new," and I'd been appeased.

Now, I'm standing in my bedroom at that same window. To my relief, the car across the street is gone, but along with that relief, the remembrance that my parents are also gone. The house, though very bright, is too quiet. No simmering pots or clanging utensils. No smell of Mom's shepherd's pie. No questions about my homework or silly banter snuggled up with Dad on the couch. I take a lot for granted.

I collect what I deem important. Cash from Mom's desk. Clothes.

Wasabi almonds. A toothbrush. I mean, if I do live into old age, I'm gonna need my teeth, right?

CHAUSIE

Online games are the only thing I have left to enjoy, and I can't even concentrate, because all I can think about is that girl. The way she'd hesitated before she'd stepped onto the sidewalk. The way she'd looked over her shoulder while she waited for a car.

I should have gone with her.

You don't even know her, I argue with myself. At the same time, my unit commander is cursing into my headset. "Pay attention, Crippled Cougar!"

"I know," I answer both him and myself. "But my gut was telling me something."

Yeah. That she was too pretty to let walk out the door, Myself says.

I act like I don't know what I'm talking about—this is getting confusing. I really need to find friends on *this* side of the country —OK, yes, I tell myself. Not out loud. *She was pretty. But there was something more. She's from the Badlands and she's in trouble. Doesn't that give me a real job to do? Doesn't that make her my duty?*

While I'm pondering that, a call comes in. I don't recognize the number, so I let it go to voicemail and ease back onto my beanbag like an old man. My hip's killing me.

The helicopter's hovering five feet off the ground, and my three virtual buddies have already hopped into enemy territory. I follow them on the screen with hips that work just fine.

The phone rings again. I throw it a disgruntled frown and tear off my headset. "Chausie," I answer, pinching the phone between my shoulder and my ear so that I can fire my weapon. In the game, we're being ambushed. Over the phone, nobody answers.

"Hello?" I prompt.

"Chausie?" asks a surprised voice. "*Leo's kid?*"

"Who's this?" I'm shooting frantically. The controller clicks under my thumbs. I nearly drop the phone as I maneuver through the firing line.

"It's Joel Redfeather." I stop firing, and I get shot.

"*Uncle* Joel?" I ask. "How do you know my dad?"

"He's rescued a number of our Tribal members through the years. Good man."

Yep. Should've stayed with her.

"How do *you* know Beam?" Joel asks. "My brother doesn't allow her to contact anyone from home."

"No, I live here with my mom. We only met today. We just happened to sit next to each other."

"That's good. That bodes well." He seems to be talking to himself.

I don't think he believes our meeting was a coincidence any more than I do.

"Is she with you now?" he asks.

"No, she's trying to get to you, I think."

There's a pause before Joel says, "She hasn't made it."

I. Should have stayed. With that girl. I can't sit. I start pacing the room and feel the hair bristle on the back of my neck. We're all connected somehow.

"Chausie, you're intended for The Outpost, right?" He says my name like he's known me all my life. He's asking if I've agreed to work for my dad back home, as a peacekeeper and a first responder in and around Badlands National Park.

"Yes, Sir," I answer. It's all I've ever wanted to do.

"You've had your training?"

Oh gah. I never should've let that girl out of my—"Yes, Sir." *All except the most important parts*, I don't add. *Because I can barely walk anymore.* "Why are you asking?"

"Because Beam is...special."

When he doesn't elaborate, I make a noise that begs for more information. "Yeah, I *got* that much."

"We need to protect her. Need to get her back home."

"*We? As in you and me?*" *Yes! Finally!* Also, Mom's gonna go ballistic.

"No one else around, Son."

"And we'll take her to The Vigilance?"

"No."

Joel's short reply gives me pause. The Vigilance has the authority to offer unchallenged refuge to any person of Tribal descent—which I had suspected and now feel certain that Beam is. The PR spin is that it's a library of Lakota customs—arts, language, burial rites—but it started out as more of a neighborhood watch—only the things being watched out for were invisible. Whatever The Vigilance is, it's sovereign in power, set apart from the US government and even from the Lakota Council of Tribes.

"Where—else would we go?" I stammer. "The Outpost? The Council itself?"

"Chausie, I don't know how to say this. We need to keep Beam off *everybody's* radar. But she has to be close enough to…" Joel silently considers more than he communicates. An interruption on his end leads me to believe someone's calling him, and his exasperated cluck says it's not someone he wants to talk to. When he speaks again, he's curt. "*You* have to take her," he declares. "Back home and up into the buttes. There's an old Oglala woman who lives there. She'll know what to do. No one will think to look there. It's a lot to ask, Son, but I think the job is yours. Will you do it?"

Will I do it? This is awesome! "Yes, of course!" I can't believe my luck.

Joel spouts off information that I have to force myself to listen to because I'm giddy with excitement. This is my chance to prove to my dad that I'm still capable. I know he's had his doubts since I got hurt. He can hardly pick up the phone to discuss it—or to discuss much of anything these days. But I mean, what with the time difference and all—and he's busy…

So *what* if Beam's uncle thinks I'm already qualified as an officer?

By the time he talks to my dad, I'll have Beam safely where she needs to go. *Nobody* knows that land as I do. I can do this. I'm gonna do this.

I tell my mom. I just say it. Tell her everything Beam's uncle said. Tell her I *have* to go and not to hate me and that there's this girl I never should've left. She takes it better than I expect. She's probably happy that I'm interacting with her for *any* reason. Or she can just see that I *am* going to do this—with or without her blessing.

I can't even think of what to bring. Mom watches me run around stuffing things into my pockets. A hunting knife. A collapsible water bottle.

She opens the closet—I think it pains her—and hands me the key to my motorcycle. "Chausie, *please*—"

"I'll be careful."

"You can't allow your anger to—"

"I know it. I promise." I seal the vow with a huge hug that visibly surprises her. She doesn't miss the opportunity. She hugs me back for so long that I begin to think I should cough or something to remind her I have to go.

"I'll let your father know you're coming," she says.

"No!" That could ruin everything. I dial back the emphatic tone. "I mean, I'll handle it."

"He'll want to meet up with you, Chaus. Help you out."

"Mom, I got this."

"OK, but Chausie?" She pins me with a look of concern. "There are things you and your dad will need to discuss."

Later on, I'll understand what my mom is trying to tell me. Right now, in my haste, I miss it completely. "Call me," she demands. "And let me know you're safe."

I swear that I will. I can't hide my smile. I speed the whole way. I don't even care.

BEAM

It's past time to meet Uncle Joel when I lock the door and retrace my steps across the backyard with a heavy book bag and a bundle of clothes. He's not going to be thrilled that I chose to stop. He made it clear that I could be a target. But it's all good now. I round the Jacksons' home with a short-lived sigh of relief.

My Uber is gone. In its place is the car I'd seen parked across the street from my house.

I recognize, at this point, that it could be in my best interest to get out of here. But I've never been much of an athlete, and you know that term *learned helplessness*? I have.

Because of my vast experience with torture in the form of mandatory dodgeball, I am confident that any evasive maneuvers I can initiate will prove hopelessly ineffective. So, instead of running, I cleverly stand in the open and gawk.

It's late evening now. The shadows blend with the general coming of night. When a flurry of wings beats close enough to vibrate my eardrum and move my hair, I spin to find a man where, for an instant, I thought I'd seen feathers. Several quick paces put distance between us.

His skin is darker than mine. The choker around his neck is six strands thick and strung with cylindrical bones, separated by turquoise beads. His eyes are so black I can hardly differentiate pupil from iris.

The way he greets me—"Summer Sunbeam"—is clipped by the same accent my father has. "I am Kanji Brings Justice, a member of the Lakota Council of Tribes. I come in the name of President Tumbling Rock, on behalf of your people."

When I was a kid, and a stranger would try to speak to me, I would cover my eyes and stand stock still, convinced that I was magically undetectable. I have the comical urge to do that now. The *president?!* The *president* sent someone all the way across the country to find *me*? And also, there's a president? What happened to having chiefs?

"President Rock sent you?" I ask. And instantly cringe. Maybe the *Rock* doesn't work like a last name. But how would I *know*? My dad never taught me. I don't wait for confirmation. "They were my dad's people," I say. "I don't really have ties there." I don't add, *Um, why are you here again?* Or, *You're not going to stuff me in the trunk, are you?* But I reserve both as options.

"You don't count us as your tribe," he says. It's not a question, and anyway before I can answer, he adds, "but the president does."

Oh. That's nice. I'd like to be part of a tribe. If it didn't involve being accosted by scary men who flap in unannounced.

Kanji Brings Justice is speaking again. "Some say that sacred visions count you as ours. Our blessing. Perhaps our vengeance. Or our bane. There is no way to outdistance sacred visions by moving across the land. And that is why I have come."

I gape at him until it's clear I have no inkling what he's trying to say. He uses a different tack. "Your father tells us that you are an omnituens and nothing more."

I don't know what an omnitu-thingy is, but I doubt very much that my father has told them *anything*. Daddy's like a graveyard where secrets go to die. A pang of hope shoots through me. "Is he *with* you?!" I search the car, but the windows are blacked out. The man tells me he is not.

"He's being hosted by the Council." I take it *hosted* is a euphemism for incarcerated. "He assures us that you would never disobey his instructions to stay put. So I've come to you. We need to know if you are an omnituens. There are expectations. And we need to know if you are anything more."

"I don't—" I'm at a loss. If Daddy really did divulge things about me, maybe he's being forced to. But maybe I'm not as scared for my dad as I ought to be. I'm starting to feel a bit annoyed with him, actually. If he survives this week, I'm going to tell him so, and I'm going to demand all information pertaining to any and all people and/or organizations who may want to *host* any of us. "Sorry," I say out loud. "What's an omni-thingy?"

"Have you not been taught such things?" the man asks.

Nope. Not sure if I should say nope. He's a little scary all of a sudden. I think he's sensitive about what's being left out of my education. Mainly, the history of half my DNA.

I'm gonna bail on the rest of our chat. "Did you send my Uber away?" I ask. I bet he did.

"We'll take you where you need to go." He gestures toward the car. "Step in."

I step back instead, right into a wall of a man who has silently advanced upon me, and I yip. I sound just like a Chihuahua. The wall-of-man shoves me toward the car with a *knife* in his hand!

Kanji berates him. "Put that away! Are you *insane?* You can't draw her *blood* here! If it comes to that, we'll break her neck."

What?! That is not the *end* of what freaks me out, though. At the same time I'm stumbling forward and hearing about the potential *breaking* of my neck, the wall-of-man gets bowled over by a speeding brown mass from the trees. I barely have time to register the footfalls before the creature is upon him. Meanwhile, the Councilman takes flight. Yes, as a bird. An American crow, to be precise.

I've observed weird things before, but I'm not allowed to talk about them.

I turn to see what, at first, I believe is a deer, because it is big and it is brown. But it does not move like a deer. It moves like a *cat*. And there are its whiskers. And there is its tail. I can't get my mind around it. A mountain lion. A sleek mountain lion as muscular and as graceful as I've never seen in the zoo. Here. In my neighborhood, in the middle of Atlanta. Which means it doesn't exist.

There are rules.

Rule number one: Do not, under any circumstance, communicate with your uncle Joel.

Rule number two: Do not, under any circumstance, communicate with (or about) creatures no one else can see.
Addendum: If no one else can see them, they do not exist.

The lion positions itself between me and the wall-of-man. I don't
know what the crow guy is doing, except that he has reformed—as a
human—over near the car. I risk a glimpse. He looks chafed, but not
shocked. Certainly not as shocked as I am. Not fearful. Not *any* of
the normal human reactions he should be having. So, the lion doesn't
exist. Come to think of it, maybe the crow doesn't exist.

I glance back in time to see the lion take note of me. *Nothing to
see here, Mister Lion. In case you're real. And not a figment of m*— He
cuts his eyes toward my house and then back to me, purposefully. I
just stare at him. So, he eyeballs me harder and then my house, like
he's trying to tell me to go there. But I do not, because I do not *accept*
communications from imaginary wild animals! I am not *allowed* to!

The lion—which does not exist—lunges for the wall-of-man, but
instead of ripping into him, the lion sweeps him off his feet. This
strikes me as a very *un*-lionish thing to do, confirming my suspicions.
When he sets his sights back on me, he unleashes a harrowing cry
which, despite its unreality, stings me with distress. This time, my
feet know very well what to do, and I run as fast as I can.

3

UNCLE JOEL

BEAM

Turns out not to be as fast as a fictitious mountain lion. As soon as I begin to flee, he's on my heels. He's toying with me. He's not even trying.

When I round the house, Uncle Joel is pounding on my front door, and I scream his name. I don't have time to dwell on it right now, but he looks just the same as he did all those years ago, and so much like a younger version of my dad. His long, black braid swings as he pivots toward my cry. His intelligent eyes, over sharp cheekbones, lock in on my...situation.

Though there is a wild animal breathing down my neck, Uncle Joel does not hesitate for even a fraction of a second. He streaks to me and throws a hand out to my foe. "Go!" he yells at the lion.

Which means he can see the lion.

Which means the lion is real.

I don't know which is more surprising, the fact that the lion is real or the fact that it obeys my uncle Joel. Springing from mighty hind legs, it performs an aerial twist and beats a path back up the way we've come.

"What. Just. Happened?!" I shriek, but Uncle Joel has no time to spare for explanations. He rushes me to the car—practically carries me—and tosses me into the front seat. He rounds to the driver's side and screeches out onto the road before he's even closed the door. I sit in wide-eyed astonishment for about ten minutes before I can breathe properly. Even now, I can't speak. My uncle's too focused on getting us out of there, anyway.

Once we're on the interstate, his posture relaxes some, and he glances over. "Are you OK?"

The question unleashes a flood within me. Words gush out like stormwater through a gully. "I'm-so-sorry-Uncle-Joel!-Please-don't-be-mad-at-me!-I-thought-I-could—but-I-almost-got-us-killed-and—"

"Whoa-whoa-whoooa." My uncle reaches across the console to squeeze my hand. "I'm not mad at you, Beam. Don't think that."

I nod. Up and down, up and down, up and down. "Two men came for me." I'm still gushing. "They tried to get me into their car and then—oh my gosh, thank you for showing up when you did!"

"That's what uncles are for, right?"

His tone is calm, but around the steering wheel, his knuckles are white. He keeps consulting the rearview mirror, and it occurs to me that my uncle has poised himself—with a second home in Georgia—for the sole purpose of showing up when he did.

"Are they following us?" I ask.

"I don't think so. We got the jump on them."

"One of the men said President Tumbling Rock had sent them. Is that true, do you think? He was a crow man with eyes so dark it was like his pupils ate his irises. He told the other guy they might have to break my neck!"

The information thins my uncle's mouth. "Kanji," he says. "He *would* be the one to show up. How did you know his name meant *crow*? Has your father taught you Lakota after all?"

"No. But when he turned into a big, huge *crow*, I decided it was a good identifier."

Uncle turns his head too slowly and looks perplexed. He didn't see that part. *Crap.* I'm probably not supposed to talk about it.

"If Kanji is able to become a crow," he says gently—probably because he fears I'm unstable—"it's a new development."

"Oh, I didn't mean he *actually* became a crow," I backpedal. "I'm sure *that* couldn't happen."

Now my uncle's voice is too knowing. "Beam, you don't have to pretend around me. I hope you know that." I nod my head, but I don't speak, so he says, "Kanji Brings Justice is an ardent member of the Council, but as to whether or not he speaks for the president, I think not. I've never known them to be confidants. I'm sure President Tumbling Rock doesn't count *killing* you among any of the viable paths forward."

"You don't *look* sure. He's holding my dad, isn't he? And he won't even let him answer my calls!"

The hard expression through which Uncle Joel penetrates me must be genetic. Daddy uses the same one. It means he's about to give it to me straight. "I'm not *completely* sure about anything right now," he says. "I always thought I'd be able to get out ahead of all this when it began in earnest."

Joel's phone vibrates from where it is upheld on the dash, and worry lines his face. The caller ID reads, *Kimimela.* He doesn't answer.

"Who is she?" I ask.

"Someone who asks too many questions. She's been looking for you for ages. She just didn't know who you were."

OK. I'm done guessing.

"There are things I need to know," I declare. This draws a puff from my uncle that I take to mean, *No kidding,* so I press on. "What is an omnitunes? Am I supposed to know every melody ever sung?"

With a hint of a smile, Uncle Joel corrects me. "Omnituens," he says. "An all-seer, or at least a more-than-most seer. The woman who called just now, Kimi, she's supposed to be one. Unlike you, though,"

—he throws a sideways glance to let me know he's guessed the truth—"it's an absolute misnomer. I doubt she can see any more than I can."

"But you saw the mountain lion," I venture.

"Right. I mean things that are invisible."

It's not usually difficult for me to discern which creatures are visible only to me, but I gotta admit, today has presented its challenges.

"I've known Kimi since we were kids," my uncle continues. "She's smart. She's incredibly well-read. But if she could ever see things that were invisible, she sure kept quiet about it."

"Maybe her father frowned upon it," I mutter, and Uncle Joel flashes his eyebrows in acknowledgment.

"Well, she doesn't keep it quiet anymore," he says. "She claims all kinds of things. Claims to be the product of a relationship between a nagi and an owl." A husky scoff reveals what he thinks of that.

"What the heck is a nagi?" I ask, but he waves it away.

"It's not true. A nagi is a creature without form. Less than a spirit, more of a...powerful personality. It often resides in an animal because it has no body of its own. Some are benevolent. Some not." Uncle Joel peers at my collar and I wonder if he's checking to make sure I'm wearing the catcher he sent. "They can ruin the hosts they inhabit—from the inside. And out," he adds. "Depending on what they make them do."

Ick. "Didn't you *know* her parents?" I ask.

"I did," Uncle Joel sings up high. "But she acts like it's all a great mystery, and only those with special wisdom can fathom it. People have bought into it. She was put in charge at The Vigilance."

"What is that?" I ask. "The Vigilance?"

"It's mainly a museum now, but it was formed to guard the Earth Gate after an Umbra, a shadow monster, was loosed into our world and nearly wiped out our whole universe."

"You're being hyperbolic."

He's not being hyperbolic. He deadpans me.

"You said she was on the lookout for *me*," I remember with alarm. "Is it because of the things I can see?"

Instead of a direct answer, Uncle Joel says, "Kimi walks a thin line between keeping the museum and keeping her secrets. There's been talk about her fascination with death and the occult. Whispers of dangerous magic that doesn't belong to us. To be fair, she's done a lot to restore pride in our culture, which is sorely lacking. She showcases traditional arts and music. She even organizes a library of folklore—in Lakota as well as English—not to mention the sacred visions, which she strives to document with pinpoint accuracy." He looks me over and his voice goes dark. "Especially the Visions of Blood." I get the feeling he's trying to ascertain whether or not those words mean anything to me.

I sit up straighter. "That crow man asked if I was *just* an omnituens. Or if I was something more."

"*Ah.*" My uncle *ahs* as if we've come to the crux of the matter. "Kimi claims to be able to see the souls of hundreds of our ancestors trapped on the other side of the Earth Gate, wandering the In-Between, unable to find rest. The Council of Tribes issued a formal reprimand for stirring up old grievances, but they have no real jurisdiction there, and anyway, her following is significant."

A growing uneasiness is stirring in my stomach. "Uncle Joel, what does any of that have to do with me?"

"I don't suppose you were ever taken back home?"

He looks for negative confirmation, which I give. "Only the once, when Oonchi died." He was there too, at my grandmother's funeral, but we could only wave to one another. Daddy hovered over me like a raincloud. He barely let me speak to anyone.

"Right," Uncle Joel says. "But surely you're aware of our history. That not a hundred-fifty years ago, our people were all but wiped out. Those of us who lived were forced to abandon our ways—were made to dress, to speak, to believe the same as the white settlers. Some of us continue to feel erased and even ashamed of our heritage, prejudiced against ourselves. What happens in history sets the stage,

you know? All the violence, the fear, the hate—that is what we are
born into. What we write our lives upon. I don't expect you to understand, because—"

"It's not like we don't have those troubles *here*," I interject. "One
time I was missing curfew after a school dance, and my date would
barely even go the speed limit. After I kept urging him to speed up,
he asked—bitterly—what I'd say if the police pulled us over to find
out whether or not I was in *this black guy's* car of my own free will. It
had happened to him before." I stare at my uncle pointedly to drive
the fact home. "We all struggle to find our place," I say. "We have to
do what we can now, in this time, to make it a home for everyone." I
sound like my mom.

"Maybe so." My uncle smiles at me. "I guess no one knows that
better than a blue-eyed Indian."

He's right. When I'd told my date that I was no stranger to
racism, that I was half Oglala Lakota, he'd commented on my blue
eyes in a way that belittled my plight.

We've been driving for a while now. We've exchanged the interstate for a narrow country road, and even neighborhood stores have
stopped popping up. We pass a solitary farmhouse every now and
again, but otherwise, it's just fields that want planting.

Nobody else is on the road until an electric-blue motorcycle roars
past doing about a hundred. That guy's not afraid to go fast.

The fields have given way to forests when Uncle Joel slows the
car and turns onto a road that I would have missed entirely, especially
in the dark. A guard greets him through the open window of his
standalone office and steps out to wheel away a tall chainlink fence,
topped with rolls of barbed wire. It's a private airport. We really are
headed to South Dakota. I can't help some excitement for that. As we
round the entryway, there's a small plane idling on a packed dirt
runway. Uncle Joel parks between two white hangers and swivels to
face me.

"Back when animosity between the tribes and the settlers was the
most volatile—I'm talking late 1800s—many Native tribes brought

back a religious ritual, a sacred ceremony called The Ghost Dance. They practiced it to seek the restoration of the land. They vowed to continue the traditions of our people and to avoid assimilation into the white culture. Most of the dances were peaceful. But a vision surfaced that called upon the dancers to draw certain symbols onto their clothing and revel until the spirits of our ancestors took notice and came to our aid, magnifying our power, wiping the white people out of our land."

"I'd never have been born," I muse. "It would have killed off the Irish immigrants who led to my mom and me."

"It was a brutal time," is all Uncle says.

"I know about The Ghost Dance," I tell him. "It sparked The Massacre at Wounded Knee. Someone began the dance in front of US soldiers who were confiscating weapons. A gun was discharged. It ended in hundreds of Lakota being slaughtered. Most of them had no weapons at all. Most of them were women and children. Right? My dad told me that much, and my history teacher practically made me reenact it in front of the class, which was horrifying."

Uncle Joel's blank response makes me want to laugh. He shakes my teacher's insensitivity out of his head and says, "There's more, though, that the history books don't reveal, and I bet my brother hasn't told you either. After the massacre, some of the young warriors channeled their rage into the worst of religion. They danced until they collapsed, pleading and chanting, bloodletting. They promised foolish sacrifices to whomever, *what*ever, would act. And they convinced a woman to join them, the Pejuta, the Elixir. Her sacred blood was what opened the Earth Gate."

"Uncle Joel?" I leave the rest of the question unasked because I don't think I want to know why he's telling me this anymore. "I just want to get my parents and come back home."

"The Earth Gate leads to an In-Between where other worlds meet. In the end, it wasn't just the gate between human life and death that was opened, nor were the spirits of our ancestors the only beings summoned. There were more gates than they supposed. Prisons for—"

I must look terrorized because Joel says, "I'm sorry to lay all this on you like this. But you have to know. It's like—there are the wars that we can see, wars we can fight. They get written up in the history books, and we think they are the wars that determine our destiny. But then there are the wars beneath the wars."

"You mean hate," I suggest. "Un-forgiveness."

"I mean real adversaries. Invisible, but real. And here is the most important thing, Beam: the one who opened the gates was born to bridge life and death, to bring healing and hope, but she was deceived and her mind was corrupted." Uncle Joel pauses to let that sink in before he says, "The Vigilance doesn't search for invisible monsters, so much as for those whose blood and light can unleash them."

"The one who opened the gates," I say warily. "She's the one who released that horrible shadow monster?"

"Yes."

"And did she really trap your ancestors?"

"I think maybe. And they're your ancestors too."

"Was she written about in those Visions of Blood?"

"Yes. Along with another who is able to reverse the damage done." My uncle waits for me to connect the dots until his phone rings again—Kimimela, again—and he rushes to say, "Beam, there is more I need to tell you. But right now I need to put you on that plane."

"With *you*, you mean!"

"I'll meet up with you as soon as I can. I promise." He exits the car, and I scramble to rejoin him.

"You can't just leave me! I don't know what to do!" He's walking too fast. I'm jogging to keep up. "I'm not supposed to be doing any of this at *all*! I am not *allowed* to."

Uncle doesn't stop for me. "You have to quit dwelling on what your father allows. That time is over. You'll have your friend to guide you to an old Oglala woman. She can advise you far better than I. She knows the history inside and out. I have to go deal with Kanji. And if Kimi is calling?" His shoulders slope. "I have to deal with her too. I think she can make a case to have you sent to The Vigilance, and maybe that's where you need to end up, but my gut says no."

I can't hear much of anything Uncle Joel is saying through the emotion I'm working to suppress. "Please!" I claw at him. "What about Mom and Dad? I only have seven days!"

Uncle Joel braces my arms and gets down on my level where he speaks to me sternly. "You have to be brave. You are a mighty Oglala Lakota, an Elixir for your people. You were born for this."

I'm too astonished to form anything more than the "Wh" of my question, but I'm reminded of a similar charge my oonchi gave to me after she died.

"The answers are coming," Uncle says, and he tugs at the catcher around my neck. "Keep it close," he whispers. The urgency in his voice frightens me. "And Beam? Go directly to the Oglala woman. Don't let anybody convince you otherwise."

I climb into the plane feeling as forlorn as—I don't know what. I'm too tired to think. The pilots are talking to each other (or two people I assume are the pilots since they have steering wheel thingies in front of them), but I'm not feeling very courteous right now. I fall onto the bench behind them and cover my eyes.

"Don't be angry, Sunbeam." It's what my dad calls me sometimes.

"I'll get over it," I mutter. But I still don't uncover my eyes.

He lingers, and about the time he begins to step away, I fling myself onto him and hug him as if he's my last tether to life. I cry. I do. I blubber into his shoulder and when I pull away, there are tears in his eyes too. "I'm right behind you," he says. "I'll catch up to you, and we'll get them back."

I nod my head and swallow a second wave of tears.

The pilot motions to a headset hanging on the back of the chair in front of me, and Uncle Joel fits it onto my ears. When I resist, he says, "You have to. Your dad's already going to kill me. Don't add loss of hearing to his list of complaints."

Overwhelmed and utterly exhausted—and a little ashamed by my emotional outburst—I hide my face and eventually fall asleep. When I wake up, we're in the air, and I feel some better. I readjust my position and notice the pressure of someone settling into the cushion beside me. He touches my headset, and now I can hear his voice.

"How're you holding up?"

In my waking state, I think it's my dad. It's not. I'm no athletic phenom, as we have already established, but I do have a pretty quick mind. Even so, I can make absolutely no sense of why I am staring into the startlingly golden eyes of my coffeehouse neighbor.

CHAUSIE

When I got to the airport and asked the pilot how we were going to pack my motorcycle, he ogled me. The plane is small. It doesn't seem much more than a crop duster to me. Honestly, if we could just stick wings on my bike, it might do as well.

"How much does it weigh?" he asked.

How much does it weigh? I thought about why that mattered. "Around two-hundred-fifty pounds." *Maybe I should leave it here.*

He sized me up. "How much do *you* weigh?"

"I'll just leave it," I declared. I'm not a heavy guy, but I really don't want to be the reason for bringing a plane out of the sky. Especially if I'm on it.

The pilot snickered. "I'm just messing with you, man. There's room in the belly."

Despite the man's odd sense of humor, we got the bike secured and ended up talking basketball while he looked the plane over and checked boxes on a sheet of paper that he then handed to a woman from the airport.

Basketball is on a short list of things that make me happy, and his Final Four predictions were spot on. But a twinge of regret reminded me how I lost the chance to earn a spot in the tournament for myself. It's my own fault. I shouldn't have gone riding that night. Mom begged me not to, but after overhearing the way she dressed my dad down on the phone—it's no wonder he doesn't call.

"You play?" the pilot asked. I've probably got six inches on him. I used to get that question all the time, simply because of my height, but no one asks me anymore, not once they see me try to walk.

"I used to," I told him and then asked about the plane's control panel just to change the subject.

When Beam arrived with her uncle, she was in no mood to chat, a feeling I understand well, so I kept my whiskers out of it. But now we're in the air and she's asleep, so I steal glances. I haven't completely messed up. She's safe so far, and we're on the way home. I smile to myself. Something brought us together. Something real and important, and I get to be part of it. This is my chance to make everything right.

Not sure when me glancing at Beam becomes me just outright staring, but when she stirs, I jerk my attention from the smooth sliver of brown skin that peeks between her waistband and her sweatshirt.

"Hey, Sleepy," I say, but either she's not quite awake or she can't hear me, so I move to sit beside her and click the channel on her headset.

The look on her face when she hears me—like she believes in me intrinsically, that I will, that I *can* take care of her—quickly morphs into confusion, and, inexplicably, I feel robbed.

"Dad?" she asks. One last attempt to hold on to the man she must have thought me to be.

"No, it's me, Chausie, remember? Did your uncle tell you?"

She shakes her head and sits up straighter, smoothing her face. "You know Uncle Joel?"

"Not really. He called me to reach you—because you used my phone at the coffeehouse."

She studies me with pale blue eyes. I swear they're lit from within. "But why are you *here*?" she says at last.

BEAM

Chausie's yellow eyes are distracting, reminding me of nights the car's headlights spot the gleaming eyes of a forest animal. Now they're scowling again, and I think I've offended him. "What I mean is—" I begin. But I didn't do anything offensive, so I just own it. "No, that's what I mean. Why are you on this plane with me?"

When he answers, his voice sounds like it's inside my head, albeit through an AM radio. "Well, your uncle believes, and I'm starting to as well, that we were put together on purpose, you and I. That we met today because we were meant to."

That takes me a good moment to process. "You mean...in a *divine* sort of way?" I ask. After scanning his long body, confined in the small space, I don't even see how we both fit onto this bench, let alone into this adventure.

He flashes his eyebrows to say *maybe so*. "I've been training at The Outpost for years—I practically grew up there—and when your uncle found out, he asked me to watch over you." Chausie leans in, his words picking up speed. "Honestly, I've been worried that I wouldn't get to finish training, because of the injury." He indicates his stiff leg. "But now I might be able to show my dad that I can keep up, and maybe even—"

He is *all* about it. His eyes are alight. I like this side of him. I hold up a finger to slow him down. "I realize that this *Outpost* must be the best thing in your world, but I have no idea what you're talking about."

"Oh. Peacekeeping. Law enforcement. We deal with remote emergencies, keep order, protect the land."

I nod like I understand, but I say, "What land?"

"The *Bad*lands," he says incredulously. "And all around there. We work in conjunction with the park." When I open my mouth to ask, he cuts in, "The *national* park. Oh my gosh. You don't know anything. Are you not from the reservation?"

"Wait. We're from the same place?"

Chausie's bearing opens up. "See? Pretty big coincidence. Right?"

"Right. I really *don't* know anything. You're Lakota?"

"No. I'm Igmuwatogla." He puffs out his chest and lifts his chin, clearly proud of his heritage. Or maybe he's daring me to challenge him. Do the Lakota and this other tribe not get along? I don't have the heart to tell him I've never heard of it.

"Tell me more," I say.

And so he opens up to me about how his dad heads things up at The Outpost and how he'll be working for his dad when the time comes, but—"My mom hates it," he confides. "Wants me to go to college before I commit to anything. She left my dad and dragged me across the country. Now I can only train during the months my dad gets me. Mom is *not* Igmuwatogla. My older brother either. And I guess she doesn't like that I *am*. But *I* do." He finishes like he has to convince himself. Or me.

"It's hard to be two things, isn't it?" I ask. "Hey, at least you *know* what you are. I'm supposed to surrender myself as some kind of ransom for my mom, and I don't understand why." Maybe *he* does. "Do *you*?" I choke out.

"I understand that you're special. Anyone can see that."

His words are soft enough to pink up my cheeks. He doesn't want me to get the wrong idea.

"Uncle Joel says so," he rushes to explain, referring to my uncle as if he's his own.

CHAUSIE

Beam has a way of mulling over the things I say before she reacts, and her unflinching eye contact is both enticing and intimidating. Instead of studying her, which I increasingly want to do, I turn to the window and look into the night. A host of tiny lights blink up at me from the ground. "We must be halfway by now," I muse. "Probably not quite. What city do you think that is?"

I inhale her before I feel her leaning over my shoulder. Sage. Sunlight. Fresh fields and flowers and...I don't know...life.

"Kansas City?" she guesses. The window is small. She has to push against me to see out properly. I like it. I don't move to give her any more space, and I bite back a smile, wondering what she'll do.

"Are you going to stay with me?" she asks. She's quiet, even with the mic on the headset.

"Yeah, that's my job," I say. "To guide you to the woman who will get you some answers."

"What will we do? Once we land. You know how to get there?"

"Uncle Joel gave me directions." That is *nearly* true. The lady we're going to see is a recluse. I think she might live in a cave. Uncle Joel gave me landmarks to shoot for and assured me she'd be aware of our arrival. I turn Beam's way, and our foreheads meet.

She isn't backing away. Her lashes flutter against my cheek when she raises her eyes. Her lips part, but she doesn't speak. Is it weird to get this high off of her proximity? I swallow. *Stop looking at her mouth.*

She chuckles and for a sickening second, I think she's responding to my thoughts.

"I think it's funny you call him *Uncle*," she says. "Like we jumped from being strangers to being brother and sister."

"Not likely," I snap—with too much energy. Enough to pop her head sideways.

The part of my body she vacates feels cold immediately. Once she's safely back on her side of the bench, she says, "I didn't mean anything by it."

She doesn't understand why I'm so averse to being called her brother, or why I would snap at her for suggesting it, but I really don't think I should explain that it's because siblings don't kiss. Not the way it had occurred to me to kiss her.

"I *liked* that you called him Uncle." Her voice is small, which confirms to me that I am an ass. "It made me feel less alone. If I over-stepped—"

"Stop." I cut her off. "You didn't say anything wrong. I never should've left you earlier. I won't do it again. I'm gonna get you where you need to go. Working on this kind of thing is all I've ever wanted to do."

She's looking out her window. I've made it sound like she's my job. Which, she kind of is. So, now I'm confused. If she's *just* my job, then I probably shouldn't be thinking about kissing her. I've gotta get it together. Everything rides on this.

"Hey." I get her attention in order to confess. "I'm not really great at human interaction. It's possible that you're picking up on this." When she smiles, I feel more relieved than I have a right to be. "Has nothing to do with you overstepping." I extend my hand. "We're part-ners now, OK? I'm in this with you."

She's searching my eyes with that same unnerving boldness. It's all I can do not to look away. Feels risky. And exhilarating. It's the same thing I feel when I refuse to brake on the curvy mountain road. I can hide behind a hard expression, but this chick can *wield* one.

BEAM

Chausie's an enigma. He's got impulse issues. That much is sure. Maybe he has a borderline personality. Yeah, I've taken college-level courses. I know things.

But then he has these sweet, vulnerable moments.

"Since we're partners now..." I venture aloud. I want to know what he thinks about the video of my mom, but I'm frightened by what it could mean. Also, I'm worried it falls under the *Don't talk about creatures only you can see* rule. I have a theory about what my second mom can be, but I don't want to say it.

My sentence is hanging out there incomplete, so Chausie prompts me with, "Yeees?"

I glance at the pilot. "Can he hear us?" I mouth, indicating the headphones.

Chausie shakes his head. "He's on a different channel."

"Good." I produce my phone. "I got this text yesterday telling me where I had to show up if I wanted to get my mom back. And there was a video." I play it for him.

"Is that your mom?"

"Yes," I answer. "Both of them are."

"There's another video?" Chausie scrolls to find out. He doesn't see both moms, one sitting cross-legged on the braided rug and one standing beside her.

"No. Just the one," I sigh. I tug on the phone, but he covers my hands to keep me from reclaiming it.

"Hang on. What do you mean?" I allow him to watch the video again. "Is there a reflection or something?"

"Which one can you see?"

Chausie regards me and indicates my seated mom.

"You don't see anything right *there* at all?" I point to the standing version. "Not an outline. Or. *Anything?*" I'm practically pleading with him to behold it. It would be such a relief if even one other person could see the things I see.

Chausie studies the video. At least he takes me seriously. "Sorry. I can't make it out."

"OK, but—" Am I really going to ask this? "Just say that there *are* two versions of my mom there. Maybe one of them is invisible." I do a reaction check with him. "What would that mean?"

Chausie sits back and brings his fist to his mouth to consider my question. His gaze falls over his knuckles, and his brow furrows in thought.

"Thanks for not thinking I'm crazy," I gush. "Or, if you do, thanks for not showing it."

Now, he slowly slides his gaze to me, rewarding my surge of gratitude with a lopsided grin. "I don't think you're crazy," he says. "Dakota's full of things that can't be explained. I'm good with mystery."

"Oh," I fairly squeak. "That's the best thing I've ever heard." I honestly feel like I could cry right now. I relax back to ponder that, careful to give him more space than I did before when we were looking out the window. It clearly made him feel trapped or something. For my part, though, I wouldn't mind being up close. It's not like it would be unnatural in this tight space. The bench is so small, and he's so lanky. I wonder what he'd do if I rested my head on his—

"What are you grinning about?" he asks. His head is tilted my way to see me better. *Busted.*

"No, um—" I laugh down at my lap. "Nothing." I'm sure my face is red as a tomato. To change the subject, I say, "Just how good of a basketball player are you?"

Guys like to brag about that sort of thing, don't they?

No. It bums him out. He looks away to say, "Not good at all anymore." He means because of his leg. Yeah, I should have thought that through. On the plus side, he slumps back into the cushion in a way that *forces* me to lean against him—if I want to obey the laws of gravity. And I do. Laws are important to me. Sadly, this has pinned his arm in an awkward position, so when he twists to extricate it, I decide I should peel myself off of him.

But he doesn't let me. "You're alright," he says and stays me with the arm he has freed, which he then lays across the bench behind me. So...this is cozy. I allow myself to relax against his side.

"How'd you hurt yourself?" I inquire.

"Motorcycle wreck." He doesn't elaborate.

"OK, well, how good of a basketball player *were* you, then? Wow me."

The shy smile through which he inquires if I really want to know is so endearing that my insides ache with the gift of it. I nod my head to tell him, yes, he has to answer. "We won some big tournament last year," I remember. "I suppose that was your doing?"

"You didn't come? The whole school was there."

"Couldn't," I say. "I had a tournament of my own."

"Let me guess. Chess?"

"Rude."

"No, it's not," he says. "You're smart. What was it, then? Football?"

I raise my head in a condescending air and admit that it was— "Mock trial. Oh-my-gosh, stop laughing!"

"I'm not laughing," he laughs.

"You *are* laughing. You're laughing right now."

"I just bet you're really good at arguing, is all." Laughing. All the way through the whole comment.

When I deadpan him, he adds, "In a good way." Still laughing.

"Basketball?" I remind him. "Did you win it for us or not?"

"Did you win the mock trial?"

"Yes, I did, actually. I *am* good at arguing."

"Of course you are," he says. It's not derisive. If anything, it's with a hint of admiration. After another moment, in which I arch my brows expectantly, he says, "I hit the shot that tied the game. At the buzzer. And I was fouled in the process, so I got to take free throws."

"And you made them," I guess. "I bet the place erupted. I wish I'd been there."

"No you don't," he chuckles.

"I do so. I mean, no, not for the game, but for you. If I had known you. If we'd been friends. You know what I mean." Apparently, my mouth has declared independence from my brain.

"Let's be friends," Chausie suggests.

It's hard to tell with a Chausie, but I think he's enjoying the direction of this conversation.

"Absolutely," I agree. "Now that I know you're a hero."

The corner of his mouth quirks upward, but he disregards his hero status. "*Was.* For like, a week."

"I bet it was a good week."

"Yeah," he says and sort of hugs me with the arm on the bench. "It *was* a good week. The team I played on before that was awful—I mean the guys were great. They just couldn't play. So, playing for this team was—it was the only good thing about having to move."

"You're dating a cheerleader, aren't you?" I blurt out.

"What? No. Why?"

I shrug. "I don't know why." I'm not even sure how that stupid question escaped from me. I wish it hadn't. "What kind of girl *do* you date, then?" Oh my gosh. What is wrong with me?

Chausie's scowling again. I'm beginning to think it's just his thinking face and not proof that he's disagreeable. "Remember those three loud girls at the coffeehouse?" he asks.

"How could I forget?" Did disappointment just leak from my voice?

"Not that kind," he says.

Oh.

Then he asks, "Do *you* know what a bun foundation is?"

After two long seconds, I burst out laughing. "Chausie! Did you just make a joke?"

"I *joke*," he says defensively. "I just haven't had much to joke *about* lately. Or...you know...anyone to joke *with*." He glances at me from underneath his long lashes.

See? This is what I'm referring to. Vulnerable. Sweet. The shy smile that does the thing to my guts.

CHAUSIE

The pilot pops onto our channel to let us know we'll be landing soon, and the message sends a jolt of nerves through me. This is my shot. I can make up for what I've done. I'll be able to move back full-time. Work for my dad.

We secure our seatbelts, which means that I can no longer enjoy the weight of Beam up against me. Which is probably a good thing. I've gotta dial it back. I've got a job to do. Get the bike. Get us out of here. I wonder if she'll trust me enough to let us get miles into the wilderness before dawn. She won't be able to see into the night the way I can.

I hope Dad's not here to meet us. Not yet. I have to prove to him I can keep up. Prove to him I'm still capable. That I can keep my emotions in check.

My knee starts bouncing and I can feel the anxiety building in the pit of my stomach. I'm gonna do this. I'm gonna make it right. To hell with what Mom wants. She's the reason I'm so mad in the first place. Even as I think it, I unthink it. I love my mom. I don't understand how things fell apart.

When we land, the night is dark, but we travel a straight line of blue runway lights. Beam's uncle told me we'd be landing in Rapid City, and I had mistakenly assumed that we'd be walking onto the tarmac of its Regional Airport. No. This is another private airfield.

The pilot jumps out to greet a man holding a flashlight and a clipboard. They don't seem to notice the black car that's creeping toward the plane without its lights on, but I do, and I begin to plot our escape. Beam's uncle had warned me there would be people out for her. I just didn't think they would meet us at the plane. How did they find out?

I can barely walk, let alone fight. Not as a man. And I can't drive a motorcycle as a—*You should have called your dad. She's more important than you proving yourself.*

I can do both. I can keep her safe and prove myself. At this point, there are no other options. I ignore the rest of what my conscience has to say and let my instincts take over.

BEAM

Something's got Chausie tense. –Er than usual.

"Wait here," he says and deplanes, leaving me alone to try to make him out through the window. He speaks to the pilot, using his height as a muscular exclamation point. The fact that he's lean does nothing to diminish his impact, but he clearly bears more weight on his right leg than his left. It must be sore from the flight. Probably didn't help that I was practically sitting on his lap. I bet it hurts him all the time.

The pilot seems to be trying to calm him. He opens the cargo bay, but by the time he invites Chausie to help him unload it, Chausie has ducked out of sight, and the pilot is left scratching his head.

"Welcome home, Elizabeth." I feel the plane rock, and now a man is blocking my path, but the greeting didn't emanate from him. The speaker is still seated in a black sedan with the door open and the interior light illuminating her platinum-blonde hair. After the man peruses the inside of the plane, he shifts to allow a better view of her.

"Or maybe, now that you're here," she says, "you wish to be called by your given name."

A pair of leopard patterned heels emerge, one at a time, to take their stand on the tarmac. The woman wearing them smooths the front of her khaki button-down shirt/dress and then lifts her face to me. Despite the unnatural sheen of her blonde bob, I can see that she's Native American.

"I'm Kimimela, with The Vigilance. We've come to bestow sanctuary."

This is Kimimela! If I weren't so unnerved by her appearance, and that of the formidable man barring my exit, I'd be *dying* to ask about her nagi and owl parents!

"How did you know I would be here?" I manage.

"We've been keeping track of you for some time. Ever since your uncle began to take such an interest in the Visions of Blood. I'm sure he's told you."

"We haven't had much of a chance to talk about it."

"Of course not," Kimimela says. "He hasn't had a lot of time for me as of late, either."

"What can I do for you?" I ask. I can still see the pilot, but I don't know where my partner has gone.

"It's more about what I can do for you. It's my job to collect and record all the sacred visions. But the Visions of Blood are of particular interest to me. *Blood* is crucial. We'd like to keep you from being drained of all yours if we can help it. Not that we'd refuse a bit in a chalice of our own." Kimimela's laughter tinkles like silver bells.

"Um, thanks." *Psycho.* I'm pretty sure this conversation would feel creepy no matter what predicament I was in. "I appreciate the offer, but I'm not going to—"

"It's not an offer, Love. We operate for the good of the people. We can't have you roaming about in the open, wreaking the kind of havoc that the last Elixir unleashed."

Same word Uncle Joel used. Elixir.

I rake the ground with my eyes. Where the heck is Chausie? He didn't leave me, did he?

"I can reunite you with your father."

I whip back to Kimimela where I freeze like an ice sculpture and feel the conflict as cold in my mind.

"With one phone call, I can have him brought to you, and you'll both be under the protection of The Vigilance."

I sip a stuttering, ragged breath. Can she? I think of how Uncle Joel warned me to go directly to the Oglala woman and not to let anyone dissuade me. But how well do I really know my uncle? If Kimimela could get my dad freed and if I could be with him, then I wouldn't have to figure all this out on my own. I'd have my dad. I'd know what was going on. I'd be protected. I'd—

"Aren't you worried for your father?" Kimimela continues. "Don't you want to talk to him? Seek his advice? I can make it happen."

Yes, I think. *Yes. And Yes.* Aloud I say, "My uncle told me to go somewhere else."

"Your *uncle* is the reason he's being detained," she snaps.

I blanch. I can *feel* the blood drain from my face while a triumphant smirk crawls onto hers.

"Something I've learned about your dear uncle, Love? He only shares what information will aid him in his own pursuits."

Kimimela does a superb job of casting doubt.

But Uncle Joel is family. He saved me before. He got me this far. Maybe she's lying.

"Look, I'm sorry you came out in the middle of the night," I say. "But I have no big plans to wreak havoc on anything. I just want to do my job and get back home to Georgia as quickly as I can, so I will not be accompanying you to The Vigilance."

"What job?" Kimimela growls.

Yikes.

I decide to seek refuge with the pilot. Maybe he knows where Chaus is. Yeah, I've been rolling around the idea of calling him Chaus. It just seems to fit, and I—

Scream. Because Kimimela's bodyguard throws a thin sack over my head. Why? Is it supposed to make me docile? It does not. I kick and I flail. And scream. As I may have mentioned. No way. No. Way. Am I getting kidnapped. I won't be able to get to my mother. And also, I DON'T WANT TO BE KIDNAPPED!

I'm more than the man bargained for. I can tell. Because he drops me. Right out of the plane and onto the ground. As I tear off the sack, I glimpse Kimimela's stupid, ugly, impractical, leopard-patterned pumps, and I run (I know. But apparently it's what is expected of one in such situations). Anyway, I *do* make an admirable attempt. But they have a car. So, that's not fair. Who could compete with that?

At least with the headlights behind me, I can see where I'm going. I make it as far as the metal hanger. Unfortunately, there are no doors on this side and no way to beat the car around the corner, so I guess my little bid for freedom has come to a tragic end. On the bright side, they stop instead of smooshing me against the building.

As Kimimela steps out of the car reciting stupid platitudes which I am not about to fall for, her henchman crowds my space. I'm trapped. I'm trapped, trapped, trapped. I'm standing face to face with this scary guy when, to my astonishment, two fury, brown mitts with curved claws fully unsheathed, wrap around him from behind and paint red stripes into his chest. The speed and accuracy with which the flesh is torn—it's artful. Calculated. I almost forget to be horrified.

What are the chances of being saved by two mountain lions in one *lifetime,* let alone one day?

The lion doesn't mean to kill the man. I don't think. But he sure as heck means to immobilize him.

I scream Chausie's name, but there's no Chausie around to hear it. Only the lion answers.

Kimimela is standing over the bleeding man, not with sympathy, but with a phone to her ear. She doesn't seem all that impressed by the wild beast, just as Kanji Brings Justice had not. Of course, right now, the lion's focused on *me,* so why should she care?

When the lion *lunges* at me, though, she's suddenly scared to death. "Don't you *dare* leave with that girl," she yells at it. "Don't you *dare*. I am calling your father right now. Do you hear me?"

The lion regards her with a snarl and then leaps at me, piercing me with one of its horrible screams along the way. I don't wait for it to land. I see an opening in the fence and I tear toward it.

I run. And I run. And I run. And always, the great cat is behind me.

He cuts me off so many times, I'm ready to give up and let him eat me. I've heard that mountain lions bury their kills between meals, though, and that is unacceptable, so I keep running, directed by his maneuvers, stumbling in the scant light that the moon provides, and wondering if anyone will ever find my body. Probably he's herding me to his feasting grounds, so he doesn't have to *drag* my carcass there. Or because I'll taste fresher the longer he waits.

Finally, I can't go on. I don't even care. "Just eat me," I tell him. "Or bury me. Or do whatever it is you do. But you should know that my parents could die too. So that's like three deaths, for only getting to eat scrawny me. And do you think that is cool? It is *not* cool!" I end up yelling at him.

The lion tilts his head in a way that tells me he's listening. I'm bracing myself, hands on knees, trying to catch my breath. He sniffs the air in all directions and then lies down, all the way down, belly on the ground.

"That was unexpected," I tell him. "Why are you doing that? Are you not going to eat me?"

He rolls onto one side and casts a look upon me which I swear means he thinks I'm dull-witted.

"You seem to exist," I say, clutching my side where it's cramping. "And yet you seem sentient. Are you the same lion who rescued me back home?" I rub my eyes. Maybe I'm an idiot. But I go to him. I sit down on my heels right beside him and ask, "Why aren't you going to eat me? Don't I taste good?'

At that, the lion licks me. A big dang lick from knee to hip. I think he's making fun of me. He nibbles my thigh. Hear me. He *actually* nibbles my thigh. Playfully (I think).

"If you're going to let me live," I tell him, "I have to get my partner back." The beast's long whiskers twitch. I think he's weighing his options. He sniffs the air again. He looks over my shoulder.

"Do you think you could help me?" I've lost my mind. "If you'll help me, then get up and I'll follow you." Immediately, he rises and plods ahead. "And stop jumping at me," I snap. "It's jarring."

The lion laughs. I realize that sounds lunatic, but the vocal thing that comes from his throat is laughter. In any language. Which means I amuse him.

I cast my eyes back the way we've come. The forest is thick with trees, and I'm pretty sure the ability to circumnavigate has *not* yet found me, but I feel certain we're marching in the opposite direction of Chausie. "Lion, we're going the wrong way."

The cat doubles back and head-butts me from behind. When I don't obey, he chomps his teeth. "If you bite me, I'll punch you in the nose," I threaten him. Not that he cares. "I can't leave my partner behind. What if he's in trouble?"

I don't know what to say, except that the intelligent look with which the big cat fixes me is enough to keep me moving. And hoping and trusting that I'm doing the right thing. That Chausie isn't trapped or harmed or—I sigh. "I keep losing people," I tell the cat.

On throughout the night we walk until I literally fall asleep while standing upright (because I'm just like a horse!). Shortly after, I collapse (because, turns out, the last parenthetical statement is false).

When I awake, the lion is lying beside me. Close and heavy and warm. It's cold out, so I'm grateful for him. I stroke his fur, and he stretches his head back over his shoulder to acknowledge me. Or to push some courage into me. Or because his ear itches.

I used to have a big black lab. He would lie against me like that. Only, this lion's probably a hundred pounds larger. And my dog was already quite large.

Above us, the spruce trees reach out to one another, creaking with comforting forest sounds. Their needles canopy us. I'm enjoying the view of treetops swaying against the brighter night sky when I become aware of faces staring down at me. They belong to gangly-legged creatures who are balancing upon the limbs. Some of them sit and kick their feet and cock their heads at me from one side to the other.

"Canoti," I whisper. "That's what they must be." The lion follows my eyes upward, but I don't think he can see them. I don't ignore them, though. I don't remind myself they're not real. Because they are. It's not breaking the rule if I talk about invisible creatures to an animal, is it?

I describe them to the lion. "My grandmother, my oonchi used to tell me stories about those creatures. Peaceful tree dwellers. They're curious about travelers, sometimes mischievous. She called them canoti."

The lion searches for them.

"They're like wispy sprites," I continue. "Long, graceful leaf ribbons. They pop into view and out again. That's why the branches are rustling."

A deep rumbly sound means my lion is impressed.

The rustling becomes a song, or I interpret it as one, and as it forms, I whisper, "Can you hear that?"

Oh, how my heart pangs with the love and the loss of my oonchi because now I recognize the song. She would sing it to me when I was sleepy. She sang it the last time I saw her. A song about becoming light. One of the lines always stuck with me: *The dove takes flight on the magpie's light where spears of frost-like flowers grow.*

The Canoti aren't singing in English, but it's lovely all the same. No wait, they are now. Or am I just able to understand them now? "'The elixir pumps through a lion's heart,'" I tell the lion. "That's what they're singing. Oonchi sang it differently: 'The elixir *owns* a lion's heart.' And here I am in Oonchi's world sleeping next to a lion. What do you think of that?"

The lion lays his big noggin down on the ground, and I stroke his ears as I listen. The elixir. Or is it the Elixir, capitalized, the way Uncle Joel and Kimimela seem to say it? And what would that mean for me?

The song continues. "Oh, and I never could bear this part," I say. "Much less tonight as I gaze between the branches. 'The stars tremble. The stars tremble in fear.' I swear I think they are trembling right now."

On that precious night, when my oonchi hugged me for the last time, it was like she hugged my very heart. She warmed me inside out and told me to be very brave. She even called me her little wichahapi, the word for star. She said that she could see with her own eyes my beautiful, bright light.

In the morning, I ran from my room calling for her. I spread the news throughout the house. "Oonchi visited last night!" Rounding the corner into the kitchen, I found my mom with her arms around my dad, both of them standing against the counter. Daddy had a phone in his hand, but he wasn't holding it to his ear. He was crying.

Oonchi's funeral was high up in the Black Hills, not far from where this lion and I lie right now. My dad was holding my hand when Oonchi stepped right out of me and went to the Wakan Tanka, the Great Spirit. Daddy felt her go, he'd said.

Uncle Joel had been watching us. "She's a gatekeeper," he'd told my dad, about me.

"For her oonchi," Daddy said. "Not for anyone else."

"Blood for body. Light for soul. She could save them all."

"Keep your voice down," my dad hissed.

Uncle Joel tried to reason with him. "She should get to decide for herself, Hawk. She should be raised with a love for her people and the wisdom of who she is." My dad walked us away before Uncle Joel could finish. I remember the smack of Uncle's hands hitting his thighs in frustration. Daddy urged me forward, but I turned to see my uncle's conflicted expression. Conviction. And helplessness.

If Uncle really is the reason Daddy's being *hosted* by the Council, maybe it's because he's sick of Daddy keeping secrets.

I fall asleep to that lovely song, and I dream of a crow, and a dove, and a chalice of blood and light. I dream that Chausie has caught up to us, and he's happy because his leg isn't hurting. He's so happy he kisses me on the lips. He keeps remarking upon it until I remember that I'm dreaming, but he still doesn't know. And now I wish, more than anything in the world, I could make him well. He's sitting on the other side of my cat. Or no, he's sort of occupying the same space. Dreams are weird. I hope he's OK.

When I awake for real it's because my feline companion is licking my face with his sandpaper tongue. The sun has risen, and it's time to go. We trudge on. I trust this cat. I know it's odd. But I do.

Soon, we're out of the forest and wading through a sea of tall grass. My phone's almost dead. There's hardly any reception anyway. I try my mom. No answer. I try my dad. I make the lion turn around so that I can take a selfie of us, and I tell him about my oonchi, and the dreams, and the flowers Uncle Joel left in my locker. I rake the long grass with the palms of my hands.

"Do you think the wildflowers miss it here when they get cut?" I ask. He doesn't know.

The lion leads me to a small spring, where we both drink for a long time, and I splash my face. "How did you know where to find the water?" I ask. If lions can be self-satisfied, this one is. He lifts his head, water dripping from his muzzle, and draws himself into the most regal of stances—like he's sitting on a throne. "You're very handsome," I tell him. "And you know it, don't you?" By the way he drops his big head, I'd think my words embarrass him—if I didn't know better.

The break's over too soon and my lion walks away, throwing a look at me to follow. I'm not sure how much further I can go. It would be easier, psychologically, if I knew how much time it was going to take. And also if I was certain that my guide was leading me somewhere I needed to go. When I don't get to my feet right away, he makes an impatient noise.

"I'm *coming*," I tell him. "Honestly. Why don't you use some of that catty know-how to find breakfast? There were snacks in my bag, you know. There were wasabi almonds." My bag's probably still sitting on the Jacksons' lawn where I dropped it when the crow man introduced himself. "I love wasabi almonds," I sigh. "Hey, can you take down a bison? I could go for a bison burger."

My lion laughs at me. He does that a lot. I don't mind.

Several more hours go by, with us traversing the vast frontier. My lion has stopped laughing. He has stopped padding in those graceful, even steps, and now that I study him, his gait seems uneven.

"Lion, are you hurt?" I ask him. I run my hand over his back hip, and he turns on me with an awful hiss, his teeth bared in warning. "Hey, that's not nice!" I yank my hands to myself to keep them from being snapped off.

When I'm sure he's not going to kill me, I say, "I was just trying to help. What's got you all hissy?"

This whole walking tour is wearing thin. The ground is hard. My legs are tired. My stomach is empty. My lion is grumpy.

"What the heck is in the distance?" I ask—if just to fill the void.

White towers, like ancient ruins, jut into the sky as far as I can see. I intuit what they are because the place has been aptly named. The Badlands. It's like a different planet. Crumbling buttes and rock spires. An abrupt end to the vegetation. I've seen the pictures, but they don't even... There are horizontal lines running across the expanse, and even though the ivory towers aren't connected to one another, the lines match up. The walls on both sides of our stairs looked that way after our basement flooded.

When I turn to my lion, he isn't paying the least bit of attention to me or to the landscape ahead. He's gone dead still, his nose slightly lifted, his ears swiveled like satellite receivers. Only his yellow eyes rove to and fro.

6
I HATED THAT SNAKE

BEAM

Suddenly, my lion pounces. On me. He winds me as he knocks me to the ground and covers me so that I'm unable to move. "Get off of me!" I punch at him, but he reprimands me with a throaty growl and flattens himself. "What are you doing?" I object. But then I hear it. A helicopter chopping the sky. And I lie still until I can see it coming this way. It's slow and low to the ground.

I squeeze my eyes shut, hoping that the lion's brown fur is enough to camouflage us. He doesn't move. I don't even think he breathes.

"Chausie. Louris," a woman's authoritative voice demands through a speaker. "Show yourself."

"Chausie?!" I shriek and squirm to escape my lion's grasp. I might as well be squished under a boulder. His muscles tense around me making it impossible for me to breathe, much less move. When I stop struggling, he gives back the hair's breadth of room I need to gasp for air, but still, his yellow eyes follow the helicopter.

It's close now. So close that I can make out a few human forms inside. If it keeps its course, it will fly on by us.

"Was it Kimimela?" I ask once it's out of sight. "They don't know where Chausie is. Is that a good thing? Do you think he's OK?"

My companion, who is still listening for the chopper, turns to regard me, and something strange begins to happen to the shape of his back, almost the way you might shrug off a coat. But that stops when the helicopter swings out wide, and now he is pushing me to get me moving. His urgency frightens me. We run.

Over the next few hours, this happens twice more—only the third time, I sense my lion's advance and raise my hand to block it. "I can get on the ground by myself. I don't need you to squash me again."

Evening arrives before we leave the grassy plains, and so it is through shadows that we enter the foreboding terrain of The Badlands. The very ground seems to disintegrate under our steps. Occasionally chasms beckon me to explore the interior of the rock. They could be openings into the grave. Or into hell. Or...I don't know, but I get all the folklore. It's no wonder this place inspires so much wonder.

We sleep surrounded by taller buttes, but under the open sky. I thought the grass was uncomfortable. Rock is worse. But it is *so* worth it to witness the glory of the night sky here. Anyway, I practically use my lion as a mattress. He allows it. I think it's his way of apologizing for nearly mauling me earlier.

I can't believe any of this is real. I take a snapshot, in my mind, of what I look like lying on a rock spire, under countless stars, on top of a mountain lion. What would my mother say?

Have you ever encountered a place and felt such a deep connection to it, that you were overcome with the sense that you belonged to it? Not that it belonged to you. But that you actually belonged to it? That's what I feel now, and a profound sense of gratitude. It keeps the overarching dread about my parents' well-being from tormenting me. I want to console the trembling stars, but I think tonight they are consoling me.

My lion is alert. I don't think he sleeps at all. When I shift my weight, he kisses me. I mean, he licks me, but it's very comforting. It fills me with longing, which is also slightly disturbing. I'm not sure I've felt as intimate with any of my human friends as I do with this animal. He nudges me awake before sunrise and insists that we get moving.

Around noon, at least I think so from the way the sun is positioned (yeah, I'm practically an Eagle Scout at this point), I hear someone playing a maraca. Does walking through a desert of sedimentary rock cause hallucinations? Who could be playing that maraca? An obscure memory comes to mind: *What to listen for while hiking. A rattling sound can indicate—* Before I can identify the diamond shapes on its back, the snake has already sprung at me. But my lion has sprung too, and the snake recoils. When it strikes again, it sinks its fangs into the chest of my lion. He doesn't whine. He doesn't move a muscle. He just waits to see what will come of this.

I flash with rage. I am livid. I *hate* that snake for striking my lion. I feel the hate as liquid fire throughout my body. It's all very unreasonable and very unlike me, but I snatch that snake right off the ground by its stupid throat, and I glare into its stupid face.

So, it bites me.

It *does* hurt. In case you're wondering. But mainly I worry I've been poisoned. I haven't. The snake seems to have been poisoned, instead. It straightens out like a stick, and I throw it down, where it kind of implodes.

"How about that?" I ask my lion, feeling quite pleased with the results of my idiocy.

But my precious friend, my lion, begins to seize. I scream out for him. I knock him over in my rush to get to him. It's also possible that he was already collapsing at the same time my small weight accosted him. I grab his heavy head and look into his yellow eyes. They're beginning to loll. *No. No. NOOO.*

"Lion?!" I yell. "Please be OK!" I search around in desperation for some way to help, but it's futile. I'm worthless. "You can't die!" I choke out, and I grab the scruff on the sides of his neck. I heave up his head. "You can't leave me! Oh God, please don't die."

In response, he attacks me. I can't believe it. He draws deep gashes down my left shoulder. I'm pouring blood. He laps up the streaming rivulets like he's thirsty as can be. I don't remember anything else.

CHAUSIE

That snake is dead, and I didn't kill it. I stare down at its mummified carcass and try to piece together what's happened. Beam passed out, and she's still unconscious. There's a lot of blood. Why wasn't I more careful? I rip a swath from my shirt to bind the wound.

I call her name. Repeatedly. I've killed her. What if I've killed her?

Also, why do I feel like I could lift up this whole mountain? Or run a lap around the world?

BEAM

I come 'round. I'm too groggy to focus. My arm's been bound. "Lion?" I call. In response, a man's voice tells me to take it easy.

"Chausie?!" I bolt to sitting, wincing from the pain in my arm, but throwing the other around his neck. "I thought I'd lost you! Are you OK?"

And here we go. The waterworks. Why do I have to sob like a little child right now? "How did you find me? How did you—" I can't finish because of the crying.

Chausie is very tolerant of my emotional state. Much like my lion. He hugs me back. When he pulls away, it's to rub a thumb over my cheek, smearing tears across what must be bite marks. He's looking at me like he's never seen me before. "I'm good as new," he says, reminding me of something I can't quite put my finger on. "Better. Actually. Beam, I think I know what they want for ransom."

I don't even know what he's talking about, but I don't have time to think about it.

"Have you seen my lion?" I sniff. "Is he OK? Have you seen him?!" I use my grip on Chausie's neck to rise to my feet, and I stagger around like a drunk person.

"Settle down," Chausie says. "You were bitten by a rattlesnake." He looks under his lids at me, to make me know he's serious.

"I'm fine," I say. "I'm fine." I glance around for confirmation that I'm fine, and that this is just a trifle.

"Beam," Chausie says, "That snake bit me. And then it bit you. And then it died. It did not die because of *me*. It nearly killed me."

"Chausie, *you're* OK. What about my lion?"

He gives me a shake with both hands. "Beam!"

"Ow!" I snap. "What?!"

When he pins me with his yellow eyes, his beautiful, strange, yellow eyes—I draw in the breath of my life. Maybe bigger than the first breath I ever drew. When I was pushed out of the womb, and all the...stuff drained out of me.

"You're *him*?!" I say. "You're my lion?"

"Yes. *More* importantly...your blood saved me."

"You're a *lion*?" I hear how incredulous I sound, and, trust me, it does not communicate the extent. "You're my lion, Chaus?"

CHAUSIE

I should have led with the fact that I'm a lion. That was an oversight. She doesn't know *anything*. And she's in shock. I study her with fingertips covering my mouth. "Yes," I say. I give it time to sink in, very much hoping that I will still get to hear her call me *her* lion after she remembers I nearly bled her to death. I worry my bottom lip.

"Beam?" How does one say this? "I'm sorry I scratched so deep."

"You're a *lion*?!" she yells.

I can't help it. She makes me laugh.

"What the *hell*!" She wriggles her hand out in front of herself. "Show me."

I do.

"Oh my *gosh*! You are *kidding* me!" She holds my feline face in her hands and searches my eyes. She's shaking her head and drawing circles through my fur, making me feel like I'm the best thing she's ever encountered. "You're my lion, Chaus?" I give way to all the catlike tendencies I've been dying to, rubbing my chin and ears against her.

"This is so cool," she says.

I resume my human form, and then she slaps my arm.

"*Ow.*"

"Why didn't you do that before and let me know?" she demands. "You should have told me!"

"I *did* tell you. On the plane."

"You did not. I think I'd remember if you said you were a mountain lion."

"I told you I was Igmuwatogla."

"You know good and well I don't know what that means. I thought it was another tribe. I told you all kinds of things, you ass." She ends up laughing. "I was *worried* about you."

"I'm sorry." I do have the sense to look apologetic.

The truth is that, at first, I had to keep her moving, and I had to be ready to protect her. I'm not as hindered by my injury when I'm in lion form. But also, I'd been surprised by the strength of my feelings for her, and I have to treat this like a job if I'm going to convince my dad I can be of use. After that, well it was just kind of fun. I rub a hand over my mouth to keep a smile from forming and tell her that—

"We need to keep moving." Which is true. As much as I'd like to take more time for this little joy-fest, there's no telling who's out to get her, or what lengths they'll go to. I wonder how they know what she is.

"Lead on, O King of Beasts," she sings.

"You need to take this seriously," I scold her.

I think I may be better company as a cat.

"I'm too relieved to," she says, but she follows after me.

"And," I say over my shoulder, "*King of Beasts* is a term used for *African* lions. It's a bit of a sore spot for us."

"*Us?!*" she yowls. So, as we walk I tell her about my dad, and how The Outpost is run by humans who can shift. There are only a few of us born to a generation, if any at all, and all of us are supposed to go through training, though not all of us will dedicate our lives to it the way I want to. My best friend, Grant, wants to study geology. He spends most of his free time underground.

She has questions.

Are you able to shift from the time you're born? No. It starts around ten years old. How do your clothes shift with you? That takes practice, actually, and there are some awkward moments. Is your mom a lion too?

My mom. I need to call her. Even though I know there's no signal, I pull out my phone to check. "No. Mom's not a lion."

I enjoy her chatter. It's *nice* to be human with her, and there are only a handful of people I can say that about. She's good-natured. She's easy. And, *gah* I just feel so *good*. I come to a halt. My hip. I work my knee up and around. There's no pain. At all. It's totally flexible. "Beam, my—" I turn to find that she's fallen behind. "Beam?"

Doubling back to her, I make her sit down. "You're pale. I'm pushing you too hard. You gotta tell me." I can feel my brow knitting as I bring out my collapsible bottle. "Rest here. You need to build back your blood supply. I'll go find water."

"No, don't leave me." She feels vulnerable. She looks it. Her voice is small.

"I'll lion up and I'll find it fast. You need it." She reluctantly agrees. I'm back within half an hour, feeling guilty that I'm stronger than ever—and really enjoying it—while she's paying the price. She's leaning back against a sad little juniper tree when I plop down beside her, dropping the bottle onto her lap, and she smiles without opening her eyes.

"You're a lion," she says. When she starts stroking my fur, I roll over onto my back. "You're more playful as a lion." The next thing I do is grandstanding. I know it. But she's so taken with me in this form, I can't resist. I lay my head on her lap and purr. She squeals about it. She actually squeals.

I drop the lion to remind her to drink. "You don't look as pale now," I observe. I'm glad to see it.

"I think I was just going too fast." She drinks, then offers me some.

"You drink it, Swee—" The word falls away as I resist the shocking urge to call her *Sweetheart*. I cover over it with, "I've had plenty."

Something has changed.

I check her shoulder wounds to keep from looking her in the eye. It isn't bleeding anymore.

"You feel bad about taking it from me," she says, "but I don't."

"How can you not be mad at me?"

"You were in pain. You were just acting out."

"I was *dying*. You were pleading with me not to. All of a sudden you were"—I try to find a way to describe it—"the way back. I smelled my own *survival* inside you. I mean, I could *taste* it. I *had* to get to it. What if I'd hit an artery? What if I'd—"

"You didn't," she cuts me off. "You didn't, Chaus. You clawed my arm. Not my neck. Not my...guts or something. I saw you do it. You weren't hunting. You didn't sink your teeth into me. You were desperate to live. And I'm glad you did it." I turn away, but she guides me back. Her face is set, stubborn, and hard, and I can clearly see her Lakota heritage now. "I'm glad you did it," she insists. "You saved *my* life. That's the only reason you were dying to begin with."

"Gah, you're beautiful," I blurt out. I hear myself and—"Sorry."

A slow smile curves her mouth. "You can say whatever you want," she tells me. "You're a *lion*."

Some kind of goofy sound escapes me that I guess is a laugh. I'm not sure how else to respond, but Beam seems satisfied. I use the bite mark on her cheek as an excuse to touch her.

"Is it sore?"

"Not really. Are you wearing its twin?"

I stretch the front of my shirt to find out, but there's no sign of it.

"It wasn't just the snake bite you healed," I tell her. "My leg. My hip. It doesn't hurt at all. It's not even stiff." I lift and rotate my leg to show her.

"Are you serious?" she asks. "That's great! You can play basketball again. You can get your scholarship back!"

I snort out a laugh. Chick's one-track about college plans.

"I mean—if you want to," she says.

"Or I could finish up here," I tell her. I can't even *believe* my luck. "Catch up with the others. Maybe start at The Outpost right away." And yet, I'm beginning to realize that living thousands of miles away from her is no longer an option. "Anyway, I guess I'll finish out the school year and get my diploma."

She nearly chokes. "You *guess?*" And that makes me laugh too.

"I will," I assure her. "I will do it. If only to maintain your ideal of how the world should be."

"You just don't really care about what you're supposed to do, do you?"

I think about that before I answer. "I just don't think that other people should get to decide what I'm supposed to do."

We sit in silence for a few minutes. She needs food. I look around for a place to tuck her away, somewhere we could risk a small fire.

"Do you think if I help you, you could climb up into that outcropping of rock? I need to get you some food, get your blood volume back up."

"I can do it," she says.

We find a small nook, and I ask her to rest while I perch above the ground. I watch. I wait. Beam falls asleep.

When she wakes up, it's to the smell of roasting hare. "I hope it'll be OK," I tell her. "It's probably not what you're used to eating. But at least it's cooked."

"It smells great. Thank you." She takes a timid bite and then another not-so-timid one. "This tastes great! Why aren't you eating?"

"I did," I tell her. I don't elaborate. Not sure how comfortable she'd be with my raw meals, even if I am in lion form. She's lucky I found somewhere to clean up. I lean back beside her.

"There's something I don't get," I say. "Your blood healed everything that was wrong with me. Why did it have such an adverse effect on the snake?"

I'm really just thinking out loud. I'm not prepared to watch Beam's sweet eyes fill with malice or hear her simple answer stab sharp as a dart.

"I *hated* that snake."

BEAM

I can't remember ever hating anything more. I mean, I've been disappointed in my lifetime. I've been hurt, indignant. But now I truly know what it is to loathe something. I'm glad that snake is dead. I feel one hundred percent justified. It could have *killed* my lion.

The further into the Badlands we climb, the more time Chaus spends as a cat. He'd be able to move much faster without me. He wouldn't have to search walkable paths for human feet.

He sniffs the air. He scratches the rocks. Sometimes he stands as still as the statue in front of the zoo. He's able to find water and, yes, more meals. It's quite an experience. I'm not sure what directional clues he discovers, but we continue for another day and a half. Which puts me three days from the deadline.

If this woman we're trekking across South Dakota for can't give me the answers I need, I'm just going to have to figure out a way to show up at those coordinates. What if Mom can't hold out for that long? What if she is fighting for her last breaths right now? Thinking about that makes me whistle like a tea kettle, and Chausie becomes a man at my side.

"What's wrong?" he asks.

"How long can a person survive without their own soul inside them?" I ask. "Because the more I think about it, the more sure I am that that's what the video reveals. Why can't my mom get back into her body? It looks healthy enough. Maybe—" I don't want to say it. "Maybe something else is living inside her."

"Like a nagi?" Chaus asks.

"That's exactly what I mean. You know about them?"

"I don't have any experience with them, but I've heard stories."

"Maybe I should have gone to the Council," I say. "Demanded to see my dad. But Uncle Joel said not to. And President Tumbling Rock seems to have authorized people to kill me."

Chausie *pffs*. "That man at your house did not speak for President Tumbling Rock. Is that what you think?"

"You don't think he came on behalf of the Council?"

Chausie shrugs. "I have no idea, but Tumbling Rock didn't give him permission to *kill* you. I've met him. I've been in the same room when he's worked with my dad. He's a good leader. Honorable. Fair. The people love him."

"Then why is he holding my dad hostage?"

"You don't really know that that's what happening, do you?"

"I know that my dad would have answered my calls if he could!" I huff. "I know that he would have tried to get a message to me."

"I think you should trust your president."

"He is not my president!"

Chausie frowns at me. "You keep saying stuff like that. Why are you so ashamed of this side of you?"

"I'm not *ashamed*." I walk ahead grumbling, "You wouldn't understand. Just shut your face." But then I dial it back. "I'm sorry. That was rude."

Surprisingly, I find Chausie holding back a grin.

"You're amused."

"Kind of," he agrees. "I haven't been told to shut my face since I was in, like, fourth grade."

"You do that same exact expression as a cat, do you know that?"

We walk on. A full minute goes by before I admit that—"You're right. I don't embrace this side of me. But I've never been allowed to. I've never been taught about it. So, I don't have the same innate sense of belonging here that you do."

Although, that's not entirely true, is it? I think about the night we spent up high, and I traveled the white roadways of the stars with my eyes. I felt as much a part of that scene as if I were born to it. Which I was.

"What's going through your mind?" Chausie asks, and I realize that I've stopped walking again. He tucks my hair behind my ear and searches my face in a way that makes me wonder what's going through *his* mind.

"Do you think we're doing the right thing, Chaus? Not going to the Council? Not fighting to see my dad?"

I really just want reassurance, but when his mouth thins, I doubt that I'm going to get it.

"I do," he answers slowly. "But this woman we're going to see... Do you have any idea how she's connected to all this?"

"No. Except that she's some kind of historian."

"Why would your uncle send you on a vulnerable trek across the Badlands when my dad's whole career has been built on keeping the peace out here? Is this lady able to protect you?"

"I think she's able to educate me," I say. "Tell me what to do next."

"And she knows that how?"

"I don't know, Chausie." I'm feeling flustered again. "It's what we're supposed to do."

"You're smart," Chaus says. "You're brilliant. You didn't question it?"

"Well, between the moment I found out about it and the moment I got shoved onto the plane, I didn't have much time to, did I?"

"It's just that—it's really important for me to do well here too, so that I can—"

"Impress your dad?" I butt in.

Chausie's ears flatten against his head—well, they would've done if he was a cat. His forehead sort of tightens and he looks a little pissed. I guess we've both touched a nerve.

"Is that so wrong?" he asks. "As long as you get what you need?"

I don't answer him, so he continues. "But the only way he's going to be impressed is if I can deliver you to the right place without you being harm—" He glances at my shoulder where blood shows through the makeshift bandage and ends his sentence with an injured sigh. *Harmed.* Without me being harmed.

"It's not your fault," I say.

"Oh, did some other lion claw you up?"

"Chausie, if you had died back there, then I would have died too. I can't take care of myself out here."

"My dad would've found you. He's probably out looking for us right now."

"But you're going to take me to the woman, right?" I ask in a panic. "It's the one thing we've been instructed to do."

Chausie peers down his nose at me. "Following orders brings you a lot of comfort, doesn't it? Do things always go right for you when you do what you're told?"

"You're not being nice."

He gentles his tone. "I'm not being mean. I told you I'd take you, and I will. Though, Uncle Joel didn't seem all that confident about it himself."

He really didn't, but I feel better knowing Chausie's not going to deviate from the plan. "It's still *Uncle* Joel?" I tease.

"Yeah. But I still don't want you to be my sister." He shoulders into me with a reluctant smile and offers his hand. "Come on, partner."

It's amazing how soothing such a small gesture can be. We walk hand-in-hand and, for a while, I breathe easier.

CHAUSIE

We're close. But there are others around. I can't identify the smell, and it makes me wary. Not cats. Not coyotes. Not bison or bighorn sheep. What in the world can be roaming these rocks that I haven't run across before? I need to get Beam to our location, but I can't run her like she's a wild animal. She's sleeping now, up close to me. I'm tired too—finally running out of that juju blood juice. We found enough dry brush to build a fire, and the warmth of it makes me drowsier still.

By my estimate, we have another half day's walk ahead of us and a climb. It can wait till morning. Give her arm that much longer to heal. I think we're safe, backed under this rock overhang. It's defensible. It's discrete. The moon's bright outside. The fire's dying. I let go of my lion and fall asleep uneasily, ears twitching.

The next thing I hear is Beam gasp. I jump into feline form and round on...nothing. I'm all senses alert. Sniffing, listening, pacing the tiny perimeter of our cave-like bed. I don't know what's wrong. I glance at her. She's glaring at me. I become myself again.

"Beam?"

She doesn't answer.

"Are you OK?" I start to fear the worst, but I can't locate the problem.

"I woke up, and you were sleeping beside me," she says.

"Yeah? And?" I've been sleeping beside her for days now.

"As a man."

"I don't understand."

She blushes and shakes her head. "Never mind," she says.

I'm at a total loss until—"You don't think I was trying to"—I wave a finger between us—"*do* something to you, do you?"

"No," she says shortly. "Of course not."

I'm at a loss. "Beam, it takes a lot of energy to maintain that form. I've been at it for days. I'm exhausted." My adrenaline rush is quickly ebbing into annoyance.

"That makes sense," she says. "I'm sorry." She takes a step toward me, but I hold up a hand to keep her from advancing.

"Just leave me alone for a while, OK?" I gruff. "I need some sleep. Don't go far. Just—OK?" I'm irritated because she scared me half to death. And I'm irritated because she doesn't trust me. And, if I'm honest, I'm irritated because she's so repulsed by the thought of lying beside me without me being some sort of a pet.

She nods and takes a seat against the rock wall, looking dejected. Now I'm irritated with myself. I lie down, facing away from her, and make a mental note to ask my dad how long he can remain in lion form.

BEAM

I shouldn't have freaked out. Whenever I wake up against the soft fur of my lion, I just snuggle into him, and I know it's Chausie, but also it's not. I've never woken up beside a man before. Except for my *dad* with whom I am inexorably safe. And I know I'm safe beside Chausie too, but...well, it's different. Not bad different. Not bad at *all*. Actually.

"Chaus?"

He doesn't answer. I get it. He feels jerked around. He thought we were being attacked or something. I probably offended him. And he does look pretty beat. I wrap my knees with my arms and lay my head on them.

"What is it?" he says, not unkindly, but without turning over.

I'm not sure what to say. "It just surprised me is all. I like being with you. I *love* being with you." I swallow. He's silent. "Look, I've never—" Why am I still talking? "You know..."

Shut UP, Mouth!

Chausie does turn to face me now. "Oh," he says too knowingly, and maybe he brightens some.

"Anyway, I'll leave you alone," I finish. Hopefully. "Get some sleep."

"Hey," he says. "I've never...you know...either. OK? And I'd never *take* anything from you. You know that, right?"

"Aside from my blood," I reason. He darkens instantly. "Chausie, I'm kidding! Please know that I'm kidding. We are so past tha—"

"Get over here," he says. The familiarity with which he demands it shows me he isn't upset. I crawl over to kneel beside him where he's propped up on an elbow. "Turn around," he says, and he draws a circle in the air to show me what to do. I start to, but he does the job for me, and tugs me against him, careful to avoid the claw marks. Now we're lying closer than before, my back to his chest.

"Is this OK?" he says.

It's the best thing I can imagine. "Yes," is all I say. "Thank you."

I feel his affirmation against my head.

"I'm gonna take care of you," he says. "And you're gonna take care of me. I don't think we need to worry about all the rest right now."

The fire pops, and the night thickens around us. Chausie's chest expands with a big inhale, and he sighs into my hair. I kind of love it.

"So, when you say you would never take anything from me," I venture.

After a slight hesitation, he replies with a guarded, "Yes?"

"You don't mean that you wouldn't take something I wanted to *offer* to you, right?"

I feel him smile in his response. "Right," he says.

"Just checking."

"But unless you want to offer me something *tonight,* you'd better let me fall asleep without putting thoughts into my head."

"I'll let you know."

His chuckle is deep and rumbly. He tightens his hold on me and kisses the back of my head. Then he pushes up to peep over at me, brushing hair from my cheek. "That was a give," he teases. "Not a take. In case there was any confusion."

It's all I can do not to roll over and kiss him right. Which is not like me at all. Maybe it is like me, and I've just never felt close enough to anyone to want to.

Chausie's already falling asleep. I try to lie still so I don't disturb him. My thoughts wind through mazes of unknowns. They look to me, in my exhausted state, to be travelers like we are, through the hoodoos of my mind.

Where the heck is Uncle Joel? Are my parents worrying about me? Are they in pain for any reason? I can't bear to dwell on that. What if Chausie hadn't taken my blood? What if he hadn't sensed that it contained what he needed, and I'd been left all alone without ever knowing he was my lion? I hug his arm to my chest.

Chausie's breathing is smooth, his body is warm, and his arm is heavily draped around me. I'm falling asleep. Strange faces morph before me. Bulging eyes and odd-angled noses. Horns. I don't mind strange creatures any more than I mind people who scowl.

Tonight, however, I can see them with my eyes closed. They take turns stooping to leer at me while I slumber. A few of them hop or crawl, and some of them glide. One slithers. More of them enter our space, and now I am growing uncomfortable with the sheer volume of them. Something's pressing on my chest.

I slide out of myself to look down on the scene from the ceiling of the shelter. I didn't know I could do that. I see myself lying next to Chaus, his face buried in my hair. There's a small creature stooping over us. It walks on two feet, but it's not human. I don't have any categories for what it *is*. It doesn't wear clothes, but it's not indecent. It doesn't have hair or fur. Its skin is smooth, and most of it is blue. It's because of what the creature is doing with its hands that I feel pressed, bracing itself to look into my sleeping face.

"Stop it," I say from above myself. "You're gonna wake up my cat, and then what will you do?" The creature yanks its gaze to where I hover, its large eyes full of amaze. I don't think it has a nose. But a small red mouth makes the shape of an O and a cute little howl accompanies the shape.

"Chenoa?" it says. Its high-pitched voice is sweet and pleading, and it tilts its head as if it's trying to surmise who I am, or maybe how it is that I came to be above myself. It follows my ethereal progress back into my body.

I'm awake now. I open my eyes.

So, I probably shouldn't still be seeing the little blue guy crouching in front of me. And I certainly shouldn't be communicating with him.

"Chenoa?" he asks again. The other creatures are no longer crowding us. Most have shuffled away. The few who remain, cautiously linger around the edges or stare out from a narrow crack in the rock.

"Don't wake my caaat," I warn in sing-song.

"Cats can't catch me," the creature brags. "Cats can't touch me." To prove it, he jumps both feet onto Chausie's side and then rebounds stiffly, falling to the ground and causing Chausie to *oof* in his sleep.

Now he's glaring up at me like I'm the one who pushed him down. "He's solid!" he says about Chausie.

"I know," I assure him. "Between you and me, I like that about him."

Chausie stirs, causing the blue guy to flinch so hard he flattens himself.

He makes me laugh. "What *are* you?" I ask him.

The creatures along the outskirts seem to take my tone as a sign they can relax, though I notice them throwing suspicious glances at my sleepy companion. Blue peels himself off the ground and moves delighted eyes around the room at them. He hasn't bothered to answer me. I'm not completely sure he understands the question.

"What are you?" I ask again. He isn't even *trying* to answer me. He reaches out to touch my nose, poking the soft part with one of four fingers on that hand. He pushes the tip down and then releases it. When my nose doesn't stay put, he blinks his enormous eyes and tries again. Apparently, my rebounding schnoz holds no small interest. I snort out of it, and he throws himself backward onto his behind—if he has a behind—which cracks me up. I keep it quiet, though.

"Do you have a name?" I ask.

The question stumps him. "I am called what you want to call me."

"How about Blue?" I ask.

"Hehehehe," he tinkles. "Hehehehe. I *am* blue!" He holds his stomach and laughs to his heart's content. Meanwhile, I stare in bemusement.

When I try to sit up, Chausie tightens his grip and mumbles, "Ten more minutes." When Blue hears Chausie's low voice, he shrieks, and Chausie tenses. I can tell that Chausie has raised an eye above my shoulder when Blue goes rigid and all the other creatures go absent.

"What is that?" Chausie croaks.

"You can see him?" I say. "I thought he might be invisible."

"Nope."

"I'm calling him Blue."

"Appropriate." Chaus sits up, rubbing his eyes. Meanwhile, Blue begins to wail like a bizarre weather siren. "Why is it making that sound?" Chausie asks.

"I sort of threatened him with your waking."

"Can you make it stop?"

"Blue, stop it," I snap. "It's too loud."

Blue chomps his mouth shut, but his eyes remain round and unblinking.

"Blue?" Chausie asks, and then he has to wait while Blue laughs his high-pitched hehehes and explains, again, that he *is* blue. "Are you a *prowler*?"

Now the azure fellow is taken aback. He gasps and squeaks, "The cat is talking to me! You made the cat to *talk* to me?!"

I shrug in response and shake my head. "What's a prowler?" I ask Chausie.

"A creature from the crevices. There are all kinds of them living below the buttes, but I've never run across one before. Some are friendly. Others..." Chausie fakes a shiver.

CHAUSIE

Telling Beam about the prowlers calls to mind some of the creepiest stories I've ever heard. The kind that used to keep me up at night, checking under my bed. Just how trustworthy is this one?

"You like Beam?" I ask him.

Blue nods emphatically. "I love light," he says. His voice is wispy and adoring.

"Yes, but, you love...Beam?" I motion to her to make sure the little weirdo knows what I'm asking.

"Oh yes. Oh yes," he trills. "Chenoa and all of her children." He lowers his voice to say, "Chenoa, the dove, she ate the Shadow for us."

"Do you know who this Chenoa is?" Beam asks and pulls out the necklace she wears to show me the dove stationed in the web.

"Sounds like one of your ancestors." Right now it's more important to me to make sure this prowler isn't going to do something horrible to us. "Blue, swear to me that you would never hurt us," I insist. "That you would never hurt Beam."

"No, I would never. I am bound to her."

"Then, swear it to me."

"It is my duty," he says.

He's not really giving the kind of pledge I'm asking for. "Swear it!" I demand and I get to my feet. "If it's your duty, then swear it to me!"

Blue is now hiding from me and quivering like a mouse, using Beam as a shield. She rubs his bald head soothingly and shoots me a look.

"I'm just making sure," I say.

"I swear it," he peeps.

I decide he's being honest. His solemn eyes spotlight me from around my girlfriend's—I mean, from around Beam's—I stifle a smile. Is she my girlfriend?

Whatever ridiculous expression is on my face, Beam questions it with a funny smirk.

"I like him," I say about Blue—as a redirect—and sit back down, causing Blue to swivel this way and that—like he wants to share this extraordinary turn of events with several others, but there is no one else around.

"Blue, what did you mean that Chenoa ate the Shadow for you?" Beam asks.

And just like that, his huge, happy eyes cloud up. "Chenoa wanted her family back. We told her noooo. We told her noooo. But *they* told her yesssss." He hisses the *yes*. "She opened the gates," he bemoans. "She opened all the gates."

Beam physically starts. "To the In-Between?!" she asks.

"To the In-Between," he confirms. "All the gates. All the tunnels. *All the prisons.*" He whispers the last.

"And the Lakota ancestors?" Beam says. "They're roaming the Earth now? Unable to go on?"

"No, Chenoa. They are In-Between. Cannot go back. Cannot go through. They linger."

It is no accident this prowler found us. Can't be. I can tell Beam thinks the same thing. "Blue, we need to know all about Chenoa," she insists. "It is very important."

Blue hops to attention, draws himself up, and bows dramatically.

From the side of my mouth, I say, "Is he about to perform for us?" And before Beam can answer, that is exactly what he does. You're not going to believe this, but he even picks up a British accent.

"In the sacred cavern," he says, "the warriors were banging their drums and dancing, dancing, dancing." With every *dancing*, Blue sways from side to side and flaps his hands. "We were all drawn to it, those of us who lived in the crevices. Your ancestors were drawn to it too." He walks his fingers across his arm to demonstrate. "Right down the tunnel, they came. Hundreds of them. Chenoa clung to the Earth

Gate and saw across to where they crowded their bars. She cried out for her parents and for the brother she had lost. Other gates became crowded as well. *Especially the prisons.*" He whispers that last part, but loudly, more of a whisper-yell.

"And then from all around, frightening creatures began to taunt Chenoa. They pled with her, lied to her. And the cavern was frantic with all the warriors dancing and drumming. She fell under the spell. She became convinced that she could rejoin her family if only she would spill her own blood to open the gates. Someone handed her the blade from which no wound can heal, and one by one, the gates swung open."

I can see that this is deeply unsettling for Beam. "She cut herself?" she asks.

Blue nods and makes a cruel slicing motion. "The prisoners trampled her down in their rampage. And when got into the cavern and saw all those young, frenzied warriors, they went on a killing spree. Do you know? The warriors kept on drumming, and dancing, and singing the whole time they were being slaughtered. I think they thought their ritual was *working*. Or maybe the prisoners were jumping around inside their bodies and that's why they kept moving." Blue pauses his remembrance to consider that.

"That's disgusting," I tell him, to which he just shrugs.

"Anyway, Chenoa came to her senses. Seeing the truth of what she had done, she fell to her knees and begged the Wakan Tanka to draw the evil creatures back to her in the In-Between. Everyone—not just the prisoners, but even the sweet, innocent onlookers like me" —*questionable*—"were compelled to appear. The ancestors slammed all the gates and Chenoa immediately wrestled the worst prisoner into her mouth, the Shadow, gagging and choking until it went down."

As if Blue has just remembered that he's on stage, he takes a moment to act out the gross process he has just described. Takes forever. Lots of sputtering and heaving. When he is *finally* finished, he says, "We had to run deep into Darkness to keep out of the way.

The prisoners make life very difficult. Plus, all your ancestors were wailing all the time. It was impossible to be happy."

"So, the In-Between is some sort of hub for otherworldly connections?" I ask. "Like a transcendental train station?"

"OK," Blue says.

"I'm asking."

"I'd like to ride a train. I've never gotten to ride a train before."

I raise my hands to question Blue's spotty ability to converse, which makes Beam snicker. She picks up where I left off.

"Blue, what is Darkness?" she asks. "You make it sound like a place."

"Darkness is nowhere. Except, I guess you could say it's where the In-Between loses its edges. It's dust. There's nothing to see. Nothing to hear. Not even your own voice. If you stay too long, you become a stranger to yourself."

"That sounds...unacceptable," I say.

"It was awful. But the ancestors became very strong and very capable, even in Darkness, and they rounded us up. Chenoa bled for ages. All the while, she wrestled the Shadow within herself, and all the while, a grandmother caught her blood so that it wouldn't re-open the gates—only they *did* open the gate to send the prisoners back. But the ancestors wouldn't free themselves. They refused to leave Chenoa, and then it was too late." Blue sniffs back a sudden sob and adds, "Chenoa's the reason they let *us* out, even though she was dying. She said they had to. They cracked the Earth Gate just enough for us to scoot into the cavern—and, oh, you should have heard the living members of your tribe weeping over all those slain warriors when they found them."

My stomach roils at the thought, and from the look on Beam's face, hers does too. The cavern must have been a bloody mess.

That space surely exists somewhere close to here, and now I'm wondering about the set of coordinates Beam was sent. At length, I ask Blue, "Where is the Earth Gate?"

"It is not where. It is when." He doesn't offer any more information than that.

"Blue?" I say through gritted teeth. "*When* is the Earth Gate?"

"When the light is no longer than the dark, and the dark is no longer than the light, and the veil between the living and the dead is thin. That's when."

"You mean Thursday?" Beam chokes out.

I peer at her. So does Blue. We seem to be having two different conversations.

"What? I'm a concrete thinker. I've been scouring the calendar since I got the text about my mom, and Thursday is the Spring equinox. Day and night are more or less equal in length."

"The same day you're supposed to show up as your mother's ransom?" I say. "That's when the gate can be found?"

"And opened," Blue helpfully offers.

A spider-like dread crawls up my spine. I don't like it. But at least now we have something to work with.

Beam is thinking along the same lines. She says, "Who would benefit from opening the gates?"

"The dead ancestors!" Blue volunteers and then lists others in rapid succession. "The dead warriors! The prisoners! The Shadows! The Shadows most of all! They need each other. They're no good apart. They were put in East and West prisons for that very reason."

Beam holds up a finger to halt his enthusiastic rant. "OK. Thank you for that. But who would benefit from opening the gates who could also have sent me a text?"

CHAUSIE

I smell them before I see them, but I don't lion up because I trust them, and because the two cats morph into human form as they enter our makeshift den.

My best friend, Grant, with his hallmark swagger, spots us and says, "Well, look what the cat dragged—"

"Don't!" Eden stops him.

"It's hilarious," Grant tells her.

"It's offensive."

"To whom?"

"To all of us, Grant. To everyone in here."

It makes me happy that some things never change. I join my friends, and the three of us press our foreheads together in greeting. It's a lion thing.

Blue is sitting on Beam's lap like a small dog—or a toddler—and when Beam stands to meet my friends, she lets him climb onto her hip.

"How long have you known we were here?" I ask my friends.

"Long enough to be burying your carcasses by now," Eden says. "You stink."

"How is *that* not offensive?" Grant asks, his hand lifted for emphasis.

"Because it's true. Dried blood and wet dog. And"—she sniffs violently—"other things."

Grant turns his attention to Beam. "Hola, Lakota," he says.

Eden rolls her eyes and, under her breath, she sings, "She's not *Mexican.*"

Meanwhile, Blue pulls himself to stand somehow on Beam's hipbone. To avoid being toppled over, Beam has to lean to one side. Now Blue is using her head as a resting place for his elbows. When Grant reaches out to shake her hand, she bunches her lips to convey how little control she has over the creature, so he pulls his hand back and then inches it forward again. It's all I can do to keep from laughing. He's not so damn sure of himself right now, as he usually is. "I'm—Grant," he stammers.

Blue makes ridiculous sucking sounds at him. It's a wonder my old friend doesn't bat him to the ground. I guess he grew up on the same scary stories about prowlers as I did.

When Beam finally manages to accept Grant's hand, the prowler nearly loses his mount, and she stumbles. Immediately, Grant steps in to bolster her and keeps her upright.

Eden looks perplexed.

"So, I take it this is the first time you've seen one too?" I ask.

Still entangled with Beam, Grant cuts his eyes at me like even *he* wouldn't have said that. He starts to speak but thinks better of it.

It's Beam who, after recovering her balance, says, "He's pretty cute, huh? Am I allowed to keep him, do you think?"

"*Chausie?*" Eden asks.

"What?" both Beam and I say at the same time. I'm answering Eden because I think she's called my name to get my attention. But now I think she's asking Beam if Beam means that *I'm* cute, and wants to keep *me.*

"Ow, Blue!" Beam interjects. "That hurts!" She grabs Blue behind the knees to tug him out of her hair, where he's trying to play swing-from-the-mast. I laugh and work to salvage what hair hasn't been ripped out by the roots. When we dislodge the little blue pixie, he folds his arms, like *he's* the one who's been wronged. "No, you don't get to sulk," Beam chastises him. "It's your own fault."

"He's ridiculous, isn't he?" I ask the room at large.

It's not until this moment that I notice the concern written in lines across the faces of both my friends.

"Chausie?" Eden asks. "Are you in your right mind?"

"Dude, we need to get you to your dad," Grant says. "Right away."

"They can't see him," Beam interprets. "They can't hear him."

"Nah," I laugh. She's serious. "Really? Blue?"

I turn to Blue for confirmation, but he's too busy pouting to give it. He pivots his seated body, using only his hands, to stare at the opposite wall.

"Remember how surprised he was when you spoke to him?" Beam asks.

You made the cat to talk to me?!

"Tell me, Blue" I prod. "Who can see you?"

The prowler huffs to show that he is not pleased. "Chenoa," he snaps. "*Only* Chenoa. Only Chenoa's children." He dismisses me with a wave of his four-fingered hand. "*You* are a fluke."

I jerk my head toward Beam. "Are you getting this?" She's cupping her arm where I scratched it. Her eyebrows are scrunched together in thought. Those creatures in the forest... I couldn't see them then. I wonder if I'd be able to now. "You turned me int—" I begin, but Beam shakes her head in a small but clear message to hush. She turned me into an omnituens, though. I search around for any other invisible I might be able to see.

"Guys?" Grant asks. "Let's get you to The Outpost before you go insane. Kimimela's coming to see your dad. She'll know what to do."

"No, we're not going to Kimimela," Beam blurts out.

"Don't be crazy," Eden says. "The Vigilance was practically *designed* for you!" Eden turns to me for backup I can't give.

"We're not going to The Vigilance," I tell her.

"OK, well, just come to The Outpost." Eden glances between us. Beam's shaking her head. "What are you even doing out here then?!" Eden snaps. "Where in the world are you trying to go?"

That is an excellent question. Suddenly, the reason that *Beam's uncle Joel told me to take her to a crazy old hermit woman* seems embarrassing. Especially compared to taking her straight to the power and influence of my own people. This wouldn't please my dad at all. It's just going to make him doubt me even more. What am I doing? Beam's watching me, and I think she can sense my inner turmoil. She's wearing the stubborn chin through which she defied me before. She's not even going to entertain the conversation again.

That stings my pride. I want to buck against her just to assert myself. I can feel my nose shrugging like I'm about to hiss when— without any warning—Blue is all up in my face. He's huge! He's grown as tall as I am, taller, and his chest broadens into a solid mass. "Her blood calls to you!" he yells at me. "Do you have any idea what a gift that is?!" It's not the chirpy voice from before. It booms and reverberates through the overhang. Even my feline friends seem to notice it. "Silence your ego and swear to me that you won't harm her!"

He's using my own words against me. I'm shaking my head without realizing it.

"I'm not going to harm her," I protest.

"Swear it!"

"I do."

"Open your eyes, *Cat!* Even your friends have her in their sights."

That works like a slap in the face. Eden and Grant have moved forward in the time it takes for Blue to scold me, and Beam observes them stonily.

"Let me get Goliath," Blue tells her. He's sitting on her shoulder again. Dude can move through space. She shakes her head. Does she even know what he's talking about? "Command *me*, then," he pleads with her. "Set *me* as your guard. Lions are unreliable, Chenoa." Beam shakes her head again.

"Chausie's not." She only whispers it.

"Not anymore," I tell her. I'm standing by her side, and I'm looking at my friends with new eyes. "Who told you we were coming?"

"We were just out hunting, Chaus," Eden says. She's lying to me. I can't believe it. I glare at her until I fear I'll do something I'll regret, my jaw clamped so tight the muscles start to complain, but I dare not relax it. I don't know which set of teeth I will bare if I do.

Turning my back on Eden, I address Grant. "Why is The Vigilance coming to visit the lions? When have they ever cared to do that before?"

Eden inhales to respond, but I round on her. "Do *not* speak to me! *Ever* again." I find myself hulking over her, pointing a finger in her face. I've never dealt harshly with Eden as far as I can recall, but I'm furious she's lying to me, and if she opens her mouth right now, so help me... She crosses her arms and remains silent. I measure my tone. "Grant?"

"They told us you were in trouble, Chaus. They told us the Lakota could be messing with your mind." Grant glances furtively at Beam. "It's not hard to believe when you're reacting to things that aren't there."

"Who is *they*?" I demand. "Who told you?"

"Your dad, Man. Your stepmom."

BEAM

I swear I can *feel* the wave of nausea my lion suffers over this betrayal. First his friends and now his dad, who hasn't come himself, but has sent these underlings to fetch him.

Instead of succumbing, Chaus stands straighter. He sharpens his focus. He lowers his voice—and says the last thing I expect to hear. "My dad got married?"

"You didn't *know*?" Grant answers.

I want to go to Chausie and comfort him. His face has gone pale. But he remains sharp as he subtly shakes his head.

"Oh, Man. I'm so sorry. I—"

Chausie cuts him off. "Tell me what you've heard about Beam."

Grant answers immediately. "That she's a threat to the peace. That she can open some kind of invisible prison that could devastate our world. She may even want to unleash her ancestors upon us."

I *pfff* at this, but Chausie stays me with a glance.

"Does everyone believe it?" he asks.

Grant indicates that not all do. "I'm not sure your dad really does. He knows her uncle. Knew her dad. But many do believe it. Many of her own people. And they're afraid of her. They want her brought before a tribunal."

I'm reaching my threshold for this *Cat's Only* conversation, and while I'm growing more and more irritated with that, I'm growing more and more frightened by what is actually being said. No wonder Uncle Joel wants to keep me secluded.

"No, I don't mind being talked about like I'm not here," I spout. "At. All. I'll just go converse with Blue."

In *all* sincerity, Chausie turns to me and says, "Please don't converse with Blue right now. That is not going to be helpful."

I hear how seriously he has taken my sarcasm, and there's a pause, after which I start to laugh. Chausie realizes his mistake, and he starts to laugh too. The whole situation is ludicrous. Grant looks like he kind of wants to join in, but he's afraid we've gone mad. The she-cat doesn't know what to do with herself. She doesn't trust me. That much is clear.

Grant turns his eyes on me. "You really have a prowler in here?"

"Are you talking to *me* now?" I say.

"I am."

"He found us a few hours ago."

"Can you command him?"

Didn't Blue just use those exact words? "Well, when he was being super annoying I told him to shut up, and he did."

Grant snickers and looks me over a little too thoroughly. Then, he bestows upon me one, great, arrogant, upward nod. "How old are you?" Chausie shifts his weight. I can tell he does not love the evolution of Grant's tone.

I preempt any male ridiculousness with—"Old enough to know that I am not about to have *this* conversation." Chausie hangs his head. I think it's to hide a smile.

"You're very *pretty*," Grant says.

"Nope." I wag my head. "Nope. I already have *way* more cat-tosterone in my life than I can handle. *Way* more. I'm invoking my right to skip this little romp down *Who's Got the Bigger Mane Lane*."

"Cat-tosterone?" Chausie asks.

"Yup."

"That's *African* lions," Grant says and traces an outline of his face. "With the manes."

"Like I don't know that."

"Told you," Chaus mutters. "The struggle is real."

"I just think you could be a little more culturally sensitive," Grant says. "That's all."

The irony of his statement is not lost on any of us. It makes all of us laugh, even the she-cat—I would call her by her name if anyone would bother telling it to me. We all regard one another, and the tension clears somewhat.

"OK, she's cool," She-cat asserts. "I get why you trust her."

Chausie pins her with a sharp stare.

"Oh, *sorry*," she wheezes. "Permission to speak to Your Royal Highness again?"

"Permission granted," Chaus allows. "You sure you're not being bewitched?"

She-cat over-enunciates her next words and points at me. "Kimimela told us that *she* was dangerous. We were trying to help you."

"*She*...is Beam," Chausie says. "Beam, this is Eden."

Eden sizes me up.

"Kimimela wears leopard print shoes," I say. "Did you know that?"

She shrugs. "A statement of style."

"Or a declaration of hierarchy," I offer.

"Whoa," Grant says. We all tend to him because it sounds like he's made a significant connection, but he stares blankly at each of us in turn and then shakes his head.

I take up the slack. "My dad moved us away when I was a toddler because he feared what his people—" I glance at Chausie, but it just doesn't feel right to say *my* people. "What they might do to me. We're trying to get to someone who can help us figure out what's going on without risking too many people knowing I'm here."

"Why don't you get your dad to talk to Chausie's?" Eden asks.

That would be great, I don't say. *I can't even get my dad to talk to me.*

The weight of Chausie's gaze falls on me. He's asking permission to divulge the truth. I nod. So, he says, "Beam hasn't been able to reach her dad for days now. And her mom's been kidnapped."

Both Grant and Eden lean in with surprise.

"They didn't tell you *that* part?" he asks. "It's why we're here. Beam's supposed to trade herself for her mother's freedom."

There's a collective pause. "Who kidnapped her?" Grant asks.

Chausie indicates that we don't know and fishes a piece of paper from his pocket. "She was given these coordinates. I can't figure out what's there, and that's not where we're headed. But, from what we can gather, it's an underground cavern." The last part, Chausie says with a knowing look and offers the paper to Grant between two fingers.

Grant. The wannabe geologist. The one who spends all his spare time in caves.

Grant takes the paper. "I kind of think her uncle might be headed that way now."

"You do?" I bark.

"He came to The Outpost to talk to Chausie's dad." Chausie shifts uneasily. "Asked me about the ceremonial caverns. I didn't have much to tell. I mean, I can talk rocks all day, but I haven't explored that particular section. It's sacred to the Tribe. I can find out if the coordinates match up, though."

"Grant, what did he tell Dad about why I'm here?" Chausie asks.

"Not much, from what I heard. Seemed like your dad was pressing him for knowledge he couldn't supply. But after he left, that's when your dad sent us out. That was yesterday afternoon."

Blue suddenly makes me jolt when he materializes in front of my face. I didn't even realize he'd gone missing, but now he's here whistling and howling and...clucking. "Chenoa! More cats! Bad cats! They're going to *make* you go with them. You should *not* go with them."

Of course, Grant does not hear Blue. He's jabbering on about caving. "Stop!" Chausie and I both say, and Chausie grabs him by the shoulders. "They're coming."

Eden's eyes slide from Chausie to Grant. Her nostrils flare as she sniffs. "I don't—did the prowler tell you?"

Chausie considers me and swallows hard. He must feel all kinds of pressure to please his dad. I can't blame him for wanting to go to him now.

Despite the fact that I haven't spoken, he consoles me with, "Don't worry," and raises his voice to address Eden and Grant. "Guys, you are my oldest friends. Please let us go do what we came to do without giving us up. Please."

He takes my hand, and both friends key in on it.

"Oh, Chaus," Eden advises. "Use your head."

"I am, Edie," he says. "You *know* me."

A godawful scream cuts through the air like a banshee, causing the half of my blood that is Irish to run ice cold. I was weaned on such stories. They scream when someone's about to die.

Chausie senses my reaction. "It's only lions," he says.

Oh. I feel better.

"Just buy us some time," he pleads with his friends.

Grant takes another look at Chausie's hand surrounding mine. "Go," he says. He morphs into a lion before the word leaves his mouth, so it ends in a growl. He's shorter than Chausie in lion form, as he is as a man, and lighter in color.

Eden eyes me in a way that means she is not as eager as Grant to leave us. It occurs to me that she and I are similar. Neither of us can bear to disobey a direct order. She takes up her lioness and trounces into the early morning light.

"We're going to have to climb," Chaus tells me. He runs his hand up my arm to check on my shoulder. "Do you think you can do it?"

"Yeah, I can do it," I tell him. I'm not sure if I can, but I have to, so what's the point? "Chausie?" What I want to do is take time to gush with all kinds of gratitude for his faithfulness to me. Time we don't have. I hope he understands how deeply I mean it when I just say, "Thanks, Partner." Standing on tiptoe, I kiss his cheek, and he drops his hard expression for a moment. *Just* for a moment. Maybe not *even* a moment. Then, he says, "We gotta go."

CHAUSIE

I'm still holding Beam's hand as we step into the first light of morning. It's barely enough for Beam to see by, but it'll have to do. I smell the wind and can discern several lions. My dad's among them. He is surely able to detect me too. Maybe not while I'm in human form.

He's *married?* To *whom?* His pretty receptionist? That's just cliché. How long had they been dating? Is *that* why my mom left? Maybe I've been too hard on her.

I lead Beam as far away from the pride as I can and still keep the course. She's been a trooper. I know she must be sore and tired, sleeping on the ground and trekking this hard. But she doesn't complain. Even the day she lost so much blood.

My hip hasn't twinged, hasn't so much as tickled since then. Two major surgeries and I still had to limp. The pain was constant. Now it's only out of habit that I favor it, not out of necessity.

Her blood calls to you, the prowler had said. *Do you have any idea what a gift that is?* A gift someone would kill for. The thought fills me with dread. Or maybe they want to keep her alive so that they can have a steady source. I nearly lion up just thinking it.

I remember the snake lying stiff and flat. If I hadn't known better, I would have said that it had been dead for months. Maybe they want a weapon.

We've come to the best way up that I can assess, but it's a steep and crumbling crag. Probably five stories tall. Though not all of it is vertical. Most of it is. If I fall, no doubt my Elixir will save me. What happens if she falls? I don't know whether to climb behind or before. I appoint her to go first. I don't want to be glancing back the whole time, worried about her. And I don't want to kick loose gravel into her face.

"Have you climbed before?"

"Yep," she says confidently. I don't think she has. She makes me smile at the weirdest times.

"Kiss for luck?" I offer.

"Don't need it." She doesn't spare a glance. She's studying the climb. Maybe she *has* done this before. "Kiss me at the top," she says, and with that, she makes her first move.

She's bold. And the holds are good. She gets stuck a few times, but she keeps her head. She finds a way to make it happen. We catch a break halfway up. There's a cleft upon which to rest. Her arm's bleeding. I'm sure I cut through muscle tissue. It undoubtedly hurts, and it hurts me to know it's my fault.

"Stop," she says, reading my mournful countenance. "There's nothing for it. I need to get this done, and I need you to believe that I can do it. If you don't, then, I don't know. Don't watch."

I'm fairly certain she can accomplish whatever she puts her mind to, but with as doleful a tone as I can manufacture, I say, "I just regret it so much."

"Chausie, this is *not* the time," she chides me.

"I should've bitten your big ass instead."

She gasps. "It is *not* a big ass!" she protests and looks behind herself to confirm it.

"It's a whole lot meatier than your shoulder." And now I have to defend myself from her blows while I'm laughing. "Poor judgment on my part. Probably an effect of the venom."

She stops punching to narrow her eyes at me. "Can we get a move on?" she asks. "Or have you decided to stay here and practice your stand-up routine?"

I pull her close and focus on her mouth. "Kiss me," I demand.

I want it. I want it so bad. I don't know why now.

"Oh you *have* decided to do stand-up," she sings.

"Just once," I bargain.

Beam points to the top of the climb. "Up there."

"Then let me kiss you."

"Up *there*," she says again.

"Just on the cheek. Like a brother."

She finally cracks up. "Why would I even want that?"

"I don't know," I laugh. "I'm glad you don't. You keep pushing for it." I present the rock wall. "At the top, then."

Stakes are higher now. I don't look down. I'm not afraid for myself. I'm not the world's greatest climber, but I'm pretty experienced, and this one isn't too hard. Beam's doing great. Three points of contact at all times. Calculated reaches. Toward the top, though, she meets her toughest challenge. She gets the sewing machine leg action going when it takes too long to find a hold.

"You got this," I call up. "Keep breathing."

"Shut up, Chausie," she grumbles. She makes a move, but as she pushes herself upward, her left fingers swing out of the grip, and I hear her cry out. I close my eyes. *Give her something. Please give her something.*

I hear large movement, feel loose debris fall over me, open my eyes. And she's gone.

"Beam?!" I scream her name. Twice. And when she thrusts her head out safely over the top, I nearly let go of the rock myself.

"Shut *up*, Chausie! There are *lions* out there."

I clamor up the rest of the wall and bowl her over when I can. "Oh my gah, I thought you fell." I'm clutching her to myself in relief. My whole weight's on top of her. I'm probably crushing her, but I don't care.

When I lift my face to look at her, she's smiling at me. She opens her hands, which is about the only thing she can do while I have her pinned like this.

"Well?" she says.

"Well?" I ask.

"We're at the top." She's leading me.

"Oh, you want me to kiss you now? After so much rejection?" Best. Climb. Ever. I try to stop smiling so I *can* kiss her, but it's not easy. Plus, I'm suddenly all nerves. It's silly, and it's clumsy, but it's...yeah. At first, it's just a peck, and then another, and then it's...more. After a minute, I roll us over so as not to flatten her, and the way she peers down at me, with her hair spilling all around, puts an end to the smiling. I silently invite her back for more. I don't think she needs me to.

Lips are cool. Sometimes soft and...sometimes not. Occasionally she makes this little hum of pleasure that sends me through the roof. I've got my fingers fisted in her hair. I can't think of anything better than this moment. I can't think of anything *besides* it.

Until the lions start keening. I haven't cried since I was five—that's not strictly true, but anyway—I swear I could cry right now. She puts her forehead to mine. It's compellingly catlike. She's a little out of breath. Which is awesome.

She tries to pull me up with her, but I groan my disappointment.

"We have to go," she says.

"I know," I sigh, but I allow my head to drop back against the ground.

The mountain lions scream like ladies being attacked. It's

unnerving, even to me. I wonder what Beam thinks of it. We help each other stand when, from further out, another caterwaul goes up. "That's Eden," I say. "She's leading them away from us."

Maybe trying to make up for the deception. *Thank you, Edie.*

I listen for my dad. I know he's out there. I hear other familiar calls and hang my head to concentrate on his, but I can't detect it. He *has* to know I'm here. Why isn't he calling for me? Of course, that's nothing new, is it? And I guess it's no wonder, what with the new wife and all. I mean, *really?* He couldn't have *told* me?

That's what Mom was trying to prepare me for. Before I left. She already knew. Has she been protecting me this whole time I've been acting like a—

Beam's watching me. And now I become aware of how deeply I'm frowning and how long I've been rooted in the same spot. I blow out a breath. I don't want to be this moody all the time.

"Are you unsure of where to go?" she asks. Her question kicks me into gear.

"No. It's this way." I do hear how weird my voice sounds. I step the way I mean, but she's still trying to decipher the shift in me.

"Do you know how long it will take from here?"

I shake my head. "A few hours." I've taken several steps when I realize she's not with me, and I turn to find her just standing there. "You coming?"

"Do you already regret it?" she asks quietly. "What we did?"

It takes me a second to comprehend what she's asking. Or maybe my brain's fuzzy with all the conflicting impulses. At any rate, it's a second that, in Beam's mind, means I regret the forward movement of our relationship—holding her, kissing her.

In the smallest acknowledgment of humankind, she more squeaks than says, "Oh," and walks out ahead of me. "We don't have to be like that," she assures me.

"No, stop it." I grab her arm, but she doesn't turn around. "Beam."

"Please let's just forget it ever happened," she implores. "And let's never speak of it again."

"Beam, turn around," I command her. She does not. "Please?" She still does not. "Oh my gosh, you are so stubborn!" I surround her from behind and nuzzle into her neck until she squirms. "I'm trying to tell you," I say, biting her ear because, well, there it is, "what you're assuming is asinine. The only thing I regret is having to stop."

Silence.

"Do you hear me?" I physically spin her to face me.

"It's OK if you're not into it," she says. "You don't owe me anything."

Pff. "I owe you my life. Look at me." She lifts her eyes without lifting her head, so I stoop to get on level. "But I wanted to kiss you before that. Pretty much since I sat beside you at the coffeehouse."

She smirks to hide a real smile. "What's wrong then?"

Now I'm the one to look away. Part of me would rather lion up and gallop out of here than voice it. I take a breath. "My dad's out there. But he's not crying for me. He hasn't picked up the phone in months, and when I call him it's like he can't get off the line soon enough. Now he's *married*?"

Beam doesn't say anything to try to make me feel better, a fact for which I am grateful. It *should* feel bad. "I've been blaming my mom, but...what if it's me? What could I have done, do you think, to make him—" I shake my head. I don't want to put words to the rest. I know what I did. I don't want Beam to think less of me.

"Now, you're blaming yourself," she says. "Which I get, because if you could just fix what you did, you'd have some control, and he'd be a good father again. But I think you should give him full credit."

"For what?"

"For acting like an asshole."

If I had a drink, I'd be spitting it out. I'm choking anyway.

"*He's* the father," she says. "He should be, you know, *fathering* you. He probably hasn't called, because he's ashamed of himself. He certainly has no reason to be ashamed of *you*."

That's not true, though. I think she can tell what I'm thinking.

"What is it?" she asks. "If you did something so awful, then let's hear it."

It's tempting. I've been limping around with the secret as surely as I had with the injury. But if I tell her, it could push her away too.

"I don't care if you did do something," she says. "You're the kid. You're not supposed to have your shit together. He's the grown-up."

Beam's got her fierce face on. I spend a lot of time lately, just memorizing her details.

"You're good for me," I tell her. "I like you."

"I like you too."

"I like to kiss you."

"OK. Can we just..." She motions to the ground ahead.

9

LAUREL FROST FLOWER

BEAM

It's past midday when we approach the landmark where Chausie believes our mystery woman to live. Sedimentary walls surround us, creating a long, narrow glen. Even though we're up high in these mountainous buttes, there's grass and a few small trees. It's the most vegetation I've seen in days. The sun's shining down, but it's still pretty chilly. Chausie tracks a crow across the sky.

"So, where to now?" I ask. There's no sign of a home. No sign of anything domestic at all. "Do we send up smoke signals?

He abandons the crow to focus on me. "Do you know how to do that?"

"No," I laugh. "Of course not." I watch him hop onto a raised rock and turn three-hundred-sixty degrees.

When he doesn't find anything of interest, he sits down and swings his feet.

"Are we taking a break?" I ask. "Aren't we close now?"

"Yeah," he says slowly. "So, about Uncle Joel's directions... I'm pretty sure we're in the general proximity of this woman's...abode, but he couldn't give me an *exact* location."

"You don't know where it is?!" I ask in alarm.

"He said she'd find us once we got here."

I huff out a breath and glance around. "It doesn't look like anyone has set foot here in—ever."

"We're OK. Hop up." Chausie pats the rock beside him and I climb up muttering, "*You're* OK. You're a mountain lion."

"Ah, but I've taken good care of you, haven't I?" Drawing my hair back, he nuzzles my neck. "Got you where you needed to be?" After a quick kiss and an impish grin, he continues to gloat about his successful mission, but as he scans the area, he betrays his own misgivings, saying, "Maybe?"

"Oh gosh, you're no more sure than I am! Actually, that makes me feel better somehow."

"I did what Uncle Joel told me," Chausie says defensively.

"I'm sure you did, Chaus. Don't worry. She'll be along. At some point. Probably." We both survey the area from where we sit.

"What do you think she'll be like?" Chausie asks. "Your uncle said she's very concerned about keeping the old rituals alive. Do you think she'll be..." He leaves the question hanging and makes a wild gesture with his head and shoulders that I can only take to mean he's a little afraid of the woman.

"I'm not sure what"—I mimic his weird movements—"means. You've lived here all your life. What do you think the old rituals entail?"

Chausie's eyebrows tell me he has no idea. "Some kind of spiritual summoning or a secret incantation? Bizarre food, at the very least."

"So, you want her to be like...a fairytale witch?"

Chausie shakes his head vigorously.

"With a big, big oven?" I continue. "And newts and rats hanging upside down?"

"No. Shut it."

"What if she's listening to us right now?" I whisper loudly. "What will she think of you?"

"Stop it," he hisses. "It's not funny."

It *is* funny—because he's the boldest person I know.

"I'm going to introduce you as *Hansel*. Do you mind?" I continue to goad him, but now I'm wondering too, what she'll be like. I feel my skin prickle. There's certainly nothing to convince me that any corporeal woman lives here. We listen for signs of life. Finally, I lean against Chaus and he accepts my weight with both arms wrapped around me.

"You thinking about your mom?" he asks. He knows I am. "We'll get her back."

"We're just kids. How in the world are we going t—"

"We're not just kids," he contradicts. "Think about all we've accomplished in the last few days. We were destined for this."

I sigh. "I hope you're right. Hey, when this is all over with and we make it back home..." What I want to ask is *Do you think you could ever love me?* What I end up asking is safer. "Do you anticipate that I'll say yes when you ask me out?"

"You think I'm gonna ask you out?" Chausie replies.

I honestly don't know. My face must say as much.

"I'm gonna ask you out every chance I get," he assures me. "Whether we can actually go anywhere depends."

"On what?" I'm staring straight ahead, trying not to express too much delight.

"On whether or not you're willing to ride on the back of my motorcycle—assuming I ever get it back."

I sit up because it occurs to me that it was Chausie who flew by us so fast—back when I was in Uncle's car. "I've seen the way you drive that thing," I tell him. "You passed us on the way to the airport."

"That's just so you'll hold on tight," he says and bumps me with his shoulder.

"It's really no wonder your mom worries."

Chausie smirks and lifts his face to the sky, scratching his neck. His beard is getting seriously thick.

"I think my dad must have been having an affair," he says.

"Though, nobody told me that. It seemed like my mom just wanted out. She didn't want me to train under my dad anymore. She began harping about college. Now I wonder if she just didn't want to sully Dad's reputation for me." Chausie turns eyes on me which are full of regret. "I haven't made life very easy for her. I've been so mad."

"She's your mom, Chaus. You're gonna go back and tell her that, and she's gonna cry over you, and all will be right with the world. Between the two of you, at least."

Chausie accepts what I've said. "She didn't even argue when I told her I had an assignment here. I think she understood that I had to do it. That it's who I am. All she wanted in return was for me to call to let her know I was safe. I wish my phone worked out here." I twine my fingers through his, and he thumps our hands down on his leg a few times. "I want her to meet you."

"I'd like that."

Our conversation is cut short when a mourning dove takes flight across what I now recognize to be an open arch in the rock at the edge of the glen, and a woman emerges. She's probably in her seventies with long grey hair and angular cheekbones. She's plenty strong and moves with grace. She's wearing a relic of Native garb, a white sack shirt with fringe and symbols painted onto the fabric. Upon further inspection, it may just be a cool piece from a high-end catalog. Other than that, she's wearing skinny jeans and sneakers. I can feel Chausie's disillusionment. He was genuinely hoping she'd be some type of sorcerous.

The woman waves to us warmly as she approaches. "How long have you been sitting there?" she asks. When she's close enough, she embraces me like I'm family. "Sister Sunbeam, I am so pleased to meet you." To Chausie, she offers her hand. "Welcome, Lion. I am Laurel Frost Flower. Come in. I've made chicken soup."

Chausie looks so crestfallen, I have to turn my head to keep from laughing. Would he have been happier to have the newt?

"Or...we could make peanut butter sandwiches," Laurel says,

misinterpreting Chausie's dismay and causing it to ripen at the same time. She gestures for us to follow her.

"Wait for it," I say under my breath. "Peanut butter is the first test of sacred initiation." Chausie backhands my thigh. "If it's chunky, we're in," I snicker. "If it's creamy, we're dead."

"If there's a big, big oven," he leans to say, "I'm going to shove you into it myself."

CHAUSIE

Beam reacts to my oven comment the way I'd hoped—fake horror and twinkling blue eyes—when Laurel pivots back to me and says, "Here you go," I sober quickly, worried she's busting me, but she reaches into her pocket and produces a telephone. How can she have a working—

"It's satellite," she explains and motions to the sky. I'm slow to accept it. She says, "Isn't it the thing you want? Won't it set your mind at ease to use it?"

"How do you know that?"

In response, she holds the phone out further and shows me how to place a call. When I take it, she directs me to remain outside, then leads Beam into her—house?—not before Beam turns back with a silent *Oooo*. Chick's not bowed by anything. Coolest creature on the planet.

I peer down at the phone. *Huh.* When I call, there's no answer, and for some reason, I feel relieved. "Hey, Mom," I begin my message. "I just now got to a phone. Sorry it took so long. I'm doing great. The weather's been really helpful, and I'm in a safe place. I saw Grant and Eden. Mom, you gotta meet Beam. I think you'll really like her. She's...well, you'll see. I'm not sure what the plan is yet or how long we'll be here, but I'll try to call again before we leave." I almost hang up, but there's more I need to say. "Hey, I owe you an apology. I'm sorry for keeping to myself so much and being hard to live with. I'm sorry for flying off the handle all the time and for making you worry. I haven't been there for you when you needed me, but I will be from now on, OK? I understand what you were going through now and how you tried to shelter me. You don't have to do that anymore. You can lean on me. I love you, Mom."

I end the call with a sense of satisfaction. Laurel was right. Getting that off my chest feels like it seals a fissure. My steps are lighter as I move toward the entryway, and I'm thinking about how pleased Beam will be when—I stop short. The entry is gone. It's just —gone. I scan the rock in front of me and go cold. Not two minutes ago, Beam walked right through this wall! Right *here!* I nearly trip over my own feet as I hurry forward to feel for it with my hands.

I turn a full circle, and now I'm off kilter, unsure if I'm even pointed in the right direction. Have I let Beam get swallowed up in this rock? What if that was the plan all along? What if Laurel was a part of the plot and we've played right into her hand? Or Blue and his prowler buddies—where has he been since this morning? Do they have Beam in there chained up, bleeding her?

I'm starting to freak out, so I let the lion take over. I can always manage my emotions better in that form. Plodding the length of the glen, I still can't find the opening.

Shit.

Shit.

Shit-shit-shit-shit-shit.

Stop it! I reprimand myself. *Are you a cat or not? Use your nose.*

I steel myself and close my eyes to raise my muzzle. Isolate Beam's scent—the sage, the sunshine, the life. *Please let me find you. Please let me find you.* And I do. I even smell the chicken soup. Her scent leads me to where I'd thought to find the opening before. Now I *hear* her too, chatting on about something that doesn't matter in the least, but it's the most important thing I've ever heard. Funny how what I deem important has shifted in the last few days. I open my eyes to the yawning archway, wide and welcoming.

Because the glen has fallen into shadow, I can see soft candlelight from within. Beam sits at a dining table, poring over an old photo album. And now I realize that there are no candles there and what I took for their light is actually emanating from Beam herself.

I pad through the opening paw by paw. From just outside my periphery, Laurel speaks to me, and I halt. Her voice is low and quiet, and I think she's accusing me. "You took her blood."

It called to me. I only think it.

"It *calls* to you," she corrects aloud. "You summoned her light. As easily as that. As soon as you asked."

I let go of my lion and regard her as a man.

"You left me outside on purpose," I say. "It was a test."

"Come and eat, Bloodkin." She directs me inside with penetrating eyes.

Inexplicably, once I pass the threshold, a homey sort of comfort immediately soothes my nerves. It doesn't *feel* like we've merely stepped into an opening in a rock. As any modern home would be, the living area and the kitchen are finished. There's an oven, but it's not big enough to toss a person into. Maybe a very small person. I shoot Beam a grin, which her happy eyes seem to question. The dinner table where she is stationed separates the cooking space from the living space. On this side of her is a sitting area, and electric lamps shine from either side of a couch. How?

"Solar panels," Laurel says, and I gape at her. I don't ask her if she can read my mind, but she shakes her head no. "It's always the same questions," she explains. But that doesn't help, because I didn't *ask* her. She offers me a seat at the table beside Beam.

"Did you reach your mom?" Beam asks.

I squeeze her leg under the table, and she smiles at me, blissfully unaware of the trial I've endured. "I left her a message."

Laurel's more of a witch than she lets on. She places a bowl of soup in front of me and three hardy pieces of bread. And honey. And butter. My stomach rumbles. Whatever the woman is, my stomach *adores* her.

We eat. And we drink. And we laugh together. More than I would have thought possible, having just met and circumstances being what they are. Beam feels kindred to Laurel, I can tell. She's open and unguarded. I find myself relaxing back just to watch her talk.

We have seconds. I have thirds.

Laurel gets us to tell her about our lives. Beam is so highly competitive, she nearly got kicked out of Mock Trial. I hold the national high school record for three-pointers scored in one season. Beam starts college in the fall as a junior. I wrecked my motorcycle into my mom's car on purpose.

Shit.

There's a stunned silence. Well, *I'm* stunned. Laurel seems pleased. She's smiling like a mother at her kid's school play. I clamp my jaw shut and glue my eyes to the wall. I can't bear to check on Beam's reaction.

"Had you planned to?" she asks.

"No, Beam. I'm not a *total* psychopath." My tone's too harsh. It's not her fault. I try to soften it. "It was a split-second decision. I'd been out riding, mad as hell. Mom had parked her car in a way that kept me from being able to pull into the garage. I guess that just made me madder still. My future was already wrecked."

A memory comes to my mind. I've just come home from basketball practice. Dad's late for dinner. Mom's upset. I tell her she's overreacting. I tell her she's *always* overreacting.

I push back from the table. In the memory. And in real life now.

"Lions *are* unreliable," I mutter and carry my shame outside.

BEAM

I watch his solid shoulders bow and fold until I'm staring at the sharp scapulas of my lion gliding under tawny fur.

"Let him go," Laurel says. "He needs to run." She clears the dishes and when I try to help, she says, "*You* need to bathe. How many days have you worn those same clothes?"

I observe myself. Aside from removing my sweatshirt during the warmest hours, I've had them on since the day I met Chaus. "Yeah, I would burn them if I had any others."

"I have some for you. For both of you. I ordered them months ago."

"You did? How did you know we were coming?"

"I've dreamed aspects of your adventure for years. I've hoped and prayed it was true."

"Laurel, what are you saying? You wanted my parents to go missing?"

Laurel chuckles. "Sweet girl, there's a much larger story being written here than your own personal crisis, as large as that is to you. There is always a much larger story."

I haven't allowed myself to think about the whole thing in light of the broader context—except for how it relates to Chausie. "Well, what is it?" *And how far will it intrude upon my own plans?* The "Northwestern" on my sweatshirt glowers up at me asserting its dominance. I feel warm. I take it off.

Laurel, whose sharp intake of breath reminds me of what lies underneath, approaches to examine the blood-caked claw marks I've inadvertently revealed. "Let's get you cleaned up," she says. "You're too tired to write stories tonight." I allow her to rub away some of the dried blood in order to assess the wounds, and I wince when she gets to the deepest track. She doesn't comment.

"I love him," I confess. I don't know why I'm compelled to tell her this unless it's to make allowance for what he's done.

"One doesn't have to be a child of Chenoa to see that much. You gifted him with sight."

"He was dying."

"He's defiant. He's impulsive. He's proud."

"Yes," I admit. "He's also noble. And steadfast. And kind."

"And a good kisser?"

I jerk my head up to make sure I've heard her correctly, and she prompts me to answer with her eyebrows upraised. That makes me smile and nod without meeting her eyes.

"I thought as much. Well, there's that." Laurel leads me down a short hallway and through another door. This door is metal, solid, and heavy. And while the living area has painted walls and a ceiling, this new area, which is shaped like an oval, was left as a cavern. A bench has been hewn from its luminescent rock walls, and they glimmer like firelight. The star of the space is a large pool of water, steaming.

"A natural hot spring," Laurel tells me. "It's all yours. Towels are there. And a robe. I'll lay out more clothes in your room. Allow yourself to rest tonight."

I let go of some of the anxiety that's been clipping my breath without me knowing it.

I undress, disgusted at the state of my jeans and my underwear. Ew. And I step into the spring—which is *quite* hot—foot over foot, down the sloping floor. I submerge my sore, tired body, and duck my head beneath the surface. Heaven. For a long time, I just float. Then I scrub my skin till it's red. Laurel has natural soaps that smell divine. And a razor. All of it.

All of it is just what I need. I don't know how much time I spend in there, but it. Is. A lot. I don't even mind when I knick my shin shaving. I watch the blood swirl in the water and dissipate into the stream that journeys out of sight through a crack in the wall. I wonder where it leads. Is there some subterranean river or an underground lake?

I hold my leg out of the water to survey the damage. Another drop falls. It'll take forever to stop bleeding. I let a little red train streak across my calf. All this fuss over something I never give any thought to. Why me? Was it just some weird genetic accident? Like my mom's blue eyes overriding the usually dominant trait of my father's brown?

While I'm contemplating that, I swear I hear snuffling sounds coming from where the stream disappears, but the moment passes, and when I finally wrap a towel around my hair and a robe around my body, my leg is fine. Right now, I am confident that life is good.

A knock on the door reveals a squinting-eyed Chausie. "You gonna hog the bath all night?"

"You're back," I say. "You can look. I'm decent."

"Then what's the point?" he jokes. But his voice is hollow. He saunters in with his head hung.

"Your revelation wasn't that shocking," I assure him. "Just so you know."

He raises his golden eyes. He's ashamed.

"I already knew you were angry," I try again. "And wild. And imp—"

"Got it," he interrupts.

"We all do stupid things. Get over yourself."

He half-smiles. "OK. Thanks."

"And I get why you're angry. You envisioned spending your life here. Your family pulled the rug out from under you."

"I don't want to be that guy, though—the kind who wrecks things and—"

"That's not who you are."

"It *was*, though. I sabotaged myself. I hurt my mom. I convinced my dad I had no business serving at The Outpost."

"OK, but also, you're the guy who raced to my aid when crazy Kanji crow man was going to break my neck. You're the guy who jumped in front of a rattlesnake for me." I don't know if he's convinced, but he seems to lift his head higher.

"Since we're confessing," I say, "I should let you know that I too have a shady past. I've cheated. I've lied."

"You. Have cheated." He doesn't buy it.

"Yes, I have. At Candy Land."

Now he's himself. More relaxed. Less self-conscious. He crosses his arms. "I'm not sure you're capable of it," he says.

"You must not yet understand how much I like to win. It required a rather sophisticated strategy. I cleverly placed the ice-cream-bar card sixth down in the pile. That way, I could jump ahead to the corresponding square on the board."

"Why *sixth*?"

"So as not to garner suspicion. Any even number would have worked as long I could get my opponent to go first."

"I don't know if I can be in a relationship with someone so conniving," Chausie says. "I'll have to think it through." He takes a step closer. "This is a good look for you," he says.

I remember now that I'm wearing a towel on my head. And, wow, was this robe as thin when I put it on? "Yeah, I should've been born an Indian from India. I can really rock a turban." I unwrap my hair and hug the towel in front of me to deflect his attention. "This place is off the charts, huh?" He doesn't deflect so easily. He pries the towel from my grasp. It's all I can do to bear his scrutiny without squirming. It helps that he so obviously enjoys what he sees. He reaches for me.

"No way, you dirty animal." I slap his hand away. "Take a bath."

"Then I get to?"

"Get to what?"

Chausie shrugs and tugs his shirt over his head. His torso is a stack of muscles I have trouble ignoring.

"Dude! I am still *here!*" I say.

"Good! You can join me." He flashes his eyebrows and holds out a hand in invitation. Is he being serious right now?

"Are you being serious right now?"

My question knocks the cocky grin off his face, and he swallows before saying, "Iiiff you want me to be?" He's still holding out his hand. We stare at one another through the possibility. Until I come to my senses.

"Come find me when you're clean," I spout. "And clothed. Wear clothes." I hurry out with a hand shielding my view of him, and I can hear him laughing.

I nearly run into Laurel who's coming to show me to a guest room, and I smooth out the stupid smile that's trying to set up residence. All down the hall, I give a prattling account about the fabulous bath and how grateful I am to be here until I find myself pausing at a certain shelf that displays photos and beaded heirlooms.

"Laurel, who is that?" The photograph in question is so old that the young Indigenous woman depicted seems to have lost her edges. The lines of her white dress are no longer distinguishable from the white of the background, and her face is solemn, giving her a ghostly air.

"Look into her eyes," Laurel says, "and see if you don't know."

"It's not—no, it can't be."

Laurel regards the young woman with what I would take for longing if she had actually known her—if their lives had been able to overlap. "That is our dove," Laurel says. "Chenoa."

"You have a real photograph of her? Uncle Joel told me you were a wealth of history. He was right. Where in the world did you get this?" I study the image until I wonder if I look as sad as Laurel did just now. I just can't imagine the grief and despair that drove this woman to do what she did.

Before Laurel can answer my first questions, I whisper the one I've been keeping to myself. "Am I going to die the way she did?"

With a heavy breath, Laurel faces me directly. "The lion was an interesting choice. He may prove to be a sound partner."

I'm trying to figure out how that is an answer to my question when she says, "There may come a time you have to trust him above your own judgment. Will you be able to do that?"

I don't know, I don't say. *I don't much like the sound of it.*

"Chenoa was vulnerable," Laurel continues. "Her parents had both been killed at Wounded Knee, and her young brother. She was deceived into thinking she could get them back."

I've never been exposed to any real violence. I've never lost anyone I cared about—except for my oonchi, but she was very old. "If it comes to it, though—" I begin. "If I'm forced to make a choice that could save my mom's life..."

Laurel watches me wrestle with the thought, but she doesn't speak.

"Other gates were opened, right?" I ask. "Other things released?"

"Chenoa *closed* the gates too, you know." The way she rushes to tell me makes me curious. Like she feels the need to defend this young woman who died half a century before she was even born.

"And everything was recaptured," I offer.

Laurel leans in. "Not everything." Her long fingers grip the leather band at my neck and lift my catcher to trace its small web, its ivory dove. "What do you know about the things that were released?" she asks.

"Only what I've gleaned in the last few days. That there were malicious spirits—nagi—who had no real form, so they sought physical hosts. But they were ruthless to those hosts. Chenoa gathered them all back. Swallowed down the worst of them—a Shadow."

"An Umbra," Laurel corrects but nods for me to continue.

"And I think Chenoa must have bled to death while she was trying to keep it from getting loose again."

"That is sort of true," Laurel says. "The Umbrae, in their own world, *shared* a physical form. But they were stripped of it when they used it to devour the light of an entire generation of young stars, and they had been imprisoned for millennia when Chenoa opened the gates, separated as far as the East is from the West. But both were summoned. And both escaped. Only one was recaptured."

"How do you know all this?"

"I have often heard it keening," she says. "It desperately longs for its mate." Her face is pinched with the remembering. Her shoulders spasm with a chill. "There is no more harrowing sound to be heard. It is utterly foreign. A demonic, guttural heaving."

The haunted way in which Laurel recounts it is harrowing enough. The lamplight flickers. Or possibly Laurel herself flickers. I blink to refocus.

"What happens if the Umbrae reunite?"

"The stars tremble. The stars tremble in fear."

"You're quoting a song. My oonchi used to sing it. Some canoti played it through the trees while I was traveling."

Laurel is nodding her head, more somber than ever. "It's from the Visions of Blood. The stars have been trembling since the Umbrae were released. Terrified that they might reunite and devour them as they did the children of their own world. Did you know that you are a star, Sunbeam? Of a sort."

"Does it want to devour *me?*"

Sometimes Laurel chooses not to answer my questions. I do not love this about her.

"You must not open the gates," she declares. "And yet I fear that you must. If you are to fulfill your destiny."

Destiny. It's one of those high-sounding ideals I've never had the occasion to believe in. Much like *prophetic visions* and *divinely contrived partnerships.*

Laurel lifts my necklace again. Tiny iridescent beads dot the web. Now they remind me of stars.

"Who gave this to you? Your uncle?"

"Yes."

"That was wise. You know, one of the interpretations points to a lion as the Elixir. It says the Elixir pumps through a *lion's* heart."

"Well, it sort of does now, doesn't it?" I say. "I mean, he drank it. My oonchi sang it differently, though. 'The Elixir *owns* a lion's heart.' Do you mean that I might not even *be* the Elixir?"

"No. You are. The visions say what the people need to hear. They're not manuals. They're more like signposts. Easy to miss. Or misinterpret."

"I like manuals," I declare. I really do. I can build a Lego set like nobody's business. Just give me the guide. "Do you have a copy of these visions? Or can I find them online?" Laurel chuckles and shakes her head. "The copies that were written are kept at The Vigilance. Sounds like your oonchi sang to you all you need to know."

She gestures into the guest room, and once inside, she points out clothes, waves at the lamp, speaks in dulcet tones that I'm not really listening to. My sleepiness is catching up with me. Laurel says goodnight. "But I have more questions," I yawn.

"Tomorrow, Sister Sunbeam," she says. "Rest while you can."

I don't notice much about the room. It's warm and dry. The bed is soft. I count it a major win. On the bedside table is a charger that fits my phone. How is that possible? I find clothes there too, clothes that fit me, clothes I would have picked for myself. I dress in a soft white t-shirt, careful to keep the catcher close to my skin, and I snug down under the covers without turning off the lamp.

Sometime later, Chausie comes to sit beside me. "You awake?" he whispers. He smells clean. He combs my hair with his fingers. I feel my smile more awake than I.

"Laurel told me not to sleep in here," he informs me. "Says you need to keep your head clear for your tasks. Whatever that means. I'll be right outside your door, OK?"

I don't respond. I'm vaguely aware that I don't want him to go, but I'm falling back to sleep.

"I don't think you'll mind, somehow." I can hear his smile through his words. He kisses my forehead. His cheek is smooth. "Sweet dreams, Beam." Chausie pushes off the bed and clicks the lamp. I hear him pad across the room.

Is being sleepy like being drunk? I ask because, as if I've said it aloud every day of my life, I now say, "I love you, Chausie Cat."

There's a moment when I think he's already out of earshot, and I'm relieved. I smile to myself that I said it. And that it's true. And that he didn't hear me. But then, from the doorway, he says, "I love you too, Indian." To make sure I know he's not just joking, he adds, "I absolutely do. Rest well, Sweetheart." And I like that better.

10

THE WAR BENEATH THE WAR

CHAUSIE

It's hard to show myself out of her room after that. We're both clean and warm for the first time in days. The bed's soft. And I'm crazy about this girl. It's probably for the best. There's no way I'd get any sleep wrapped around her tonight. There's no way I'd let her get any. I'm grinning to myself like an idiot. I can't remember the last time *that* happened.

Leaving her door cracked open, I scan the large living room. What keeps people—or animals for that matter—from sauntering through the open, archway entrance? Not even the cold comes through, though, and the light from the inside doesn't spill out. I toy with the idea of sleeping as a lion on the floor of Beam's threshold. But there's a couch nearly as close, so even though Laurel has offered me a bed—how big is this place?—I crash on the sofa in human form.

I wonder what kind of tasks Laurel has in mind. We came here to get answers, not assignments. I wonder if it's anything like what she's already put *me* through—leaving me outside to find out how connected I am to Beam and enticing me to divulge my culpability in the wreck.

Even though my brain's working overtime, I fall asleep hard for several long, necessary hours of oblivion.

Not long enough.

"Kit-ty *Cat!* Kit-ty *Cat!*"

It's not the high-pitched words that bring me fully awake. It's the fact that my guts are being trampled by the speaker, who has launched himself on top of me to perform them.

Oof! "What the *heck*, Blue!" I chomp my teeth at him and he flinches even though I'm in human form. "Can't you just tap me on the shoulder like a normal...demon? Where have you been?"

"Hinto."

"What?"

"Blue's name is Hinto."

Why he's speaking about himself in the third person, I do not know.

"What's *Hinto* mean?" I ask. To which he replies—wait for it—

"Blue."

I rub my eyes and laugh in spite of myself. Hinto takes this as an invitation to use the couch as a trampoline. Bounce. Bounce. Bounce. Fliiiiiip. Bounce. Bounce. Bounce. Fliii- I snatch him from the air around the middle.

"Stop. Why are you here?"

"Are you commanding me to tell you?"

"Don't you want to tell me?"

Blue nods his bald head emphatically.

"Then tell me."

"Chenoa sees the war beneath the war."

I pinch the bridge of my nose to keep my head from hurting. "Blue? Could you please, just this once, try to be a little less cryptic?" I wonder what time it is. When I yawn, the prowler leaps to the ground with a yelp, apparently terrified of being eaten, though I'm only inhaling. "You're a weird little thing," I tell him, but the image of how very large and intimidating he can be flashes through my mind.

With an abrupt hardening of tone, Blue screams, "How's this for clarity?! Beam is surrounded by ruthless prowlers who have hijacked her mind and are trying to convince her to pour out her blood."

I don't understand what he's saying, but my heart kicks into overdrive. I charge into Beam's bedroom. She's not there. "Where is she?!" I yell and lunge for him. When he streaks across the room, I streak right after him, becoming lion along the way and knocking over the table with shocking noise.

"At the spring!" Blue howls.

"What's wrong? What's going on?" It's Laurel. I don't have time to reform or explain.

I practically take the metal door off its frame. Beam is standing on the far side of the cavern, leaning over the pool. At first, I don't see anything else. But I hear things. The sound of bubbling water. The hissing of steam, like from old train engines. And I smell things. Something rotten, like when leaves sit too long in a pond.

And then I do see. I don't know why it took so long. The space is full of prowlers, but not like Blue. These are menacing and malevolent. They're hovering around Beam, taunting her. A few of them lift their heads as I come roaring through the door, but not one of them is concerned.

I remedy that.

Leaping into the fray, I snap, slash, and trample everything in my path. I have one thought. Get to Beam. Laurel shrieks from the doorway, horrified, I think, that I'll massacre Beam in the frenzy.

They go down. Everything between me and her. It's clear that I have the advantage. None of them believed I could sense them, let alone rip them apart. As they die, they disintegrate into thick puddles, frothy like sea foam, and sort of shiny like an oil slick.

The others take notice. A general alarm goes up. One tries to attack me, and I welcome it, reading his steely glint like an invitation to ride. When he jumps at me, I meet him in the air and rip his throat out.

Any prowler left in existence, save Blue, vanishes down a crack in the wall. Blue is gaping at me. I'm a mess with the flesh of everyone

I've mauled and whatever it is that makes up the foul puddle in the end. Bending to my front elbows to thrust my head and neck under the water, I give myself a quick wash. But I glance up to find Beam still fixated on the water, tears running from her eyes and her face screwed up in anguish. After a vigorous shake, I rub my head and neck against her, but she doesn't move. She's holding a blade by her side. No idea where that came from, but the sight of it sends a sting through my spine. It's a wicked-looking thing. Like something out of the old stories in which a sacrifice is required. I let go of my lion to grasp the hand around the knife, gently so that I don't startle her, but firmly enough to keep her from slicing one of us.

"Beam?" It felt better when I had a more obvious role to play.

She's trembling. She won't look away from the water. Or she can't. I am violently seized with a new kind of fear.

"Laurel?!" I hear the tremor in my voice. Laurel must have been waiting for the invitation. She moves into the water fully clothed. As she disturbs the surface, Beam's eyes rove the way they might if someone has blocked the TV. Then, when Laurel reaches the point of Beam's focus, directly underneath her and chest-deep in the steaming pool, Beam says to her, shakily, "You're not well."

"No," Laurel agrees.

"You're fading."

"Yes." Laurel's voice is placid, her face pleasant. "And I'm at peace with it, Little Sister. I do not ask you to spill your blood for me. Nor would I accept it."

"I can make you well. I can make all of you well." At this, Beam searches the water again. Laurel turns her gaze to me in question, so I search the water too, and what I see makes me stiffen. There are forms in the water all around Laurel. Some are lying on the bottom, still as stone. Some are kneeling, clutching themselves. One man looks an awful lot like Uncle Joel. The woman next to him has long red hair and Beam's blue eyes.

"Her parents are in the water," I infer. "I mean, a vision of them or something. And other people. Everyone is sick or suffering. Some are bleeding. It looks like her dad is—" I don't say it. *Already dead.* His eyes stare up without focus.

"Sunbeam," Laurel says, calmly. "You're being tricked, just like Chenoa was."

"I can make it stop," Beam says. "The spring will carry my blood into the earth where it will make everyone well."

"Not even your strong blood can do that. The truth is it will only reopen portals that took too great a cost to close."

Beam tenses against my hold. "I can *do* it," she says through gritted teeth.

"I'm not going to let you cut yourself, Beam," I tell her.

With a sudden frenzied look at me, she draws a quick breath that sounds like a whispered *haaa.* "*You* could do it. Like you did before, Chausie. Tear me open and drain me into the water." She sounds eerily un-Beam-like, and her request is so morbid it ties knots in my guts.

"What have they done to her?" I ask in a panic.

"Chausie, you have to summon her light and draw her out."

"I don't know what you're asking me to do."

"She's losing herself. You have to bring her back to the surface."

Blue, who has been hovering behind Laurel, now shows up in my face. "Command *me*, Cat!"

Beam narrows her eyes at him. She looks hungry. Cunning.

"She made you a son of the blood," Blue tells me. Beam is listening. He purposefully angles away from her and lowers his voice. "I will answer to *you*," he says through his teeth.

"I don't dare command you. I don't know what you'll do."

"I'll do what you say!" Blue screams. He's growing larger as he did before.

"If *I* command you, Hinto," Beam says, with the quiet creepiness, "you are *bound* to obey me?" I don't know where she's heard him called Hinto before, but Blue's face fills with terror. He keeps his eyes on me and yells, "Now! Before Chenoa can!"

It occurs to me what Beam will command him to do. Take the

knife. Slice her open. She tries to lift it to him, but I'm forcing her arm to remain by her side.

"Take the knife!" I scream at Blue. "I'm commanding you! You're in my—" I don't know how to bind him to me. "Service," I guess. "And not Beam's," I quickly add.

It's done. He's as good as a genie. He pries the knife from her grip.

"Now destroy it!" I say.

He shuts his fingers around the blade, rolling one hand around the other. Instead of it cutting into him, it disappears—like a magic trick. "I cannot destroy it," he says. "But I can put it back."

Beam is furious.

"Chausie!" She sounds utterly betrayed. She's weeping. She falls on her knees and feels around under the bench, maybe for the knife. Or maybe for pieces of rock that have chipped off. She means to spill her blood any way she can. Suddenly she stills, rises to her knees, and uses her fingers to expose the shoulder I wounded. She's going to claw the scratches open.

"Chausie, look for her light," Laurel urges. "You have to find it. Do not let it fade." The sorrow in her voice draws my eyes.

"How do I do that?!"

"The same way you did when you couldn't find the door. Let her blood call to you. Ask for it. Plead for it."

Laurel means to remember what I did when I thought Beam was trapped inside the mountain and I was desperate to get to her. I kneel before her and wrench her wrists in front of her, cuffing them together so she can't do any harm. I don't lion up this time, but I do put my forehead to hers, and I close my eyes to try to push into our connection. I reach for her. I don't know how else to put it. With all that I am, I reach for her. She stops struggling, but she's rigid.

What I begin to see behind my closed eyes is horrific. Not just from Beam's point of view, but personally devastating. I've fallen into the vision in the pool, and I'm unable to look away. I force my feet to move past each sick or bludgeoned person, but it's like I'm trapped in some kind of macabre maze. I stay engaged by singular focus. I'm hunting. I'm stalking. But the more suffering I pass, the angrier I become. And now anger is all that I am.

Not all that I am. I finally catch a glimpse of Beam standing in the vision, wide-eyed among the carnage, and I want her to be OK so much it hurts. How can I be so full of love and so full of anger at the same time? I lift my foot, which is a paw, to step over what is, oddly, the snake that died because Beam hated it. It's as empty and as dead as the last time I saw it. Prowlers are gathered around us, watching to see what we'll do. I hate them. But not just in a vacuum. I hate them because I love Beam.

I sense someone else too, from outside my line of sight, like someone driving a car in my blind spot. I think it's someone in the real world with the power to look into this scene. I don't take my eyes off Beam, but I try to catch their scent. I can't tell if they're orchestrating the vision or merely spectating.

I'm losing focus. I begin to turn my head.

"*Stay,* Chausie!" I hear Laurel's voice as if from a dream, and it snaps me back to the task at hand and somehow breaks the connection to our voyeur.

Beam is with me in the real world, kneeling before me, her head to mine. She's also with me in this vision, where I close the distance between us. I'm embracing her. Vowing to take care of her. To fight for her. To bring her back. Whatever else is around us dissolves into light, and the vision dissipates.

I'm not sure how long we sit like that, but at some point Beam's muscles relax, and I become aware that I can see her light without opening my eyes. I think I understand what's going on. "None of it's real," I tell her. "Not yet. And none of it's your job. It's a trick to overwhelm you, to get you to reveal what you are. Or to get you to do their bidding. But I'm not gonna let that happen."

I'm not sure who *they* are, but I think I'm right about the rest.

Beam is watching me. She's so full of sadness that tears prick my own eyes. She pushes taller onto her knees and wraps her arms

around me. "You came for me," she whispers. "You saw what I saw?"
I nod against her head.

"They were all around you," I tell her. "You burned them up."

"*You* burned them up, Chaus. You were a lion. But you were light."

Laurel has wrapped a towel around herself and has joined us, sitting on the bench, where we sit on the ground. "You did good, Cat," she says.

Beam feels fragile in my arms. Over her shoulder, I tell Laurel, "I really don't give a damn about your tasks. I'm not letting her out of my sight from now on."

"You've already completed the tasks."

(Remember when I said that she was part witch? Accurate.)

"You *orchestrated* this?" I spit.

"Of course not. But I thought they might reach out for her. And I knew this would be the safest place for you to learn how to find her."

"Why did you separate us?"

"They can't get to her as easily with you around."

"Are you out of your mind?"

Leaving my question adrift, Laurel says, "Little Sister? Do you know why you're called Beam?"

Beam hasn't let go of me. I think she's traumatized. It's probably the only thing keeping me from shutting down. I answer for her. "It's short for Elizabeth somehow."

"No. Your dad told you that, I bet." Laurel responds to Beam like she's the one who answered. "Because he was afraid the truth would get you—"

"Where she is right now?" I snap. Laurel ignores me.

"When you were born and your father presented you to the Council, a Lakota prophetess spoke out to say that you would be a light to your people. I was there. I heard her say it. You were named Summer Sunbeam because of it. Your father didn't think it meant more than that you would be a gift to us, a leader, or an artist. A gentle blessing. But the prophetess met with him privately to tell him she'd kept some of her words secret. That you would also prove to be the next Elixir, both blood for body and light for soul. And that was not welcome news. The Vigilance was already a sovereign power by that time and treated anyone with *gifts* as a threat. Your dad was afraid it would turn into a witch hunt."

Laurel is shivering now. Beam has finally let go of me and is watching her.

"Chenoa's blood made her the target of obsession," Laurel says, though her chattering teeth make her hard to comprehend. "She was deceived, and her light lost within her."

"We need to get her warm," Beam says, her compassion for Laurel superseding her shock for now, though it doesn't mine. I knew people in the pool too. Intimately. But I can't give in to that part right now.

I help Beam to her feet. "Who else knows what the prophetess said?" I ask. "Who else knows for sure that Beam is the next Elixir?"

Laurel looks me in the eye, but she's in no shape to discuss this anymore. "The Visions are ambiguous," she manages. "Thank Creator for the clever mercy of a lion." She can hardly finish for coughing, and Beam urges me on, so, with my thoughts racing, I carry the older woman to her room, and while Beam gets her into bed, I make us all some tea. We sit with Laurel in heavy silence until she stops shivering, and she sleeps.

BEAM

Once we're back in the kitchen, Chaus and I lean on opposite counters. He's wearing blue jeans that sit low on his hips and a navy t-shirt that hugs his torso. He's barefoot. It's well into morning now—hours since he saved me from being—I don't know—deceived? Corrupted? We're simply sipping hot tea, just two friends hanging out after a nearly fatal psychological ordeal.

Over my cup I say, "Laurel was strong when we got here, wasn't she? I mean, I know she's getting older, but until the"—I visibly chill

—"incident, she didn't seem sick. She certainly didn't seem to be...dying."

"She's going to get much worse before the end," Chaus says, "if the visions in the pool are true."

"No, they can't be true, Chausie. All those people aren't going to — Why won't she just let me heal her?"

Chausie is troubled. "I think she was me," he says.

"I don't understand."

"She didn't mean that Chenoa's light was lost. She meant that *she* lost it. Chenoa's blood called to her as yours does to me. She couldn't hold onto it. She couldn't shut out the demons."

"Chausie, she'd have to be hundred-seventy-five years old. No. *More*."

"It's strong blood." Chausie presses fingers into the top of his leg, below the hip bone. "Two surgeries since the wreck. And a third one scheduled."

"I know. I saw you in pain."

He looks at me hard. "She was me."

"If that's true, then do you think—are you going to age more slowly than I am?"

My question doesn't make him happy. He chews on the answer like it's sour. "I hope not. It's no wonder Laurel lives like this. Everyone she knew and loved is gone. I wouldn't want to just hang around under *those* circumstances."

"Chaus, you don't think I *cursed* you, do you," I ask in alarm. "*Did* I?"

He sets his cup down to hug me close. "How can you ask me that?" he consoles. "No. I was desperate to live. You saved me."

His chest is warm to my cheek as I ride the rise and fall of it. Two breaths. Three.

"And you don't mind that the only reason I kept you alive was to make out with you?"

Chausie pulls back to observe me while I do my best to keep a straight face, and then he narrows his eyes. "Prove it."

He's the best kind of drug. I can't remember anything that's wrong while he's kissing me. His hands are on my face. He's pressing me into the counter and telling me how good it feels to him without stopping to form the words properly.

It's perfect. Even so, I jerk my head back. "Stop."

"Wha—really?" The chagrin on his face makes me giggle—and I do not giggle as a normal mode of communication.

"I'm sorry." I hold on to him to keep him from feeling rejected. "I heard something."

He listens, but says, "I doubt very much that your ears picked up something mine—" But at that moment, his sentence is punctured by a man's voice yelling his name.

"See? It's coming from outside in the glen."

Chausie listens more intently and nods in tiny increments. "It's my dad. I should go to him."

He sounds decided, but he's also asking me what I think. Then he looks down at us, me in his arms, and breaks into an unexpected smile.

"Why are you grinning?" I ask though I'm on the verge of a giggle-palooza myself. It's totally juvenile. We may be in real trouble here.

"Because I'm afraid my dad *will* think you've spelled me. And he won't be wrong." Chausie pops me with another kiss. "I should speak to him. He'll listen to reason."

"Yeah," I assure him, but I'm sobering now. "How does he know we're here, do you think?"

Chausie chews on the inside of his cheek. "Uncle Joel?" he guesses and then raises his head to bellow, "Blue!"

Our prowler appears, puckering as profoundly as his little red mouth will allow. I guess he's making fun of us for kissing. "Yes, Master?"

"Don't call me master."

"All right, *Cat!*"—I flinch when Blue screams the word—"What should I call you?"

Chaus ignores that. "How many people are outside?"

Blue glances around. "I don't know. How many?"

"Go find *out*!" Chausie hisses.

"Now *that's* how you voice a command!" Blue says. He nips outside and is back within fifteen seconds. "Just the one man," he reports.

"OK. Thanks." Chausie moves toward the door.

"And a lion who is a man right now."

Chausie stops. "So, two men. And one of them is not a lion?"

"Neither of them is a lion right now."

Chaus sets his jaw and through his teeth, he says, "But only one of them is *ever* a lion?"

"Correct." Blue starts cartwheeling across the floor.

Chausie's thinking. "Is the other one Lakota?" he asks.

Blue stops to regard him. "What's Lakota?" We both stare at Blue to make sure he's being sincere.

"Does he look more like me or more like Beam?" Chausie asks.

Blue considers this. "He looks more like Laurel. He's not as close as the cat, but he's driving a beeeeeeeaaauuutiful motorcycle up the trail. And cats can jump. So the cat doesn't use the trail."

"It could be Uncle Joel," I say.

Chausie's dad can be heard calling for him again, closer now.

"It could be *any*one." To Blue, Chausie confirms that—"The two men are the only people out there?"

"Yepperrrrs!" Blue croons.

"Don't ever say that again," Chausie says. "Stay with Beam, and come get me if anybody—or any*thing*—tries to get close to her. Got it?"

Blue salutes like a US soldier and a Lakota warrior at the same time, using both hands, and then turns to me saying, "I think we'll make something of him yet."

After Chausie steps out, I try to see through the opening, but he must have rounded the corner. The morning is bright. The sun is reflecting off fresh snow.

"Blue," I ask. "Who controls the prowlers that got into my head?"

"Nobody. People *think* they can control them, but no."

"So, Chausie doesn't really command you?"

"*We* are bound to Chenoa."

I wonder who *we* are, but finding out about the prowlers in the pool seems more important. "So, they just came to me on their own?"

"You summoned them. I watched you summon them."

"Nope. I'm pretty sure I did not."

"You sliced your leg and dripped your blood into the water. And that is where they came to find you. You summoned them, but you don't control them."

I'm not going to think about why he was watching me bathe without me knowing he was there.

"Are you saying that when I cut myself shaving, that tiny amount of blood called out to things that live inside the earth?"

Blue answers yes with great sweeping arcs of his big head. "They can't be commanded, Chenoa, but they *can* be lured. They like the patterns in the drums and the chants and repeating images. They like human blood because Creator places such a high value upon it. They like the frenzied activity that makes people weak. And they like empty bodies—well, who doesn't like that?"

11

THE FATHER CHAUS AND THE DEAD GUY

CHAUSIE

It snowed last night. Everything's bright and white as I walk out into the soft, powdery stuff with bare feet. "Dad?" I shield my eyes.

"Here!" he says. And then I spot him. He's wearing a dull brown coat over his uniform and cargo pants stuffed into his boots. It's been months! I sort of gush inside at the sight of him.

"Dad!" I begin to trot in his direction, but then I remember he's married and he hasn't bothered to reach out to me, and you know what? He's the whole reason Mom and I have struggled so much. So, I restrain myself. All to say, I end up tripping over my own feet and falling face-first into the snow. Not exactly the first impression I wanted to make.

My dad hurries to help me. "Son, you can't even walk. How have you made it this far?"

He assumes my injury is what caused me to faceplant. I push him away with a testy, "I'm fine. I was just being a klutz."

When I rise to my feet, Dad's yellow eyes meet mine and for the first time, I realize he's having to look up at me. "You've grown," he says and pulls me into a long hug. I'm not gonna lie—I sink into it and have to flick a tear away when he pulls back.

"Where's the girl? How is she not freezing to death?"

"She's fine. She's inside."

"Inside where?"

I gesture toward the opening, but he can't see it. "Just—come," I say.

When we cross the threshold into Laurel's house, my dad scans the area in disbelief and stamps the snow from his boots. "Tell me about the leg. How's your range of motion? Have you been devoting yourself to therapy?"

I don't have time to explain before Beam's sharp intake of breath draws my attention. She recognizes my dad. I wondered if she would. He was one of the victims in the vision in Laurel's pool. One of the most gruesome. Ripped apart. Bleeding out. Stuck halfway between human and lion.

"This is your dad?" She manages to keep her voice even, but her eyes are saying more than the words are. Namely: *why in the world didn't you tell me that you watched your dad dying in that pool?* I duck the question, though I think she gets it. The sympathy in her eyes says as much. Still, I avoid them. Not because I don't trust her reaction. I just don't trust my own.

"Dad, this is Beam Redfeather," I say.

She moves forward to offer her hand, and I'm thankful that she pushes through the revelation without addressing it.

"Beam, this is my dad, Leonhard Louris."

"Mr. Louris." She greets him warmly, her straight black hair falling to either side of her ice-blue eyes. She's very grown-up all of a sudden. "Your son has saved my skin at least once a day since I met him. You must be very proud of him."

I'm proud of *her*. I watch her steal my dad's favor with her courtesy and charm. At the same time, she's sizing him up. It's intimidating. Was I really just kissing this woman?

Meanwhile, Blue has taken to bouncing around the living room while he mimics my dad and hugs himself too fondly. I shoot him a look and mouth, *Stop it.*

Apparently *mouthing* a command holds no power. I'm not at all sure about the rules of this relationship. I don't even know if there are any.

"Indeed," my dad answers Beam. "It's a pleasure to make your acquaintance."

Dad's like me, tall and sinewy—most lion people are. He always stands in a strong stance, and he wears a hard expression. Even so, Beam challenges his statement. "Really? I was worried you might have bought into all the hype about how dangerous and enchanting I am."

She looks my dad directly in the eye. I think he's surprised she's so bold. Instead of holding her gaze, he scans the house, and I bite my lip to keep from smiling.

"It's homey in here," he says. "Completely unexpected. Who keeps it up?"

BEAM

"Are you even listening to me?" Chausie's arguing with his dad, who thinks I should go straight to The Vigilance. I'm just standing here. So, once again, cats are debating what to do with me, and I'm not part of the conversation. It doesn't matter. They can come up with whatever they want, and I'll do what I think is right, regardless—unless I'm *forced* to do something, which I guess is also a possibility.

Turns out, I don't have to worry. Chausie keeps advocating for me. I wonder how much longer we'll be able to remain partners. He did what he was supposed to do. He brought me this far. His angry tone pulls me back to the debate.

"The *Vigilance* wants to use her as much as the people who have her mom," he argues. "Hell, Kimimela may *be* the one who has her mom. Beam's not safe there while that crazy woman is in charge."

"Don't be ridiculous," his dad scoffs. "Without Kimimela there would *be* no Vigilance. She works tirelessly to protect her people. Including your new friend here."

"Kimimela is not trying to protect her, Dad. She's trying to imprison her. At the airport, she—"

"Please don't tell me that was you. I assured Kimimela that my son would never have attacked one of her people."

Chausie doesn't drop his head, but he seems to be fighting the urge. "They were trying to *kidnap* Beam. They nearly ran her over!"

"Don't be so dramatic."

"Dad! They were trying to force her into their car against her will. That is all kinds of illegal, even if you work for The Vigilance. I could've done worse to that man and you know it. I showed restraint, just like you taught me."

"If Kimi has an interest in the girl, then what is that to you? She's built her whole career upon that which *this* girl"—he points at me—"may be able to tear down."

Chausie hears more than his father is saying. His defense of Kimimela is personal, and it occurs to both of us, I think, whom his father has married.

"Dad, just how well do you know *Kimi?*" He says it with a special emphasis on the shortened form of her name. His dad doesn't answer. "Grant mentioned to me—assuming, of course, that I already knew—that I had a stepmother. That would have been a nice thing to find out from you before the rest of the world knew. Is it true? Is it Kimimela?"

His dad gives a curt nod. "I was going to tell you, but you showed up unannounced."

"You didn't think that maybe you should have told me before you were actually married?"

Silence follows. Then Chausie raises his head to listen to something my ears can't pick up. "Is that my bike?" he asks. His sudden childish enthusiasm works through the room like Christmas magic. "You got it from the airport?"

Mr. Louris nods in affirmation. "*Kimi* retrieved it for you. On her behalf, you're welcome." Christmas magic broken. "I want you to ride to The Outpost this afternoon. Leave the girl to me."

"No, I'm not going to do that," Chausie balks. "Are you *kidding* me right now?!"

Mr. Louris' chin advances and his voice drops. "You will ride out, Chausie, if I tell you to, and you will wait for me there. You're not going to let this girl dictate what you do. She has no experience with the land. She's not even one of her own people."

He practically sneers at me, the *girl*, and even though I'm not used to being referred to as a woman yet, I decide I'm going to demand it from now on. I've stayed out of this discussion so far because—well it's Chausie's dad, and I thought I should just let him handle it. But I'm forming a fairly intense rebuttal when Chausie launches his own.

"Beam has more guts and more brains than any of us. If I hadn't listened to her, she'd be in the wrong hands by now, and I'd be dead."

Mr. Louris regards Chausie, then me. With condescension dripping from his words, he says, "Chausie, I'm sure the two of you have shared a great deal in the last few days." He may as well have said, "Chausie, I'm sure the two of you have allowed teen idiocy and hormones to cloud your judgment."

"But you're just a kid," he continues. "You haven't even completed training. And now you're practically crippled because you can't control your impulsivity. If you have any hope of a position at The Outpost, you'd better get your priorities straight."

I gape at Mr. Louris. "Did you *really* just use Chausie's injury as a weapon against him?" I ask. "He has been tied up in knots trying to figure out how to please you. You are his *father*. You're supposed to—" I'm at a loss. "He's not even hurt anymore!"

Chausie stays me with a raised hand and responds, not in his own defense, but simply with a calm and certain declaration of what is going to happen. "I'm not leaving her, Dad. There's no convincing me. Or ordering me. Or shaming me. You're wasting your time."

Chausie is my hero. I mean, he is actually my hero.

"Then you're wasting *your* time with any future plans at The Outpost. *My* people obey direct orders."

Chausie's hurt, though, just like when he found out he had a stepmother, he does the opposite of what you'd expect. The muscles in his face relax, and he stands tall like he's making room for the sword to completely sever his life's ambition. His dad can't be serious. It's all Chausie's ever wanted.

His dad says, "Look, Son, your faithfulness is admirable, bu—"

"I'm surprised you can *recognize* faithfulness." Chausie literally growls it. And there it is. The burr that's been riding in his fur since he found out his dad remarried. Another war beneath the war. Mr. Louris bristles. Chausie doesn't back down.

I've learned to see the beginnings of the transformation. The twitch of muscle beneath skin. The hyper-focus behind the eyes. But neither of the men let go. They remain fully human.

Finally, as if it settles the matter, Chausie simply says, "Beam's blood chose me."

A new voice corrects him. "*Chooses* you." It's Laurel, who has entered the room without us noticing. She looks better. Much better.

"Right," Chausie agrees. "And I choose her." His words sink into me. He means to see this through no matter what the personal cost. "Laurel, this is my dad."

Laurel doesn't seem that interested in his dad. She lays a hand on Chausie's shoulder and admires him with enough pride and pleasure to make him squirm. His cheeks blush red.

Alternately, Mr. Louris goes white. His lips frown and twist. I can't tell if he's concerned about the blood comment or if he's upset with Laurel for some reason. Either way, he doesn't greet her, which is rude, since he's standing in her home.

Very quietly, he says, "Chausie?"

CHAUSIE

The way my dad says my name sets my teeth on edge. He's creeped out, and that creeps me out. I don't understand why he hasn't acknowledged Laurel. Maybe he was dreading the same magical reception that I was when I first came, but I don't have time to think about it, because the sound of my bike stops right outside the door. I go with my dad to vet the new visitor and then rush back inside.

"Beam," I call excitedly and step aside to let her see her father for herself.

Her reaction is not what I expect. She comes forward, encouraged by the way I've announced the visitor, and offers her hand. "I'm Beam." She looks expectantly at the man, and when he doesn't say anything, she looks at me. The man's tongue pops out and licks over his lips. That's not right.

"Dad?" I ask. He glances at me and we both round on the stranger, pushing Beam back behind us. The man's Indigenous. Seems about the right age. Looks enough like Beam's dad in the vision. But by Beam's reaction, he is clearly not her father. I'm about to ask who he is when something glides across the film of his eyes the way a reptile blinks its third eyelid. The only reason I'm sure it really happened is that I hear Beam gasp from behind me.

My dad doesn't notice the eyeball thing. I know, because all he says is, "Beam, this isn't your father?"

"Dad, you need to step back," I tell him. I don't recognize it at the time, but with that one brusk imperative, our relationship becomes an adult. My dad falls back and waits for further instruction. He's flexed, ready to follow me into a fight.

The man who is not Beam's father has yet to speak. He's focused on Beam whose face he can likely spot between my father and me. I move to close the gap and block his view.

Blue picks this moment to loudly whine and repetitively lament, "He's a *prisoner!* Your dad is a *prisoner!* Your dad is a horrible, awful *prisoner!*" He won't stop with this sort of thing, wailing like a siren, grating on my last nerve. "Your dad's a—"

"Shut up, Blue!" Beam and I both shout. "It's (He's) not her (my) *dad!*"

My own father flinches. He doesn't know whom we're berating or why. I will never understand the physics of this. How can he not hear all that screeching? I don't even think he can sense Laurel. I haven't worked that one out yet.

"Let me go get Goliath," Blue pleads—as if I know who the heck Goliath is. Or, for that matter, what the heck *anything* is that comes out of his mouth. Such as this last statement: "The prisoner has to come out of her dead dad!"

BEAM

"There's a prisoner inside him?!" I'm asking Blue, but I'm staring at the creepy man whom Blue just described as dead. "Why can't I see it? Can *you* see it, Chaus?" Chausie shakes his head without looking at me. He and his dad are poised to pounce.

"Just the eyeball thing."

The man takes a stilted step toward me. And now I have two lions in the room. Chausie pins the man to the ground with a paw on his chest. His dad's growling, but Chausie is silent, searching for a sign of life in the man's eyes, or maybe for a clue as to what to do next.

Scream. Is what he does. His frustration must have peaked. He howl-screams in the man's face, and to my surprise, it's Blue who responds. "Goliath can do it!"

The man's weird eyelids slide sideways for a second time and his tongue pops out. Chausie, as a lion, screams again. He's communicating with Blue, and Blue understands him. Blue says, "*No* one else can. Certainly not *me*."

"Yes, you can," I contradict him. I can see that he's lying about whatever Chausie has asked. But my words get lost because, at the same moment, Chausie emits such an earsplitting command that it must surely rival the sound of any other lion—on this continent or across the world. I cover my ears.

Without further argument, Blue shoots into the man, our new visitor—who, now that I look at him, does seem a bit grey—and he disappears.

A wrestling match ensues within the man—only, any parts of the two prowlers that remain inside his body are invisible to us, so all we see is an appendage here, a face there, nipping out of this poor guy's dead form. Chausie's gone whole kitten. He hunkers down on his front paws. His whiskers twitch. His eyes dart to the flailing prowler parts wherever they emerge.

When he attacks, it's to chomp down on a red and yellow tail and drag a long salamander-type prowler out of the man, slinging its body around the room. The prowler whips through Chausie's father, who is slack-jawed, even as a cat, because all he can see is his own son savagely—joyously?—romping around with...nothing.

But, oh, the stench! Surely Mr. Louris can smell that.

Chausie repositions his grip, and the prowler gets free. In the room, it grows to three times the size it must have been inside the man's body. This doesn't affect Mr. Louris or the body on the floor, both of whom are able to coexist in the same space as the creature. But the rest of us are crowded, and we retreat into the kitchen to get a handle on what we're dealing with. Blue is hiding behind Chausie's hind leg, holding on for dear life.

"You should let me get Goliath now," he whimpers.

The salamander, or dragon, or whatever the prowler is, considers each of us in turn. I swear, it's looking down its nose at us. Its eyes are intelligent. I don't think it wants to eat us. I mean, why travel all this way on a motorcycle in a dead man's body just for lunch? Seems like overkill.

Poor choice of words.

Two things I've noticed about prowlers: One, they're curious. Two, they can't resist showing off. When I was a kid, if they suspected I could see them, they'd strike up a big performance for me. It's probably exciting to be seen when you're used to being invisible.

"You are the definition of majestic," I flatter the prowler. My lion cuts his eyes to me in question, or maybe to check my sanity. "And your prowess is unmatched. How did you shrink yourself to fit into that small man?" I hope it understands English.

The scary salamander regards me from on high, a shadow of satisfaction possessing its brow. "I am Baalesh," it says, as though the name carries enough weight to crush us all.

"Oh!" I gasp because I think it's the right way to go. Not because I've ever heard the name before. And apparently, it is the right way to go. Baalesh hums a low note and lifts its head even more.

The tip of Chausie's tail flips this way and that. Otherwise, he's unmoving.

"Why can the lion see me?" Baalesh inquires. Its voice is slow and rich as chocolate.

"I get asked that a lot," I say. "You wouldn't believe..." I wave my hand to show how incredible it is, how much I get asked that. "He can see you because he drinks my blood when it suits him." Chausie's dad makes a noise. I think he may have gagged. Perhaps I should stop with the hyperbole. But Baalesh seems to respond to it, and anyway, Baalesh licks its lips, like the man did when it inhabited his body.

"You can't have any," I tell it. "I hope that's not why you've come?"

"I'll devour you whenever I please, while you are still wriggling if it suits me."

Chausie checks the beast with a snarl, and Baalesh's narrow eyes shift toward him.

"Unfortunately," Baalesh says, returning its gaze to me, "I've been sent to retrieve you whole."

"Like a bird dog," I offer. (Stupid.) Baalesh snorts with indignation. Chausie's hackles couldn't be raised higher without lifting him off the ground.

Blue pipes up. Covering his eyes, he squeaks, "Truly, O Mighty,

Baalesh, like the noble bird dog, you are among the most cunning creatures in the world."

I snap my fingers at Blue like he's won a contest. "Right!"

Blue's caught on to the game plan. "The one who chose you was both wise and discerning," he says.

Oh, that's good. Blue has his moments...

"Who was it, Baalesh?" I ask. "Who told you to say you were my dad?"

Mr. Louris is pinching his lip in thought. It's the same thing Chausie did before he apologized for clawing me so deeply. He knows. Or he suspects.

"The woman with the bodies," Baalesh answers. "I get to keep that one if I bring you back."

"Oooooo," Blue sighs with envy. I don't think it's part of the strategy. I think he's genuinely jealous.

"Enough!" Baalesh bellows. "Come with me, or I tear your lion apart." It swings a fist at me. I think it's going to grab me like King Kong grabbed the little blonde lady, but Chausie launches himself onto Baalesh's back before it can close its fist, and he sinks his teeth down, jerking his head back and forth to rip into the thick skin. Baalesh jerks back in pain, inadvertently scraping my shoulder wounds open. I fall back a step, instinctively covering the wounds with my hand.

The two go rounds. Baalesh is gigantic, but Chausie is agile. And smart. He's back and forth with quick, light steps, anticipating the monster's attacks. But Baalesh gets lucky. Its beastly tail thumps Chausie off balance and roils until it pins his neck to the floor. Chausie emits a sharp high-pitched whine. Have you ever heard your own beloved pet cry out in intense pain? It makes my blood boil. I have to force down the volume of my next words, not against fear, but against the rage that threatens to consume me. "I do *not* give you permission to touch my lion."

"*Baalesh*," it says, an edge to its voice and emphasis on its own name, "does not need your permission. *Baalesh* does not answer to you." To prove it, he grinds his muscles into Chausie's neck. Chaus kicks to get free, but now he's having trouble breathing.

"You misunderstand," I say, cooly. (I don't know what comes over me. I'm not ordinarily a hothead or a courageous warrior or anything, but I just get so angry when snake-like creatures harm my *cat*.) "I'm not commanding you, *Baalesh*. I'm giving you notice. Release him, or I will send you to hell."

It doesn't release Chausie, but I do have its attention. I feel so hot that I strike Baalesh in the throat with my fist, following in to grab the soft parts underneath its massive head. "I said, *release* him!" I stare into that stupid face without a trace of unbelief. I *will* send it to hell. Baalesh doesn't attack me as the snake did. It just starts smoking underneath my hand. It's being scorched. It writhes, but it can't break out of my hold, and it looks as confused as I'm beginning to feel. I glance around for the source of the flame.

"It's you," Chausie chokes out. He's a man again, on his knees rubbing his neck. Blue's ogling me, his eyes even larger than normal. I'm still seething.

"I'm going to release you," I tell Baalesh, "so that you can spread the word that my *cat*"—I see Blue out of the corner of my eye—"and our *prowler*"—Blue postures delightedly—"are off limits." I jerk my hand away and a clump of Baalesh's flesh comes along, falling to the floor with a wet-sounding thunk. *Nasty.*

Baalesh lets loose a throaty cry and flees, not out the entrance, but to Laurel's spring room. It bangs open the door and scuttles across the rock. Chausie watches it go and then eyeballs my bleeding arm, but I'm peering at my hand, the one with which I tore off the Prowler's flesh. It's smeared with my own blood along with disgusting morsels of Baalesh. I wipe it on my pants.

"You OK, Chaus?" I ask without looking. My hand's still gross. Chausie's leading me to the sink by the elbow and runs hot water to cleanse my shoulder.

"Yes, Ma'am," he says, soaking a towel and gently scrubbing me. The Southern accent he employs makes me smile. I wonder if he knows he's using it. When he's satisfied with his work, he kisses my shoulder, gives me a wink, and tells me to wash my hands, which I do.

All this time, Mr. Louris has been silent. The man's probably in shock. I try to think of what it must have looked like to him without being able to see Baalesh, and I'm seized by another fit of inappropriate giggling. I steal a glance at Chaus, who wants to share whatever I'm amused about, but of course, I'm not going to say it in front of his father.

"Chausie, can you track it?" Laurel asks. She's gazing at the clump of Baalesh I flung on her floor. And left there. My mouth tics an apology, and I move to clean it up, though I'm not exactly sure how to go about it.

"With that wretched smell?" Chausie answers. "Yeah, I can track it."

"Then I think that is your road." Laurel sets about the kitchen. "Take supplies." She quickly procures a sling bag that is already packed with bottles of water and two flashlights. Next, she makes peanut butter sandwiches and zips them into tight, little baggies like my mom used to do. "Should I include some of the newts and rats I have hanging in the attic?" she asks.

Chausie's lips pucker in knowing. She *did* overhear our conversation.

Laurel sobers. "Hold on to each other," she tells us. "May Creator guard your ground and sky."

Chausie's dad, who has been shifting his weight from foot to foot, also shifts his attention—from the spring room which, to his eyes, has thrown itself open, to his son, who is bantering with what I'm beginning to think he sees as flying articles of food. He clears his throat but then shakes his head to indicate he doesn't know what to say.

"Laurel?" I ask—and trust me, this ranks among the growing list of words I never thought I'd hear myself say—"Are you already dead?"

Mr. Louris stills.

"I am," Laurel admits. "And cremated long ago, so...none of that." She wags a finger at the dead man's body.

Just like the disgusting part of Baalesh, the body is *also* sprawled on Laurel's floor. I'm not at all sure we'll be invited back.

"I'll fly away, Little Sister, when the story comes to a close. In fact, I think I may be bound to roam above the Earth for as long as Chenoa is trapped beneath it." Laurel finishes packing for us and hangs the bag around my neck and my good arm. "It's just a theory."

Sadness must show on my face, because Laurel touches my cheek and says, "It's not a bad existence. I have a part to play, after all."

She embraces me. In the vacuum of my mother's presence, it fills me with unlimited affection for the woman. "I'm grateful for your part." I hope Laurel hears how much more I'd say if my throat wasn't stinging with emotion.

I've been treating this whole event like my life was the only one interrupted. Do blue-eyed girls from Georgia really get asked to make an impact for the greater good? If so, will I be brave enough to do what's needed when the time comes? I was *given* this blood. I didn't earn it.

Chausie is with his father, explaining our course of action. This is punctuated by comments from Laurel who wants Mr. Louris to understand that the Lakota have long respected his people. "But you don't allow your cubs to teach you anything," she says. "Your son is answering a sacred call. *Magnificently.*"

I'm the one to convey Laurel's words. "He really is," I add. "He didn't have to."

"Alllright," Chausie puts an end to the praise. "Trail's going cold."

I'm concerned with the way Mr. Louris is now appraising me. Like I've gone from being *the girl* to *the queen*. I'm neither. *Woman* is just fine. Maybe *lady*. I'll have to think about it. You know what? Let's just stick with *Beam*.

"Dad, don't tell Kimimela more than she needs to know," Chausie says. "Not till we know who all the players are. The priority is to find Beam's mother. Time is running out. And...take care of that for Laurel, will you?" Chausie motions to the body. Mr. Louris says that he will.

CHAUSIE

I'm a laundry load of emotions churning. Last year, my dad dropped the floor out of my world, and I didn't even know he was the culprit. No wonder I've felt so volatile. Don't think I haven't noticed the uncomfortable hesitations or the half-ass excuses either. There's more he's covering up.

Now he braces the back of my head. "I'm sorry, Chaus. I should have been the one to tell you."

"Dad, I can't do this now." I push back against his hold. It's more than his new marriage I'm worried about. It's the creeping dread that he's tangled up in something truly awful. I don't want to ask, but we have to know. "Where did the body come from?"

Dad steps back. "It found its own way to The Outpost."

"How?"

Another shifty-eyed pause. "You saw him, Chausie. You didn't know he was dead either. The Outpost is where Beam's father *should* have come for help in finding her. I thought he finally had."

"On my bike? You said Kimimela—"

"No, she had already returned that to me. It was all my idea for the man to ride it here. I thought you'd need something to ride back, and honestly, I thought it would help persuade you to come. The— dead man—who I thought was Beam's father—just wanted to reach her as quickly as he could. Which seemed legitimate to me at the time."

I stare at him hard. *Can I trust you?* I want to ask. But he's already given me the answer to that, hasn't he? Along with a new life for my mom and me without him in it. I don't have time to interrogate him. I shouldn't have to.

"Blue!" I call. "Are you coming?"

Blue's been dangling his feet from the cabinets. Now he rolls his head away in a melodramatic attempt to shun me. No idea why. I roll my head with the same energy, to solicit help from Beam.

"Why aren't you talking to Chausie?" she asks.

He turns his back on both of us.

"Come on, Blue," I say. "We don't have time for this. What's wrong?"

"I've never ridden a motorcycle before," he says to the wall. And that's all he says.

Beam says, "Why should that make you angry with Chausie?"

"He didn't even take me into consideration!" Blue huffs. "Just told his dad-the-lion noooo, noooo, I'm not going to ride my bike."

Beam covers her mouth and turns her smiling eyes on me.

"Blue, I'd be happy to take you for a ride," I assure him. "When all this is over, let's make a day of it. What'd you say?"

"Promise?"

"Yeah, Man."

He scrutinizes me. "Just the two of us?"

I am strangely uncomfortable with this proposal. "I guess?" Beam stifles a laugh when I consult her with a shrug of my nose, and Blue answers without further sulking.

"OK, I'll come. But you are *really* going to need Goliath."

12

TUMBLING ROCK

BEAM

According to Chausie's nose, the crack in the spring room wall is in fact the exit through which Baalesh fled. But it is far too small for us to enter, so here we are, all packed up but with no door into the secret halls of eroded sandstone. Basically, we're trying to crawl into the earth's crust. Does it make any sense? No. Not in the life I led up until a few days ago.

After sniffing the spring room, Chausie sniffs the whole house, including cupboards and closets. It's his dad who finds an entryway. Having searched outside, Mr. Louris now calls to us from the glen. He has cleared the snow and some of the soil around the base of the butte, revealing a small hole. Chausie immediately begins to claw at it, and his father joins him, their strong feline muscles flexing through their fur.

Soon, the earth crumbles away to reveal an opening wide enough to enter, and Chausie bounds through it while the rest of us wait to see if it's a viable path. I'm shivering with cold by the time he jogs out.

"This is it. I found the scent and it's walkable—at least as far as I went."

"It's very dark in there," I comment. Now that it comes to it, maybe the freezing cold out here in the bright sunshine isn't so bad.

"Here." Mr. Louris offers a small flashlight from one of his pockets. Seems puny for someone whose job it is to roam the wild.

"We don't usually need extra light," he explains. "Our night vision..."

"You have to stay here and take care of the dead guy," Chausie reminds him.

"I know." His dad looks him over. I think he'd like to hug him again, but he doesn't. "You really are healed," he says.

"Yeah. Don't spread it around, OK?"

"I won't. But I'm so glad." He glances at me and back to Chaus. "Go do your job."

Chausie nods, pride working its way into a bashful smile. It was probably the exact thing he needed to hear.

"Ready?" he asks me, and off we go, Chausie first so that he can help me down into the hole. *Oh, dear.*

Always, there is this feeling that we're being watched. And often, the narrow trail is bordered by sudden coveys into darkness. When I run a hand along the cool, stone wall, which I do in an effort to feel grounded, any unusual gaps make me paranoid that something is hiding just out of sight. Speaking of which, where does Blue go when he vanishes?

Chausie is a cat. This limits our conversation. He understands what I say, but all I can do is infer his intentions from his whiskers and his tail—which *is* quite expressive. He's able to see far better than I, so, even though I have a small flashlight, he moves more quickly than I'd like. When he turns to me, his yellow eyes are lit, and he drops his lion to procure his own flashlight and point out spiky, chandelier formations hanging overhead.

"Is that not the coolest?" he asks.

Apparently, he doesn't share the same aversion to our surroundings.

"It is pretty cool," I admit. "What makes the different shapes? Why are some parts pointy like that and other parts smooth like petrified bubbles?"

"We'll ask Grant. He spends inhuman amounts of time crawling through these things. Sometimes there's only room for him to snake through on his belly."

"There's no way," I tell him, but Chausie mutters, "That may be *exactly* what we'll be doing."

"*I* won't," I say, but I know that I will—if it means getting my mom back.

"You wouldn't mind it if you were a cat." He paces onward, but I hang back.

"Do you wish I was?" I ask. I don't say the next, but ever since I met his friends I've wondered if he'd rather end up with a fierce little lion lady.

"A cat?" Chausie spins, and his flashlight makes me squint. "Sorry." He drops it to his side.

"Yeah, I mean," I play it down. "I don't have whiskers."

"I like that you don't have whiskers."

"I don't have an expressive tail."

He peers over my shoulder. "I beg to differ."

"I'm serious," I say with a slap. "I can't keep up with you. I can't challenge you—"

He cuts me off with a snort and resumes his stride. "You challenge me just fine. I've never met anybody who knows her mind so well." When I don't follow, Chausie stops again.

"Does this really bother you?" he asks.

I say no, but I mean yes, and he stares at me, bemused.

"What?" I demand.

"I don't want you to be anything but Beam." When I remain doubtful, he crosses his arms. "You know? You're a complex, little woman. How can you trash-talk a maniacal dragon demon one minute, and then feel insecure around *me* the next? You make me *really* happy—just by being you. I haven't been happy in ages."

When I crash him into a hug, he chuckles. "But if you'd like a more honest evaluation of your tail, I'd—"

"Shut up," I say into his chest, so he kisses the top of my head and tells me he loves me like it's a secret.

I thought it would be cold inside the cave, but it gets warmer all the time. And all the time, our path slopes downward. We march on for a few hours—probably feels longer than it actually is—and there's often something jutting up, or out, or down, something on which to bang my knee or some other body part. At some point, though, I become aware that there's more light to see by. We take a left into an open cavern that glows red and I nearly gag as the stench overwhelms me. I cover my mouth and nose while Chausie directs me against the wall with a nod of his feline head. When he morphs into a man, his voice is low in both pitch and volume. "Baalesh is somewhere in there."

"No kidding," I say from behind my hand. "Why doesn't Blue stink like this?"

Instead of answering that, Chausie does the scowling face at me. But now I know there's something behind it, something he'd like to say. "Yessss?" I ask.

"I think we should keep exploring the path we just left."

"But Laurel told us to follow Big B."

"I know. But there are people down that way. I'm sure of it. And I can smell new construction. I can't imagine what that would be unless we're really close to the outside. My gut says we should go. Anyway, it's not far. We can double back."

I'm aware that I'm a rule follower. And I am willing to consider that—at times—perhaps—I take it too far. Directions, instructions, maps...all friends of mine. Are they friends of Chausie's? Not so much. He's willing to—and let's be truthful—he'd much *rather* reach the goal by any other thrilling means available.

"What *is* the goal?" I ask aloud. I actually want to know. It's broader than it was when we left Atlanta.

"Toooo find your mom?"

"That's what I want it to be. But Laurel says we're part of a broader story. Even you say we were put together by some divine appointment." I thrust my head back the way we've come. "Let's follow your gut."

"Yeah?" Chausie answers with surprise. "Cool."

"Am I *that* rigid? Honestly. It's not like I just follow the rules *blindly*."

"As I said, you know your mind. Come on."

About thirty minutes later, we find a dry recess in which to take a quick break, and I sit against the rock with a sigh of relief. "I've never had to concentrate so hard just to walk," I say. "My eyes are as tired as my legs."

"Am I pushing too hard?" Chausie's bending over me, rummaging through the bag that hangs at my chest.

"It's just good to rest."

He hands me a peanut butter sandwich. "It's not wasabi almonds," he says, "but it'll have to do."

"Oooo. I'd eat 'em up."

Chausie sits back too. "When we get out of here, I'm gonna get you a life's supply."

"All at once?" I ask. "Or year by year?"

He replies around a big bite, "Did you just propose to me?"

"Yeah, if you'll keep the almonds coming."

We like to flirt with this idea that we'll stay together past the adventure we're having. But I know where Chausie's heart lies. Here. In the Badlands, having adventures every day. Freedom to be his lion self. And I start college in the fall. Hopefully law school after that.

I've never had much sympathy for those high school couples who struggle with what to do when their lives lead them apart. I mean, if it doesn't propel you toward your life's goals, stop whining about it and get a move on. But it's not that easy, is it? Not when you really start to care about somebody.

"What happened?" Chaus asks. "You went dark."

"Just wondering if they'll deliver those almonds to Chicago," I say.

"*I'll* deliver those almonds to Chicago. And force you to relax your genius brain with long day trips around Lake Michigan. I've already thought it through."

When I crane my neck to read his expression, he says, "You're not the only one who plans ahead, Beam. When it matters." He pops the last bite into his mouth, brushes his hands of crumbs, and adds, "I've already ordered your motorcycle helmet."

Gah, he makes me smile. "There's no way you could've done that."

"Oh, yes I did." He scoots closer. "It's pink camo with the words 'Chausie's Chick' printed on the back." I snort at that. "Oh, and a bristly pink mohawk." Chausie feels the air above his head to indicate where the mohawk will be stationed. "'Cause, you're an injun."

"Oh my gosh," I laugh. "You did not just say that. That's not even what the Lakota do. They keep their hair long."

"How would *you* know?" he teases. He's very close to me now and kisses me through a smile. Who would have thought he'd prove so extraordinarily gentle?

"Do you *really* want to make this work?" I ask.

"Oh, I'm *gonna* make this work," he declares. And then, not so confidently, he adds, "Don't you want to make this work?"

"I do." I can't believe I'm saying it. Not because I'm not head over heels for the guy, but because it throws such a wrench into my tidy, well-organized plans. "I do want to."

"Right. Good. Well, let's get you out of *this* mess first. You ready?"

He helps me up, and we begin again. It isn't long before we come upon the framed-in skeleton of an unfinished room, made right into the rock. It's not huge, just the size of someone's living room, and it's empty except for a few saw horses. The sub-floor looks like cork, and the whole place smells of wood shavings. Black plastic sheets divide this room from the next, but natural light can be seen where the dividers meet. Chausie flashes his eyebrows in expectation and hurries to find out what's on the other side.

"You're such a cat," I whisper and try not to recite what curiosity does to one.

Shifting the plastic partition aside, we blink because daylight spills in from a row of windows far above us. A wide ramp leads into this much larger, deeper, and taller space. It seems that we are only mice exiting our hole.

From the ramp, we have an aerial view of what is part library and part museum, but I get the feeling this section of the building is for staff only. There are drawers at ground level, labeled to declare their contents and shelves of books that line the walls. There are glass cases displaying a host of items that I can't make out from here.

"The crow man is down there," Chausie whispers. "Or has been."

"How do you know?"

He touches his nose and begins to descend. "Hang on!" I clutch his arm. "Where are you going?"

"To find out what this place is."

When I realize he's left me behind, I jump to catch up, and for the next few minutes, we scan the collections. There's a rack of antlers from which leather purses hang, decoratively woven with porcupine quills. I only know that because of the description card. How in the world can they be so intricately crafted? Over my shoulder, Chausie says, "Whose job was it to collect the quills, do you think?"

A vision of a timid, young barber comes to mind, amidst several angry porcupines. "That's funny, Chaus. I'm glad you're taking this all in stride."

Next to the bags are masks. Macabre, eyeless bird faces with long hard beaks. A coyote head whose paws and fur were made to drape a person like a sweater. "What's this one?" I ask. I think it must be some sort of hag. There's long hair flowing over its head and shoulders.

"Chiye Tanka, I think." When I lift my eyebrows in question, he says, "The Elder Brother."

Still doesn't help.

"Bigfoot?" he tries.

"Oh. Yikes."

"It's just a mask. I think it's horse hair. Look over here." He bends over the next table where there are bones and dried-up carcasses. A dove. A rabbit. Several large, severed wings. *Ew.* Black feathers have been ripped out and collected into bags while the naked wings remain in piles. Many more wings fill a small trashcan to overflow. "This is more workstation than display table," I observe. "What do you think was going on here?"

Chausie leaps back, dropping something onto the table with a thud. A large, decapitated head, covered in yellow fur, its dead eyes staring up at us.

"Chausie, that's not—it's not—"

"It is," he replies.

"But just a regular mountain lion, right? Not a human."

Chausie's watching the head like he's waiting for it to speak to him. "See the way the bone extends to make room for more brain?" He points to the apex, his lips curled in revulsion. "This was a shifter." The canines are missing, and there's evidence that they were pounded into dust.

"How do you think she died?" I ask.

"She?"

"The head's smaller than yours. I just assumed."

"This place gives me the creeps," he says.

The next counter we come to holds dozens of books, some of them opened or marked to specific passages. Some of them are upheld on stands as one might position a recipe book while cooking. Many of the volumes look ancient, with worn leather and yellowing parchment. Some of them aren't even bound. They're just stacks of brittle pages written in languages with which I'm unfamiliar.

Chausie reads a few of the titles. *"Ancient Death Cultures. Rites of Passage. Necromancy?"* He turns to me with the question.

"Has to do with consulting the dead."

"I know what it means. What's it doing here among all the Native artifacts? It's just a disturbing hodgepodge of the occult and world religions concerning death. *Yie!* Look at these."

He flips through pen-and-ink drawings of gruesome scenes. Romanticized, but very graphic portrayals of women being slaughtered and bled into jars, or over volcanoes, or spattered against walls. The dates vary by hundreds of years and the locations by tens of thousands of miles.

"Why is it always women?" he asks and glances back to the lioness's head.

"Misogyny's nothing new."

"Yeah, but *why?* Don't those men have mothers? And what the is *that?*"

The last drawing is truly horrific. It appears to be some tortured soul hovering above her own body, clawing to get back inside. It describes a process by which her blood can be used in the making of a talisman—I think—because someone beside her is clutching a bracelet and staring into a bowl full of liquid that appears to be dripping from her body's hand. There's a list of ingredients and creepy icons sketched at random intervals beside the words. But there's also a small scene being played out in the reflection of the blood.

Whatever the end goal, the process seems to necessitate the ousting of the woman's soul from her own body. Looming behind everything, what at first I disregarded as a storm cloud, because of its colossal size and billowing darkness, now strikes me as a malevolent being without enough physical definition to name. The whole thing is just oppressive. "What do you think it means?" I ask, resisting the thought that it has to do with my mother's condition in the video.

"I think it means that somebody's into some dark shit." He's leaning in now, pointing at the bowl, his brows knitted together. "Are you seeing this?"

Another sweep of the illustration makes my blood run cold. I clutch the counter for support.

"How?" he whispers. Distributed through the liquid of the bowl are the exact images we saw in Laurel's spring—as if the bowl is the spring itself. The carnage of our own friends and family stares up at us in inked images.

We slowly turn our attention to a real bowl that is perched upon an adjoining counter. "I felt someone watching us," Chausie says. "They were using that bowl to scry on us." He searches the room as if that person is about to materialize when—*Thwack!* The counter's front end lifts and bangs to the ground on its own, sending ripples throughout the nearly gelatinous contents of the bowl. Chausie jerks me back by the arm as other sounds emanate from inside the cupboard, knocking like small fists pounding upon a door. Perhaps the strangest thing of all is that there are also high-pitched voices from inside—shouting obscenities.

"Something's trapped," Chausie says and bends to reach for the latch.

"Chaus, are you sure you want to do that? You don't know what's in there."

"I know if it's trapped in *here*, it needs to be freed."

He opens the cabinet, and out pop three small prowlers, no larger than Blue, but each is green. Well, one is kind of yellow. They brandish curled fists, reminding me of the fighting Irish leprechauns from the University of Notre Dame. They're furious, and they're cursing, but they're so cute I want to squeeze them and dress them in small top hats, like the guy on the cereal box. I hold up my hands to show I'm not a threat, but all three of them narrow their eyes at me, making them appear comically suspicious. (I heard it too, but I'm not going to rhyme it. OK. *Magically delicious.* But I'm not going to sing it. *Dammit.*)

Chausie clears his throat and our new acquaintances nearly leap out of their skins. They shriek and swear some more.

"What were you doing in there?" he asks. They pretend not to hear him. Or maybe they think he's talking to me. "Hey!" He pokes one of them, sending it fleeing behind the others, and they jostle for who gets to stand in the back.

"The lion man (expletive too strong for civilized company) touched me!" the one wails. "He acts as if he can (expletive, expletive) see me."

"I *can* see you. What were you doing in there?" Chausie inspects the inside of the cabinet. "Why couldn't you get out?"

None of the creatures look at him directly, though they sort of throw sidelong glances, the way my dog used to do when he thought he was in trouble.

"Hey, Guys?" I ask gently and get down on their level. "Were you being held captive in there? Can you get back to where you belong now?"

"You are letting us go?" The one Chausie poked now steps forward.

"*We* didn't keep you in there," I say. "Do you know who did?"

"We were just minding our own (expletive) business!" declares another one. "When we were (expletive) sucked from our (expletive, expletive) crevasse." I can't relay the rest of what he says, because it's so filthy and shocking.

"Were you raised by pirates?" I laugh. They find this highly offensive.

"I'm sorry. You're just so—"

"Hush!" Chausie hisses and spins toward a door we have yet to breach. He throws an arm in front of me like a seat belt, which sends the prowler boys scampering up the ramp where they disappear into the cave.

Even though I don't sense anything, I wait for Chausie's instruction. He's listening. He's sniffing the air, and now I realize that a new smell is permeating the space. A sweet, earthy incense. I hear something too. A low voice droning. Chausie stalks toward the sound, his human face set like the predator he is, though he's still in human form.

I become aware that I'm not as apprehensive as I ought to be. On the contrary, the sweet smell and the droning song are attracting me, drawing me out. I follow Chaus into a small office. Nothing more. A desk, a chair, a filing cabinet with drawers. Have we missed something? I retrace our steps to the main room, but Chausie whistles me back. He has swiped aside a wall covering to reveal a closed pocket door and now he slowly slides the door, peeks through a tiny crack, and then opens it fully, onto another wide room.

This room is sparsely furnished with a couch and two rugs bearing angular patterns. Up high is a loft with a railing around the perimeter—and rafters above that. Behind the railings, the loft is segmented into stalls.

The droning is sung by a man with his back to us, and he waves a burning bundle of twigs which he follows forward like it's a divining rod. After a short pause, he steps back to the center of the room and then bends to float the smoke around his feet. Rising again, he wafts the smoke to his face and breathes it in. The whole process gets repeated on the next wall.

I turn to Chaus, my brow bent in question.

"A smudging ritual," he murmurs. "The sage is supposed to purify the place of evil energy."

Whether or not the man notices our presence, he continues to chant, and I find that I am in love with the song. Though I don't understand the words, they're delivered with much passion and little tonal derivation. It's a prayer. Or an incantation. He begins to move the smoldering wand up and down, back and forth, like a paintbrush, or like he's sweeping away cobwebs. His motions ride on the rhythm of his voice. When he's finished with that wall, he turns toward the one from which we are spying.

I would normally apologize for such an intrusion, but he's so fascinating, I'm too absorbed to feel self-conscious. The man holds my gaze and then Chausie's, but continues to sing and wave. He wafts the smoke around his feet and up to his face. I find my own nose pushing forward.

Suddenly, with the clatter of a dislodged pail, there's a floundering of black feathers from the rafters above, and a huge crow falls out as if it is being shaken from a blanket. It stumbles to the ground and hunches into its wings where it grows two times, three times, five times itself, and becomes a very disgruntled man, the same man who took a crow's form at my house. I fail to stifle a cry, but Chausie remains collected and poised to pounce. Likewise, if the man performing the ritual is shaken, he doesn't let on. Rather, he observes the burning sage with satisfaction like it's a job well done.

Instead of addressing Kanji Brings Justice, the man speaks to Chausie. "Master Lion," he says and Chausie dips his head. "Will you offer a chair to our guest?"

Chausie is quick to comply. He wheels the desk chair from the office and stations it behind Kanji. When Kanji doesn't sit, Chausie lays a hand on his shoulder. I imagine there's some heaviness to it. Then Chausie gives a kick to the back of the man's knee, and he buckles into the chair where he fixes me with a poisonous glare. I forgot how full of darkness his eyes were—like they are all pupils.

"President Tumbling Rock," Chausie says, "Did the ritual reveal this man?"

What did he just say? My eyes go wide and land on...the president? And now I'm nervous. I'm nervous all over. I thought that if ever I came face to face with this man, I'd give him a piece of my mind. But now that it comes to it, I can't think of a word to say. I find that I have questions but not accusations and, above all, a growing sense of wonder. I thought he'd be, I don't know, all the stupid stereotypes people think *I* should be, I guess. Instead, I find that he's some sort of holy man, a singer, a believer. But the most shocking part? He's peering at me through the kindest eyes—of blue.

"Evil hearts and evil magic have a low tolerance for the smudging, Master Lion. Will you remove the bones?" How Chausie knows what the president is referring to, I'm not sure, but he scoops the crow man's long hair aside and unties the man's choker. Kanji's pupils recede to reveal normal brown irises, and he slumps forward like he's been unplugged.

When Chausie offers the necklace to the president, he declines with a flash of his palm, saying, "Shifter magic is beyond me. I leave its fate to you."

Chausie looks perplexed about what he's supposed to do with it, so it hangs from his outstretched hand until he eventually stuffs it into his pocket.

I think some of the bones are the hollow shafts of crows' feathers, so I guess now we know what the wings in the other room were used for.

"President Tumbling Rock," Chausie says. "This is Beam. Beam Redfeather."

Kanji, meanwhile, is sneering at me again. He says, "Her father assured us she wouldn't come. And now here she is, an abomination within our land. Cut her and see."

Before the words are out of his mouth, the president lets the sage fall to the ground and drops Kanji as well—with his fist. It took three paces across the room and a devotion to...me? I remind myself to breathe.

The act strikes Chausie differently. He's got his lips pursed like he wants to laugh.

"Kanji Brings Justice," the president scolds, "your name has become a lie and a disgrace. From now on, you will be called Kanji Self-Righteous."

Out of the corner of my eye, I see the rug is catching fire, so I snatch up the burning bundle of sage and grind my shoe into the live ember on the rug. When that's out, I can't help myself, I waft the smoke into my face for a long, soothing toke.

When I open my eyes, all three men are staring at me, and I'm a little embarrassed. I may have just transgressed a sacred object or a cultural norm. I shakily extend the sage to the president, but it's the crow man who reacts, shrinking back like I'm brandishing a weapon. Chausie snorts out a laugh. "Yeah," he says mockingly. "*She's* the abomination."

"Summer Sunbeam," the president offers, "will you place that into the bowl for me?" His loose gray hair falls well beneath his shoulders. He's several inches shorter than Chausie, which still puts him taller than me.

After I locate the stone bowl and deposit the bundle, I find my voice. "It's an honor to meet you, Sir." I find that it truly is and catch the wink Chaus throws at me from over the president's shoulder.

"It's not the first time we've met," he says. "Though you were too young to remember it. When you were a baby, your father organized an old-fashioned naming ceremony, and because I was the medicine man at the time, the honor fell to me."

"*You* named me?"

"I came very close to naming you after the color of your eyes." He steps closer as he says it, and the mutual dominance of our recessive trait connects us.

There have been times, if I'm being honest, when I've felt—less than whole. I mean, imagine that the chorus of your identity all your life is that you are *half* of something, *half* Native, *half* white. It's easy to feel reduced. But now, looking into President Tumbling Rock's blue eyes, I'm struck with the idea that having genes from all over the globe makes me *more*.

"What made you change your mind?" I ask.

"A holy woman came forward to share a vision she'd been given, and I knew that you would become for us a brilliant guide. You were born in August, and it pleased us to call you Summer Sunbeam."

The crow man makes a derisive whistling sound that draws the president's attention back to him. With a deep sigh, Tumbling Rock says, "Kanji, what you have done is too shameful to mention, yet too vile to ignore. Is life so small a thing that you felt authorized to end it? You have lifted yourself above Creator, and have brought guilt upon your Tribe. The blood of the dead cries out to the heavens. Would you fly through the noise on the wings of the lives you took? You heap curses upon us. By your own deeds, you will die. But there may still be redemption for you. Tell us what you know of Maggie Redfeather."

My heart skips at the mention of my mother's name, and while Kanji stares at the president in surly silence, I study his face. *What do you know?*

13

THE CATACOMB

BEAM

When it becomes apparent that, despite the president's prodding, Kanji isn't going to reveal anything, the president says, "Enough wasted time. Let's confine him to one of the upstairs rooms."

Chausie and the president escort the crow man up a flight of steep narrow stairs, along the balcony, and into one of the stalls on the end. I follow at a distance, and when I top the stairs, the first open doorway stops me in my tracks. The room is hauntingly similar to the one in the video. I choke to recall who recently possessed it. The standing lamp. The humble desk. The minimal camp bed. The braided rug. There's a closet with another pocket door, and I shove it open in haste. It's bare. I circle the area twice. I comb the floor for clues, for anything to tell me that I'm correct, that this is the room where my mother was held.

Down the hall, a commotion breaks loose. There's a sound of a struggle, a man's cry, and a sickening thwack. I thrust my head out in time to see Chausie exit a door and gape over the railing. Fear of what I'll find keeps me from doing the same. The crow man takes advantage of Chausie's distraction.

He dislodges the choker from Chausie's pocket, but Chausie takes a swing that connects with his cheek. As Kanji reels from the blow, he spots me and dives in my direction. Man becomes crow. Chaus becomes lion. Crow flies at my head—his sharp beak on target with my eyes. But Chausie's teeth are close behind, and he snarls a rebuke.

Whatever the crow may have wanted to do to me, he thinks better of it and veers away half a second before Chausie's jaws clamp down like a gunshot in front of my face. The crow swoops over the railing. Chausie dives after him.

I get to learn what it means to *hit the ground running* because that is exactly what my lion does. They vanish down a hallway. That crow had better hope to find tall ceilings if he's going to escape with his feathers intact.

But now I remember the horrible thwack, and I look over the railing to find what I'd feared. "President Tumbling Rock?!" Kanji must have pushed him over while Chausie was securing the room. He's lying in a fetal position with both his hands cradling his head. I bound down the stairs and run across the room to kneel beside him. He's not moving much. "Sir, how bad is it?"

His eyes search for me for a long moment, and I worry he's unable to think clearly. Then I worry he's playing me to get a taste of my blood. Then I don't even care, because what if he is really incapacitated, and I'm the only one who can help? I'd much rather be wrong about his intentions than withhold the thing that may be able to save him. "I'll give it to you if you need it," I say. "I'll cut myself right now if it will save you. Can you tell me?"

He answers much the way Laurel did, although with a weaker, raspier voice. "I wouldn't ask it of you. Nor would I accept such a sacred gift."

"Why not?" I ask. And then I sit back on my heels to scrutinize him. "You're not already dead are you?"

He chuckles in response and comes to a seated position with a groan. "I don't think so. Maybe a bit concussed."

"I have water." I unzip my bag. "I have—" The president stops me with a hand on mine.

"Summer Sunbeam," he says. "Ask me what you need to know."

"Is my dad OK?"

"Yes."

"Why did you detain him? Why did you keep him from speaking to me?"

"It was your father who refused to speak to you. Refused to take your calls."

"I don't believe you," I tell him. The only thing is...I do. "Why would he do that?"

"To keep you as far removed as he could, I imagine. To keep anyone else from confirming what you are. He came to us to solicit help in finding your mother and refused to leave until he got that help. Treated it like a hunger strike."

Now, *that* I can believe. "I think she was kept up there, my mother." I point to the stall I mean. "But she's not there now."

"I think you're right," the president says. "I need to ask you something about that, but first—"

"Do you think I'm a danger to your people?" I blurt out. It is suddenly very important to me what he believes—like it will establish what is true. "I would never hurt anybody, not on purpose. I know I have to keep my—" I was going to say *my power in check*. And now I feel as if the paradox of my life has surfaced. For all intents and purposes, I've been led to believe I have no power. That the things I see don't exist. That I should keep quiet about them because they're shameful or because they'll put me in danger. And yet I've been treated like a ticking time bomb. I am the danger.

The revelation is shocking, but with the sort of satisfaction of fitting the final puzzle pieces. I haven't been protected all my life. I've been neutralized.

"If I doubt you, Sister Sunbeam, it is not the strength of your heart. I do not see cruelty there. I see a fierce protector. Only, I wonder to whom that protection extends. The sage drew you to itself, revealed you as a daughter of light. I am confident that your light can reach into the darkest corners of this universe for the good of my people. But only when you can also call them your people."

He allows his words time to settle, then says, "But no matter. You were born to us. And what kind of tribe would we be if we did not aid you in your time of need?"

CHAUSIE

The president was hurled over the railing before I could do a thing, and now I am chasing a crow down a long hallway where he is soaring as high as the ceiling will allow, careening from side to side. I bounce up the walls after him. I could have chomped down on his backbone twice, but both times I only yanked out feathers instead, worried that I'd do irreparable damage.

Coming up fast, at the end of the hall, is a double metal door. Time's up for the crow. He reaches a wing to punch it open as he's in flight. Wing becomes hand. Hand becomes arm. Arm becomes man. But he's in motion, so he somersaults over himself. I slow to keep from crashing, giving him time to pop up and shove the door open. He launches himself through, again as a bird, and anger shoots needles down my spine. I should've dug in when I had the chance.

The door leads into a cold, dark room. Cold enough to be a refrigerator. There's a water source, a stream winding through the middle, and I think the water must be what's cooling the place. We're back inside the earth now, so calling this a room is generous. It's a limestone cavern, dimly lit with soft blue bulbs laid in paths at ground level. There are couches carved into the rock walls. Tens of couches, maybe upwards of a hundred. They're stacked like bunk beds, four, sometimes five tall.

The crow has hidden out of sight and keeps very quiet, but I'm distracted by the couches, or rather, by the forms which occupy them. As I walk the width of the space—it's kind of an eggplant shape, curving this way and that, and so the couches curve too—as I walk across, I have to traverse the stream on an ornamental wooden bridge. This is a tomb. Like the ancient catacombs. There are well-preserved bodies lying in repose, clothed in ceremonial garb. Most of them died when they were old, but there are some children too. What *is* this place?

The crow seizes the opportunity to streak from one of the couches. I make a bid for him, but I miss, and before I can mount another attempt, he is soaring up through a smooth cylindrical chamber, cawing with delight. At first, I mistake the chamber for an enormous elevator shaft. But when I look down, I see that it's just more of a dark hole. Why would anyone drill into the earth right here? Gold? I can't see the bottom.

I've lost the crow. I study the empty shaft going up. There's no telling how far it extends. Ten stories? The faint scent of fresh air comes to me, and I can see a small circle of daylight that is the open sky. I hate to give up, but the crow has clearly escaped, and I don't want to be gone from Beam any longer than I have to.

Dammit. That crow is the key to this whole thing and I let him get the drop on me. That's what I'm thinking as I stare around the creepy, blue-lit morgue. It's quiet in here, except for the stream, and yet I get the sense that I'm not alone. There are heartbeats. Breaths being held. I wish I hadn't been so quick to dismiss my dad.

When I fail to locate anything alive, I decide to stick a pin in it for later and head back down the hallway where it dawns on me what this place is. We're in The Vigilance. We just didn't come through the front door the way I have in the past, and this part is off-limits to the public. There would surely be an outcry over the things I've seen here today.

One of the doors proves my assumption correct. I've been here on field trips. I quickly wander the familiar exhibit room past pipes with beaded handles, traditional garb on manikins, and a long timeline of Indigenous tribes going back further than woolly mammoths. A huge taxidermy bison—the same one, I smile to remember, that Grant and

I got in trouble trying to ride—guards the library where, admittedly, I never spent much time.

I tiptoe through now as a means back to the hallway, but on one of the round tables as if a careless patron abandoned it, lies one thin, hard-bound volume entitled *The Sacred Visions of the Oglala Lakota*. It's written in both the Tribe's Native language and in English. A pen and several notecards a scattered nearby. On one of them is a working interpretation of what appears to be a problematic line.

The Elixir owns a lion's heart. The Elixir pumps a lion's heart. Pumps THROUGH... The Elixir is a lion and SHE is the Elixir. The Elixir is a lioness???

The Vigilance appears to be closed today. Whose work is this, and why has it been left? Maybe Kanji? I don't have time to spend on it. I have to get back to the real thing. So, sniffing the air and smelling no one, I allow the scent of smoldering sage to guide me back. When I find Beam sitting on the floor with an unharmed president, I stop at the doorway until they lift their eyes to me.

"I lost the crow, but I do have information."

Once I share with them what I've found, Beam remarks, "The woman with the bodies." She's quoting Baalesh. I thought the same thing and felt ill as I worked out who that woman must be and to whom she is married.

"It's Kimimela," I say. "She's the one who runs this place. She's the one who told Baalesh to pose as your dad." But she must be using *my* dad—because he wasn't in on it. I truly believe that he was deceived. That gives me some hope that he's not as deeply involved as I feared.

Beam's eyes widen. "Are we inside The Vigilance right now?" She looks to the president for confirmation, which he gives.

"Hang on—" Beam asks the last question I expect to hear. One that never would've crossed my mind. Not, *So Kanji Brings Justice is working with Kimimela?* And not, *Did they kill a lioness to make shifter magic?* Not even, *Where are the visions about me located?* No. She chooses, "Isn't this place a sovereign entity? Are we even allowed to be in here?" She glances over her shoulder like *now* she's afraid. Not because some crazy bird dude wants her dead, but because she might be infringing upon official guidelines.

I've seen the president discuss things candidly in the middle of debate between strong personalities who strongly disagree. I've seen him present proposals and enact regulations. I've even seen him joke around. What I've never seen is the confounded expression he's quietly wearing right now. But leave it to Beam to let concern for the rule of law interrupt someone's ability to process communication.

"She's the product of two attorneys," I offer.

When the president has recovered his faculties, he says, "No, that's good. She'll need a mind dedicated to what's right and true." To Beam, he says, "The Vigilance was set up to protect the Oglala people."

"Yes, but the Lakota are—"

"The *Lakota* are seven tribes. The *Oglala* Lakota is one. The Council represents all seven of us. There was blame. The one who opened the gates was Oglala. And when another Elixir was foretold—"

"The Vigilance was given sovereignty to protect Lakota from Lakota?" Beam asks.

"Yes. But the visions were ambiguous. They weren't clear if that Elixir would be Oglala specifically, or Lakota, or of some other descent altogether. And *you*, Beam, are both. And neither."

"Well, visions aren't manuals," she says. "They're more like signposts." I run my bottom lip through my teeth to suppress a smile.

The president nods in agreement. "Being above the law corrupts the law, and the sovereignty afforded to The Vigilance is no exception. Things have been happening here, hidden from the tribes. I'm afraid to know the extent of it. And yet I must, in order to protect my people. *All* of my people." The president peers pointedly at Beam who seems to accept his inclusion of her. "Anyway, I do not accept sovereignty that extends to criminal acts. Kidnapping. Murder. Lies spread through the whole community. I am well within my action-able duty, if not my legal right, to be here." The president reveals a cloth notebook with a soft yellow cover.

"Where did you get *that*?!" Beam asks.

"I found it upstairs tied to the underside of the bed. I wonder if it will be better served by your eyes. I can't make any sense of it."

Beam is clearly familiar with the notebook. She hugs it to herself as a welcomed friend. She pages through while I look on, but it may as well be in Cantonese. I can't make any more sense of it than the president can.

"It's Mom's shorthand," she says. "But I know it. We used to write notes back and forth, and sometimes we'd make up more complex codes and equations to decipher, and—" When she realizes she's geeking out she ends with, "Anyway, I can read it."

For the next few minutes, Beam puzzles through her mother's words and offers us pieces of information. "The name of the friend who solicited Mom's help was Esther. Esther's elderly father had latched on to Kimimela's ideals about the preservation of the earthly body in the hopes of a resurrected life here on Earth. But Esther found out that the future resuscitation of the body required an infu-sion of other kinds of creatures until the body's true soul could be found and the two reunited. The bodies are not holding up to that." Beam looks up to say, "Do you think that's why the prowlers are being trapped?"

I frown at the page. "You got all that from those little marks and circles?"

She ignores me. "There is some backstory on Kimimela. It says her father died when she was thirteen. Her mother was addicted to alcohol and severely depressed until her own untimely passing. By then, Kimimela had managed a scholarship to the University of Washington where she earned a degree in Native American studies. She got married, pursued her master's in education, had two children, and became a professor. Then she sought a doctorate in what began as American Indian Customs and Languages but ended up in a broader degree of Death, Religion, and Cultural Rites.

"Oh no," Beam reacts to what she's reading. "During that same time, her husband and children were all tragically killed in a car wreck. Kimimela was in the car too. She was in a coma for days, so her *husband's* parents made all the decisions about preparation, ceremony, place of burial, all of it. When Kimimela woke up, they were already buried. She sued her in-laws and demanded the remains be transferred to Lakota burial grounds.

"She didn't work with The Vigilance at that time, but she sought their help, leveraging their political power so that, in the end, she was able to have the remains of her children exhumed—not the husband—and brought directly to The Vigilance."

"I saw the bodies of children in the tomb room," I tell her.

"You did?"

"I don't think Kimimela and Kanji are after the same thing."

"But they are clearly working together from here." Beam flips through the last pages. "It doesn't mention him anywhere."

The president weighs what we say without comment, while Beam continues to read. "This is where things get super sticky," she says.

"Your mom wrote *super sticky?* Show me."

The look of disdain with which my girlfriend blesses me makes me grin. "The translator's allowed certain liberties," she says. "The more my mom's friend Esther found out what *really* goes on here, the more she questioned her father's end-of-life plans. They became convinced it was *not* in keeping with Lakota customs and, further, that it was a violation of the natural order of Creation. Esther's father withdrew his permission for his remains to be kept. But guess what. After he died, Kimimela had his body moved here anyway. And that's when Esther called my mom."

Beam reads the rest silently. Before the end of it, her brow is furrowed, and she wipes a tear from her eye.

"Are you OK?" I ask, drawing invisible lines onto her thigh. She nods without looking up, and the president wanders to the far corner of the room, suddenly interested in a tapestry.

"The things I read to you," she says, lifting the notebook and then allowing it to fall to her knee, "were written before she was held here. Written during interviews with her friend and during research. But this note to me was written after she found out that she wasn't going to be allowed to leave. It says the stuff you say when you don't think you're going to see somebody again."

"But you *are* going to," I tell her. "Because we're gonna go find her. And to that end...." I stand and raise my voice to include President Tumbling Rock. "Sir, we were told to track a certain prowler, and his scent is leading us deeper into the earth. I think that's still what we're supposed to do. Do you advise us differently?"

"Who told you to follow the prowler?"

"Laurel Frost Flower."

I'm pretty sure we're setting the record for the number of times the president has lost his ability to speak.

Finally, he says, "Laurel. Who has been dead for..." I think he's trying to do the math.

"Yes," I say before he can.

"The one who played your role in the first act of this play."

Beam catches my eye. "Yes," I admit, though I'm not sure how he guessed the connection that Beam and I share.

"Then, I think you must follow her wisdom. We have people searching for your magpie from this side."

"My oonchi called Mom that too."

President Tumbling Rock smiles at Beam and places a hand on both her shoulder and mine. He blesses us, saying, "May Creator guard your ground and sky."

14

A WOMAN WAITS TO BE FREED

BEAM

He's my president. My chief. That's what I'm pondering as Chausie and I jog back up the inner-butte trail. He's someone I believe in. Someone to whom I could offer my allegiance. I recall the way he clocked Kanji on my behalf. That was pretty cool.

The only sounds, besides my thoughts, are my shuffling footfalls and the occasional water droplet smacking the ground. But when Chausie considers me past his whiskers, I realize that those noises are being replaced by low, throaty, very spirited voices. I can't catch the words yet. It's like one voice is recounting something, and then several others react to what it's telling. Must be a marvelous story.

Chausie drops his lion. "It's Baalesh. Can you hear what he's saying?"

I shake my head.

"He's talking about us. His audience can't believe what you did."

"Should we confront him?" I ask. "Find out what he knows?"

"Yeah, let's do it." Before he can lion up again, I grab hold of him. "Will you stay like this for now?"

"Sure." I think he likes that I asked. He squeezes my hand and leads me onward, taking care to stay close to the wall as we round the corner. This is where we stopped on our first trip before we decided to follow the trail to The Vigilance.

As we progress, the curious red light grows brighter, and the space heats up. We find ourselves in the middle of a profound subterranean room. The ceilings are too high for the light to reach, but from the darkness, a waterfall spills, creating a vast pool and a slight breeze. We round the perimeter to find a larger area still, and the source of the red light, a formal stone fireplace—which is beyond odd —with enormous, white, marble bison on either side to brace a thick hewn mantle. A fire is blazing from within—no idea how it's vented— and it's around the fire which the prowlers are gathered, guffawing loudly, sitting in huge leather armchairs, and discussing...us.

I wonder if this is where they were stationed when the stream carried evidence of my shaving debacle.

This whole time, I kept wondering if Blue was nearby, though he hasn't spoken and I haven't seen him. Now, I whisper his name, and he appears, the red firelight making him purple.

"Are these some of the dangerous prisoners from Chenoa's jail-break?" I ask. "Or are they just regular prowlers like you?"

"There are no *regular* prowlers," he responds. "But these are not the worst."

CHAUSIE

When I clear my throat to announce our arrival, all five enormous, multi-colored prowlers crane their large heads. But when Baalesh spots us, he jumps to his feet, screeching the chair on the floor and causing all of his brethren to do the same.

After no small amount of cajoling, Beam convinces them that we are not here to annihilate them and to please sit back down so that we can talk. We learn things. Most importantly, "Down *that* path is the sacred hall. A woman waits to be freed. We wanted to sneak in to listen to the drums, but the big guys scared us away."

"Big guys?" I ask, trying not to betray the fact that they them-selves are larger than any other beings I've encountered in my life thus far.

"Yes," they say.

It is less than I'd hoped for.

"Baalesh?" I want to question the prowler about Kimimela, but Baalesh physically shuns me—the way Blue might.

"I was going to get to keep that body," he sulks. All his prowler buddies murmur sympathetically.

"But you did get to drive the motorcycle," Beam volunteers.

Ooohs and *aaahs* follow her statement along with a *tch* of malcon-tent from Blue. I redirect the conversation before he can go off the rails. "Baaelesh, is that sacred hall where you were supposed to take Beam?"

"I just like the drums," he says unhelpfully. "I was going to go to the party anyway."

"But is that where the woman with the bodies wants to meet Beam?"

"Well, my body is gone, so what's the point?"

"*Mmmmmmm*," the others console him while Blue rolls his eyes.

"This is impossible."

Baalesh and his buddies have exceeded their tolerance for this conversation, and I don't like the way the one closest to Beam keeps eyeing her. He's drooling. "That's enough," I say. "We know what to do."

Beam wants to run, I can tell. And that makes me laugh. I've seen her run. It's not pretty. But it's pretty cute. She's doing this half-step/half-hop thing that horses do when they're not given enough rein. *A woman waits to be freed.* Are we finally closing in on her mom?

I move with confidence, but inside I'm a bit squeezed by doubt. All we have is Laurel's word that this is our road, and I hate to say it, but Laurel always seems to have a hidden agenda. We could be with my people right now and Beam's uncle, approaching this place from the light of day.

Blue isn't helping. He's very frazzled. He keeps releasing agitated puffs and sighs at regular intervals. Beam and I exchange sidelong glances, but neither of us is willing to ask what's the matter. Finally, he hisses, "Are you insane?!"

Instead of addressing him, I say to Beam, "Why can't he just state his business?"

"Blue?" she asks. "Would you like to voice your thoughts in a more productive way?"

"You have no idea what you're dealing with," he spits. "There are monsters down there. There are *fire* demons. Your blood won't hurt them. Won't even tickle them." He pins me with his big-ass eyes. "And your cat-crobatics won't do anything but piss them off. They'll drop you both through the ground, as close as we are to the In-Between."

I turn to him abruptly. "How close are we?"

Blue just eyeballs me like I'm an idiot until I voice my own concerns. "Beam, what exactly do you think Laurel wants us to find down here?"

"Information," she answers. "Right? What Baaleash knew about my mom's whereabouts? Isn't that where we're headed?"

"But it's all part of a larger story to her. What if this is another one of her twisted exercises?"

"Don't say that, Chausie." She hugs her stomach.

Why didn't we ask more questions? We were so elated that Baalesh fled from us, it seemed reasonable at the time, to track him down. We didn't consider what other monsters might be waiting for us inside the mountain. I don't say any of this out loud.

"Don't worry," I tell her, and my voice comes out steady somehow. "If I *did* learn something from Laurel, it's to hold on to you." I put my forehead to hers. "Just stay with me, OK? Right here." I wrap my hands around her head to indicate our mental proximity. "And right here." I pull her up against me tight.

When I'm satisfied we're together in this, I say to Blue, "How will we know which ones are fire demons?"

To which Blue replies, "*Pff.*"

I guess we'll just know.

So now I'm leading Beam into what may be the worst situation we've encountered yet. I try not to think words like *into what could very well be our deaths* or, God forbid, something worse. In order to lighten the mood, I say, "Tell me about your mom. What's her name? Maggie? Magpie? I have her to thank for your blue eyes. But her hair is shockingly red."

This gets us moving again. "Because she's Irish," Beam says. "But, you know, like generations ago. When she's around, you can bet my dad is smiling. They joke all the time. I can make him smile too, but otherwise, he's very serious. They met in law school. Moved out here afterward. Mom loved it because where in the world is the fight for civil rights more important than here? She stays incredibly busy. Probably why there's only one of me."

A thought pops into my mind. "Hey, let me see the video *now*." Sure enough, this time when I see Maggie sitting cross-legged on the woven rug, I also see her standing beside herself, arms crossed, watching. "That's just creepy."

"You can see both of them?"

"Yeah. Your blood did that for me."

"Uncle Joel can't see anything invisible."

The implications of her comment make me suddenly and intensely hot up the back of my neck. I have to resist the urge to lion up. It almost happens anyway. "Your uncle drank your blood?"

"He wanted to know if it was true—that I was the Elixir. I didn't understand it then. But Daddy had just broken his nose for cutting me, so he got to test out the healing properties right away. Wow. I haven't seen you glare that hard in a couple of days."

I am glaring. "I would have broken his nose too," I declare. I kind of want to right now. Of course, I nearly drank her dry myself, but she kindly neglects to address the fact. She says, "But the point is, he can't see the things you can see. I don't think my blood *calls to him,* as Laurel says."

That makes me feel a little better.

"Chaus, something has taken over my mother's body. Like in the pen-and-ink drawing we saw."

"Yeah, but she doesn't look too bad for it." That probably didn't sound as encouraging as it did in my head, especially since I'm running my fingers around the neckline of her shirt to check for her necklace. "Your uncle told me this catcher protects you from a very bad thing."

"I know," she says softly. "It's the Shadow Blue told us about. It wants its mate. It needs me, specifically, to open the gate."

"Then why the hell did Laurel send us so close to it?" *Because she wants something too.* I halt and my jaw clenches. If Beam was trapped In-Between, as Chenoa is, I'd do anything to get her back. "Is there *anyone* who doesn't want the gate open?"

Beam suddenly cries out and seizes my arm with enough force to bruise it. "What is it?" I yank my head up—and do you know? Blue's *pff* was perfectly played. There is no mistaking fire demons for anything other than what their name suggests.

Three enormous beings of fire spring up on the path ahead. It's hard to define their exact shape because the flames jump and shift. But each has legs—sometimes two, sometimes three—and each has a massive torso and a head like a ram—only, the horns keep forming and reforming so, like the legs, it's difficult to discern the number of them. What remains constant is that all of the fire demons appear to be more than capable of destroying us at any time. And, though their bright forms are startling, it's their horrible noise that is unbearable—like seismic waves crashing and shattering bones in the process.

If Beam's blood holds no power against them and if my strength doesn't faze them, then do we stand a chance by simply turning back? Maybe they're agreeable, and they'll just let us leave.

It should be impossible for the demons to walk side by side in the narrow corridor, and yet somehow it works. As they advance, their fire simply morphs in and out of one another, as well as through the walls and the ground.

"Let's run for it," I suggest. "Back the way we—"

"Don't do that," Blue cautions. "Their prey drive..."

"Look!" Beam says. Right through the fire demons, emerge my two feline friends. They pad up the path offering cheerful cat calls, one hundred percent unaware of the inferno they've just traversed. The demons also seem unaware, or just unconcerned, about Eden and Grant.

"You're seeing this, right?" Beam asks.

"Yep."

My friends drop their lions as they approach. "You guys smell so much better now," Grant says, but Eden picks up on our abject horror and spins to find out why we're peering over her shoulder. "What is it?" she asks, turning back to us none the wiser.

"Grant?" I say, loudly enough to be heard over the noise he can't even perceive. I have his attention, but I just shake my head. "Beam? Is there any way you can make them able to see?"

"If there is, I don't know it. But wouldn't that also make them vulnerable? I mean, they walked right through unscathed."

Grant and Eden stare at us blankly.

"What's beyond them?" I ask. "Where did you come from?"

It's Eden who answers. "The coordinates you gave us. It's a huge cavern, some kind of tribal meeting space. There are symbols painted on the walls and a whole lot of human footprints on the ground like a rave took place."

"Or a Zumba class," Grant offers.

"Chausie!" Beam yells. The light flickers and suddenly the demonic fire is barreling toward us. Again, it's the thunderous sound even more than the heat that overwhelms me. I throw myself onto Beam, but she's ripped from my grasp, and as the demons fall upon us, the ground ceases to exist.

15
INTO DARKNESS

BEAM

I'm falling. It doesn't take that long. It's not like ages and eternity and all that epic awesomeness of fantasy movies. It's more like getting shoved off the front porch and landing unceremoniously on your rear end. The ground is hard, but I'm not hurt. There's a lot of dust, but I don't cough. There is utter silence. And there is utter darkness.

"Chausie?" I call for my lion, but I can't hear my voice. I can't even feel the vibration of it in my skull. "Blue?" I swipe the dust only to find more dust. It's several inches thick. I scoot around to try to make sense of my surroundings. There's nothing. Just emptiness.

"Where are you?!" I yell without hearing it. It all gets swallowed up before it leaves my throat. My breath, my voice. I scream as hard as I can. *Nothing* makes a sound. *If you stay there too long, you become a stranger to yourself.*

"Was I the only one who fell?!" Though there is no noise here, that thought rings through my mind like a gong. My trembling fingers bump on the hard round case of my flashlight, and I frantically flip it on, but it produces no light. *No-no-no-no-no! I don't want to be the only one in the pitch-black, dark silence.* Maybe I'm asleep.

Wake up. Wake up. Wake up. Or unconscious. Still, *Wake up. Wake up.*

In truth, I know I am awake.

The fire demons sent me *below.* I fell into Darkness.

Breathe. Breathe-breathe-breathe. I'm starting to hyperventilate. That's not going to help.

Well, it's probably not going to hurt. My body can't panic forever. I mean—just physiologically. Eventually, it has to settle. Right? That's what they taught us in speech class. I give myself permission to panic. Ironically, this calms me down.

Pulling my knees to my chest, I close my eyes. Not that it matters. It's all darkness either way. I reach out for Chausie. I silently call to him. Open myself to him. I imagine his forehead to mine and, for a moment, I am seized by a desperation that does not belong to me. It eases the moment I feel it. I hear my name like a distant echo.

"Chaus?" I answer. And I can hear myself say it. So I say it again. "Chausie?" I gulp a breath. Tears of relief sting my eyes. "Where are you?"

I rise to my knees and crawl around the space, feeling frantically for my lion. I move in what I hope are spirals so that I can cover all the ground close to where I landed—to where Chausie must have landed. When my hands finally fall on his soft fur, I throw myself on top of him. "Oh, God. Oh, Chaus. Thank God."

Something's wrong though. He's as solemn as a sack of sand. He's not breathing. I shake his heavy body. I burrow my fingers into his fur, but underneath, his skin is cold. I place my ear on his chest. No heartbeat.

No heartbeat.

Now, I wonder if the feeling of desperation I took for Chausie's was merely a premonition of my own impending despair.

"Chausie?!" I scream. I can certainly hear my voice now, but it's absorbed by the dust as soon as it leaves my throat.

"I'm here, Beam. Talk to me." I tilt my ear toward him. His voice didn't come from his body. It's only in my head. I can't reconcile what that means. Or I don't want to. Tears push against the back of my eyeballs with flood-force strength, but I'm not having it. I squeeze them as tightly shut as I can and sniff back a sob.

"Get over here," he demands. Just the way he did that night we sheltered in the rock overhang. The night he slept next to me without being a lion and we promised to take care of each other.

I don't understand. But I lie down on top of his lion's body and try to go to him in my mind.

"Hey," he says. I can see him now, behind my eyes. He has tears too, and his voice is thick. "You stay with me. Do you understand? Do not leave me. Do not go out."

I don't think he knows he's dead. I can't bring myself to say it. "I'm not ever gonna leave you," I say, though I don't know how I'm going to keep that promise. I'm only speaking to him in my mind now, but I surround his physical form and stroke his fur. I swear he's smaller in death.

"I need you to shine out, Sweetheart. You gotta reach down into that well of light you draw from so that I can find you. Can you do that? Call out to me as you did before, with your light."

I do. I'm not sure how. Only that he wants me to. My light fills up the cavern causing the lion's copper fur to shine. He's no less dead, but...he's much less mine.

CHAUSIE

When the demons bowl up the path, I seize Blue and yell in his face. "Get Goliath!" He doesn't wait for the command to leave my lips before he's gone.

Grant and Eden take up their lions.

I said that Blue is gone. That is true. But the thing that takes his place is also blue. And it is also Blue, I think. He becomes a massive strong man, a genie, a sail. He grows and the muscles in his chest and arms bulge. The cool blue of him takes on its own meteorology, becoming a swirling force of ice and snow.

As the demons fall upon us, they also fall upon him. The floor gives way. Eden tackles me through the colliding storms of fire and ice, to the ground on the other side. When we land, we roll over one another. But she rights herself and drags me by the back of my shirt several yards further—in the direction from which she and Grant have come. I scream for her to drop me. I swat at her behind myself to get free.

The lioness is a force to be reckoned with. I can't convince her to let me go, and struggling doesn't help. Finally, by becoming a lion myself, she has to drop me, and I scramble around to see the two storms swallow one another. No smoke. No water. Just one terrific roar like the build-up of a bomb, and then nothing. No explosion. And no Beam.

Eden and I let go of our lions again and stand alone in the long, underground hallway, me with fingers tented over my nose and eyes probably as wide open as they'll go.

"What just happened?" Eden says. "Where'd they go?"

Think. I have to think. I'm pacing. I'm straining to control the flood of emotion threatening to incapacitate me. Eden's instincts were spot on. She did exactly what needed to be done, and the only clues she had to go on were the ones Beam and I gave as we reacted to what we saw. Still, I'm burning with an anger I have to wrangle to suppress. By saving me, she also separated me from Beam.

"Did you feel the ground fall away?" I ask. There's no chasm now. No hole.

She shakes her head. She yells for Grant. "Chaus, where'd they go?"

I'm afraid of the answer. I channel my fear into summoning our prowler. "Blue?!" No answer. "Hinto! Be! Here! *Now!*"

I hope the reason he's not answering is not that I've gotten him killed.

Eden is sniffing around, listening, checking the walls to make sure there are no hidden tunnels.

"We can't find them that way," I tell her. "They've fallen." *Shit.*

They've fallen. "Give me a second to—" Eden is regarding me skeptically. "Just give me a second."

BEAM

With my own light to see by, I study the dead lion, but I can't figure out why he died. I think of Laurel, and I call out to him. "Grant? Are you still here?"

Grant appears as a man, well, as a ghost, sitting against the wall on the other side of his body. He wraps his arms around his knees like he's cold. "Where are we? It feels like a prison."

I look around. "It is a prison," I agree. "But not for you." As soon as I say it, I know it's true. I don't see a gate. But I *become* a gate. I hold out my hands to him, and he hoists himself up, all arms and legs the way teenage boys can be.

"What are you, Beam?" He examines me and the area all around me. "You're shining like an angel."

"I'm not sure what I am."

"I couldn't find a way out until you called to me," he says. "And then it was like when you sleep past ten without meaning to, and you wake up to a sunny day already in progress."

I'm sorry that I won't get to know him. I didn't take him for a poet, but now I get the idea that's part of who he is too. I'm sorry he has to go.

"Why are you sad?" he asks. "*I'm* not."

"When you go," I confess, "I'll be here all alone. I don't know where Chausie is. I don't know how to get myself out."

Grant shrugs and takes a step back. "Then I'll stay. Can I?"

"I don't know any of the rules. I guess?"

"I sort of picked up on the vibe that you wanted to hang out with me, back the first time we met. I have a gift with the ladies."

"Indeed," I smile. I'm touched by his offer to hang back, and even more that he's trying to make me laugh when he's the one that's—

"Are you uncomfortable?" I throw a glance at his body, which he follows.

"It's a little odd," he says.

"Is that Grant?" Chausie's voice rings in my head, full of relief. "Are you together?"

"Chausie's asking about you," I tell him.

"Give me the phone." Grant beckons with the fingers of an outstretched hand.

Maybe we *can* loop him in somehow, though I can hardly bear for Chausie to find out that his oldest friend is dead.

"We are, Chaus," I answer. "And he wants to talk to you. But, Chaus?"

"Yes?" He knows it's bad.

"It's going to be like talking to Laurel," I say deliberately. "Do you understand what I'm saying?"

CHAUSIE

From where I kneel, focused on my connection to Beam, I raise my eyes to Eden.

"What's wrong?" she says. I only shake my head.

"Oh, Chaus," Beam comforts me inside my head. "I am so sorry. He's right here, though. He's as flirty and as cocky as ever."

Eden's eyeing me. I turn my back to her. "How did it happen?"

"I'm not sure. We fell. He's still in lion form. He's—"

"Let me talk," I hear Grant say.

"Put him on, Beam."

"Why do you both act like I'm a telephone?" Beam's voice gets more distant like she *is* holding out a telephone, and then I hear Grant close up.

"Chausieee," he sings, "have you seen this woman's light?"

I sniff and laugh at the same time. "Yeah. I have. Is this for real?"

"'Fraid so. But I'm gonna stick around. Keep her company. Keep her safe. And warm." He adds the last just to rib me.

"Hear me," I threaten him. "If you hit on her, even from outside of your body, I will kick your ass."

Telling Eden is not that fun. She takes up her cat and sprints away from me. I chase her. When she slows to make a turn, I tackle her but fall back when she kicks me with her fast hind feet.

"Stop it, Eden," I tell her. "We have to compartmentalize until we have time to deal with it."

She takes back her human form, but she doesn't get up. She lies on her side, curled up like a fetus, and starts to cry. "I'm sorry, Edie," I tell her. "I'm so sorry."

"This is *your* fault, Chausie. You should have turned her over to us."

"No it's not, Chaus," Grant assures me. "It's not your fault. Tell that cat she only purrs when she gets pet."

"No, I am not telling her that."

"Just do it."

Eden's glowering at me. "Grant says you only purr when you get pet. His words."

Surprisingly, she huffs a laugh, then cries. And then both at the same time.

"You're such an asshole," she says.

"Me?" Grant and I both ask.

"Grant," Eden answers. She wipes her eyes, but they fill up again. "Are you sure?" Her voice is thin and pitched too high. It forces my own tears to flood their banks. I nod my head.

"I hate this," she says.

"I do too," I tell her.

"I'm surprisingly OK with it," Grant says.

Eden jerks herself to sitting. "I can hear him. How can I hear him?"

"Beam's a telephone," Grant says.

After sounds of shuffling, we hear Beam say, "Grant, what do you think you're doing?"

"Trying to get better reception."

"Putting your hands there is not going to help with that."

"Grant, I swear—" I begin. But Eden is laughing.

"I'm just joking! There's not much else to do down here, though. It's fairly grim. And it's kind of hard to ignore my body lying on the ground apart from me. As devastatingly hot as it is. Any ideas on how to spring us?"

"How about this?" Eden says. She puts aside her grief and regains the authoritative disposition she normally possesses. "We all just sit still and listen for three minutes."

BEAM

To me, it sounds like a death sentence. Because I am in a sensory deprivation tank. A supernatural prison.

Of Darkness.

Grant watches me with a commiserating smile. "Maybe someone *not* in hell should time it," he suggests. I stare at him for the length of a heartbeat before snickering. Honestly, he's decent company as far as dead friends go. He offers his hand for support, and I accept it with gratitude. We bow our heads to listen like we're praying.

One...two...three...

"There's nothing to hear down here," I blurt out. It's only been about twelve seconds. "It's absolutely silent. Part of the whole *fallen into Darkness* schtick."

"She's so snarky," Grant says. "She'd make a great cat."

"That's exactly what—" Chausie's voice cuts off.

"Chausie?" I ask.

"Quiet," he barks. Grant and I exchange a look. Reaching into our connection, I listen for whatever Chausie and Eden are tending to. I can see, from Chausie's point of view, but the light's all wrong. Instead of the natural orange and red hues cast from the rock, everything is shades of blue.

"Where are they?" I whisper. "Why's everything purple?"

It takes Grant a moment to suss out what I mean. "Oh. He's a lion. Colors are different from that point of view. He's stalking something. Do you smell that?"

"No."

"Smells like you. Without the fields and flowers."

"*Human*, you mean? Or Lakota? Or like it could be my mom? Are you actually smelling what Chausie is smelling?"

"More closely related to you than just human. And yes. He's following his nose."

It's like watching a scary movie at a part where you can only hear the breath sounds. At a bend in the path, the view stills, then sloooowly we see around, first with the left field of vision, then the right. Nothing down that corridor. Chausie advances and so does our view. Occasionally, he rotates and we can see Eden, also a lion. He's checking in with her. Eventually, the view opens out onto a huge cavern.

"That's where we came from," Grant whispers. He has his forehead to mine, the way Chausie does sometimes. "The open cavern with the symbols on the walls."

There are large, navy circles painted with arrows crossing in the middle, and there is at least one lion depicted. Several drawn birds are standing in the sky on the wall without any sort of tree or perch. A crow. A magpie. A hawk. A dove. There are stars and moons.

Chausie must be crouching. The view from his eyes angles up steeply and then we're soaring into the air so fast and high, it takes my breath. It's incredible that he's capable of such a leap, even as a mountain lion.

"Oh!" I exclaim. "That was awesome. I wish I could have seen him do it."

"I can do that," Grant says. I inadvertently glance at where his body lies. "Well...I could," he says.

I hate this for him, but he doesn't act too bothered by it. At any rate, he stays on point. "Where is he now? Eden and I totally missed that ledge."

It's an overlook. A long balcony of rock recessed above the open cavern. Chausie scans the whole empty space below and then turns to observe the nook he's found. I don't see the cudgel until it's already swinging. Everything goes black.

"Chaus?!"

I wrap my hands around Grant's head and my own, to try to keep the connection from escaping, but it's no use. It's broken. We can't see or hear anything from Chausie.

Grant's wide-eyed shock must mirror my own. I draw a big breath to freak out loudly, but he both anticipates and forestalls it. "He's tough," he claims quickly. "He's nearly as tough as I am."

Again, I refer to Grant's body as a visual reference.

"Not the point," he says. "He's been through a *whole* lot. He's tough."

"I have to get to that room," I say.

Grant's focus drifts beyond me.

"This Darkness thing," he says, indicating the room we're in. "It's not just a basement, is it? It's an exact copy of the part of the cave we were in."

I turn full circle, trying to assimilate what he's saying.

"Without the appropriate sounds and light," he continues. "But the shape of it is the same."

"I don't know, G. Everything about this place looks the same to me."

"You gonna call me G now?" He gives me the sort of know-it-all grin that tells me it was only a matter of time before I fell for him. How can someone so irrepressible be dead?

"Dude, eyes on the prize," I remind him.

He points down the hallway. "That's where Eden and I came from," he declares. Then gesturing to our feet he says, "This is where you and I were standing when all of a sudden we weren't."

I try to remember what it looked like. "All I can remember are fire demons. It *could* be, I guess. You think it's the same place, just on a different *plane* or something?"

Grant shrugs. "Why not? Eden and I took up the same space as your demons did, right? Maybe they had the power to switch the playing field altogether. Let's walk that way, and see what happens."

"What if we need to be right here? What if this is the Earth Gate?"

"Do you *see* an Earth Gate?"

I admit that I do not. "More like a trap door," I mutter and look up. Even with my own light, I can't make out anything beyond the darkness.

"Walk with me. We won't have to go far to test the theory."

CHAUSIE

The sound of crashing into my mom's car is what I hear, instead of the shattering of my ocular orbit. The way her tires bumped on the driveway. The way my body crunched between the metal and the bike. The way the window's glass gave way to my helmet.

My mom had my bike fixed for me before I ever got out of that first surgery. Her car's still banged up. It's funny what goes through your mind when you're being knocked in the head with a club. I should have taken care of that car for her by now.

16

THE IN-BETWEEN

BEAM

Grant and I walk side by side, and he keeps pointing things out to prove his theory that we're in the same cave, just on a different onto-logical plane. I'm too stricken to concentrate on most of what he says. It's not until we come to a place where the path bends that I get excited about the possibility that we might not be far from Chausie at all. "Chausie went this way," I tell him.

"I know. That's what I've been trying to show you."

"No, he really did. Remember? When he peeked around the corner, and we could see from his point of view?"

"Honestly, for someone so magical you're not that bright. Not that smart," he corrects. "You're very bright."

"This is great, *G!*" I emphasize the *G*, and he snorts a laugh.

"I hope so. Can you dial him up yet?"

I can't. I give my head a little shake and keep walking. There's not as much soft dust now. The landscape seems to be solidifying. In all the time I've been with Grant, I haven't had to breathe. Or, I haven't noticed it. Now it's all I can think about. The air feels thin. Like there's not enough of it, or like there are too many people vying for it in close quarters. I find myself working to fill up my lungs. After about the fourth enormous breath, Grant says, "OK, why are you doing that? Are you just showing off? Because, you know, I don't partake in oxygen anymore. Sort of on the wagon."

I yawn without meaning to. Then Grant does. When I cock my head in question, he simply shrugs his shoulders and says, "Did you know that chimpanzees also contagious yawn?"

"Really?"

"Yeah. I tried to make my *dog* yawn once. I can't make him yawn, but he can make me yawn. Hey, don't get snagged." Grant redirects me, around a gnarly...tree? We stare at it.

"I have no categories for this," I say.

"It's a helictite bush," Grant offers.

"Oh, OK."

"You don't really mean OK, do you?"

"No, Grant. I do not. Because I am not a spelunking nat-geologist."

"You're throwing around some big words there, Sister, but the one you want is speleologist. Helictite bushes are speleothems. Things formed in caves by mineral deposits. I've never seen any as magnificent as these."

"It's like walking through an orchard after Tim Burton got a hold of it." I follow Grant through the skeletal bushes. I should be thankful he knows real facts about this place. It would be easy to get caught up in the graveyard feel.

The space widens into a larger cavern, and as we wind our way through, I can feel eyes upon us. Eyes that briefly shine when I crank my head in either direction.

Tens of human forms silently progress along with us, just beyond my field of light. They're wearing white smocks that seem to glow. If I stare at them, I'm not sure I see them at all. But if I look just to the side, I can make them out.

"Hey!" Grant exclaims. "Frostwork!" He gallops down the hall—abandoning me—and pulls up short where the room narrows.

"Grant!" I whisper yell and catch up as quickly and as sneakily as I can. When I rejoin him, he's perusing a wall of silvery spears that grow out like translucent thistles, like flowers made of ice.

"I bet you feel better in here, don't you?" he asks, oblivious to our spectral company. "Frostwork grows in areas with more airflow. It's not really frozen, you know."

"Grant," I whisper. He takes my tone for reverence.

"Yeah," he whispers back. "They're incredible, aren't they?"

I lay a hand on his shoulder while looking back over my own. The figures are boxing us into this passage. "Grant," I try again.

He misunderstands my breathlessness. He *way* misunderstands it. "I know, Babe," he says and smoothes my hair. "But...*Chausie*..." When I turn back, his mouth is practically on top of mine.

"What are you doing?" I snap. "I am trying to tell you that there are ghosty-type-people-thingies surrounding us."

"My bad," he says and draws himself up to search for the ghosty-type-people-thingies in question. "Oh."

I take that to mean he's spotted them.

The ghosty-type—I'm just gonna call them people. They're approaching us slowly like the zombie apocalypse, though they're quite graceful. No lurching or losing body parts or making weird grunting noises. Probably they're not hungry right now. Or they're just not all that enthused about the number of brains between the two of us.

Meanwhile, my grandmother's song is niggling in the back of my mind. *Where spears of frost-like flowers grow...*

CHAUSIE

I groan as I come to, bracing my fractured head where I was just knocked senseless and back into human form. I'm overlooking the room with the symbols on the walls. I guess it's lucky I didn't get pummeled right off the ledge. People are entering the cavern below.

They're a little see-through or maybe that's the head injury. I blink and immediately regret it. *Gah, that hurts.*

Eden sounds like she's about one second away from tearing someone's throat out. She's standing between me and my attacker. I should take up my lion to help her, but I feel sluggish. Still, I manage to flip over to see—through the eye that is not sagging into my mouth and swelling shut at the same time—Beam's uncle standing behind the man with the club.

"Uncle Joel?" I ask though it's garbled beyond comprehension.

"Good lord, Hawk! You've walloped Leo's kid." He rushes toward me, but Eden rebukes him with a wild, throaty growl and a snap of teeth. So he halts.

"Isn't Leo married to the woman working with Kanji?" Hawk asks.

I spit blood out of my mouth and manage to sit up, not without a grunt of pain. "It's OK, Edie," I mumble, my palm to my eye socket. She allows Joel to come to me, but she rumbles all the while, and Joel holds his hands up in surrender as he kneels down. With his fingers, he presses around the orbit of my eye. I'm actually starting to feel better. I push his hand away and work my jaw.

"What are you doing here?" I ask testily, not only because it hurts, but also because I'm mad that this *Hawk* fellow got the drop on me. I should have been chomping on that guy's neck before he even knew I existed. Joel doesn't answer me. He's still studying the part of my face that was bludgeoned.

Hawk comes closer without saying anything. He's not a big man, but he's every bit scrappy. I really don't think he's as apologetic as he should be.

"Chausie, this is Hawk," Joel tells me.

"Yeah, I got that much." I'm not being as polite as my upbringing demands but under the circumstances...

"My brother," he adds. Something about that unsettles me. "Beam's father."

"*Shit*—uh—*Sir!*" I jump up. I practically salute, but thankfully I jerk my hand to a shaking level. "Chausie Louris."

Eden snickers a hissy cat laugh. She doesn't even pretend to hide it. But when she becomes a woman, she sobers. "Hello, Beam's father. I'm an officer with The Outpost. Why don't you respectfully keep your distance till we can assess Chausie's condition?"

This sucks.

No, it doesn't. This is great. Beam's dad is here. She'll be so relieved.

Yeah, that part's good.

Why do you talk to yourself when you're nervous?

"Shut up," I say out loud.

"Excuse me?" Hawk says.

I pucker my lips to keep from speaking out of turn. "Blow to the head," I offer, by way of excuse. "I'm feeling way better now. It's not nearly as bad as I initially thought."

"Right. Don't spring on people like that." Hawk's low voice is as serious as his countenance. "I'm not sure who can be trusted."

He throws a glance at Joel, and I believe that uncertainty extends to his own brother.

Unfortunately, things get worse, not better, when Hawk says, "You were assigned to my daughter? Where is she?"

BEAM

An older woman steps out in front of the rest of the ghostly crowd. She reminds me of Laurel. She addresses me and then smiles broadly as if she's pleased to hear her own voice. I know the feeling. It occurs to me that I'm looking at the Lakota ancestors right now, those who were trapped In-Between. And that must be where we are. I try not to dwell on the fact that they've been here for over a century. I'd like out much sooner than that.

The grandmother, bolstered by her own noise, stands tall and swings her arms as she speaks words of welcome and introduction.

Well, that's what they sound like to me. They're not in English. She waves to the people on both sides of her. They're all Lakota, as far as I can tell.

Now, the old woman pauses for me to respond, and I bow my head in what I hope is a show of respect. "Do you understand what she's saying?" I mutter to Grant.

"You're the Indian, Muchacha," he mutters back, followed by, "Oh my gosh, you look just like Eden right now."

He's right. I can feel it on my face. The conflict between exasperation and comic relief.

I clear my throat and speak out. "Friends..." I begin.

And Grant adds, "Romans, Countrymen," out of the side of his mouth.

It shouldn't surprise me that he knows Shakespeare, I guess, but it does.

"My mom teaches theater," he says.

The woman advances toward me. "I'm sorry that I don't speak your language," I tell her. Why didn't I make dad teach me that? "My father is *Hawk of the Mountain*." I know that much. "Hawk Redfeather. I don't suppose any of you speak English?"

Instead of replying to me, the grandmother takes my hand and leads me further into the frostwork hall. I catch a scent of something my oonchi used to use, some kind of herb maybe. It's pleasant. Familiar.

The others tread behind us. I do not love that part. I want to be able to make a quick escape back into the open. Though Grant is right—it *is* easier to breathe in here.

Up till now, the passageways have been wild, meandering tracks that could hardly be called paths. They were the product of subterranean rivers, Grant said. Sometimes we had to navigate big rocks with no sure footing. But this is a true hall, carved with forethought and great care. The frostwork decorates the walls like an ice garden. And it lights the way.

At the end of the promenade—it's a few dozen yards—one giant, frostwork bouquet has been gathered into the hands of a corpse.

I do a double-take. She looks like one of the mummies in the *Pharaohs of Egypt* exhibit, except that her clothes are Lakota. Not the white smocks that the others wear, but a longer one, sky blue. Magpies and stars decorate the garment. Circles that represent eternity, or maybe the sun and moon. It's a Ghost Dance smock but, in keeping with the way most of the tribes carried out the ceremony, there are no emblems of war. No, that's not true. There *were*. There were arrows. They've been rubbed off, but I can still make them out. The corpse's hair has been brushed into silky black strands that rest on either side of her head. There is a cloth draped across her lap, and it is upon that which the frostwork is gathered. She herself has been placed upon a dais of stone.

Behind this dead woman, evenly spaced into the curving wall of the cave, are several gates. They are the most beautiful works of art I have ever seen. While admiring them, I get the same blanket sense of belonging that I did that night on the butte with Chausie under the wide-open sky. The gates are made of frostwork, woven as wrought iron in the hands of a master smith, both intricate and imposing. Only, they sparkle like stars, casting soft light into this dark space.

Grant is gaping. "Have you ever seen anything so incredible?" he says.

CHAUSIE

Joel is fingering my cheekbone again.

"It's fine," I tell him.

"It's better than fine," he says. There's a quiet edge to his voice. "It's like it never even happened." He straightens up and crosses his arms. "How did you know her blood held power? She barely knew it herself."

Hawk bursts between us, shoves his brother aside, and yanks me off my feet by the collar. "What have you done to her?!" He slams me into the side of the cave and pins me there with his arm to my throat.

"Nothing!" I choke out. "Nothing." I'm sure he thinks I bled his daughter dry and discarded her body somewhere.

"You drank her *blood?!*" he roars.

"It called to me," I defend myself. "It was days ago. And she's fine! I was *dying!*"

"He's telling the truth," Eden says. "Let him go." She's not pleading. She's commanding, and she's taking up her lioness.

"Eden, no." I don't think Beam's dad is going to back down. His hold is strong. I'm not going to lion up against him. I'm concerned I may have to lion up against Eden.

"Mr. Redfeather, Beam and I take care of each other." One of my hands is held up to keep Eden from advancing. The other is wrapped around Hawk's forearm to keep him from strangling me to death. He relaxes the pressure somewhat.

"Then where *is* she?"

Well, that's the question, isn't it?

Over Hawk's shoulder, my small blue friend appears, hanging by one hand from a stalactite. "Where have *you* been?" I huff, but I'm so relieved to see him that I could hug him.

Both Hawk and Joel glance around to find out to whom I'm talking, and Hawk backs off of me.

"Is it time to go ride yet?" Blue asks.

"No, *Blue*. It is not time to go ride yet. My oldest friend is dead and Beam has fallen into Darkness." I brush off that last bit with a wave for her father like it's no big deal. "I've talked with her. She's fine." To Blue again, I say, "If you want to ride my motorcycle, you have to help me find her."

Blue crosses his arms. "If I find them," he insists, "I get to *drive* it."

"No, you're not driving it."

"You let Baalesh!"

"I did not let Baalesh. That was not my idea."

"You're upset. We'll talk after we find your Beam." He pops out of sight.

"You can't even reach the handlebars!" I call after him.

He pops back long enough to grin and say, "*Goliath* can."

Beam's dad is inscrutable. Uncle Joel is puzzled. People are arriving. They stream into the cavern below and mill about, greeting one another. "Everybody sees the people, right?" I ask.

"They're real," Eden says and backs out of sight. The rest of us follow suit.

Beam's dad is sizing me up.

"I understand you not trusting anyone," I venture.

"I know the visions, *Lion*." The way he says *lion* carries weight, but not in a positive way.

"We saw President Tumbling Rock earlier," I say. "He found a notebook that belongs to your wife."

He must already know. He says, "Why didn't you end the crow when you had the chance?"

I can feel shame burning my cheeks. "Because he's human?" I answer. "Because he was flying away from m—"

"He was flying away so that he could end my daughter's life at a later time."

I really don't think this conversation is going well. I'm worried that Hawk doesn't distrust me in a *general* way, but actually thinks I'm no good. Or worse, that I'm complicit in the plot on Beam's life. His next words convince me of it.

"If Maggie was held at The Vigilance, then your *stepmother* was involved in her kidnapping, and she and Kanji Brings Justice are in cahoots."

"You're right," I say. "But I don't even know Kimimela."

"Speak of the devil..." says Uncle Joel.

Kimimela strolls into the cave wearing those stupid-ass leopard-print heels.

"I have no affection for her," I say. "I certainly have no allegiance to her. I didn't even know my dad had married her until yesterday."

This is the night of the ritual. Here. In the place where Beam is supposed to show up. Kanji and Kimimela orchestrated this. I think of the violent drawings we saw at The Vigilance, the mutilated wings with chunks of flesh still attached, the severed head of the lioness. What the hell has my dad gotten himself into?

BEAM

The grandmother woman leaves my side to comb the mummy girl's hair with her fingers. I kneel down beside them. I notice that the girl's left wrist is bound with white cloth and I sniff back sudden sorrow. She bled herself to get her mom back. She thought she was saving her, but she ended up trapping all these people and killing herself. Without Chausie, that could be me.

"Chenoa?" I ask. The woman raises sad eyes and moves her head in acknowledgment. Chenoa is more than this woman's *people*. She's her daughter. Or her granddaughter. Or maybe that's just what it means to be part of a tribe. To own each other as family.

That triggers another thought for me.

"Oonchi?!" I cry out. I crane my neck to find her. "Oonchi?!" There's a murmur throughout the crowd as I leap to my feet. My eyes dart from face to face, but no one comes forward. The woman speaks and makes signs to help me understand. She's saying that my oonchi's not here. She's saying that my oonchi has gone on to the heavens. I remember my oonchi walking out of me, and I accept that this is true, so I kneel down where I had before.

The woman asks me to do something for them. But I don't know what. She begins to sing. Her raspy, old voice carries the melancholy tune around the cave where it swells and resonates.

I've heard my oonchi sing this song. I've even heard my dad when he's had a drink or two. Oonchi used to say that when a Native heart sings a Native song—not the silly ones about gambling or ballgames, but the real, transcendent, universal songs of spirit and animal and life— then Creator hears and sings along.

CHAUSIE

We're backed against the wall of this overlook to keep out of sight of the gathering crowd below. Joel is peering at them and jabbering about who's showing up. I'm assuming Beam's mom is not among them, or one of the brothers would have said so. And I'm pretty sure her red hair and white skin would stand out in this crowd.

I raise my hand to silence Joel. "Do you hear that? The singing?"

It's clear that no one does. "The singing?" I ask again. "Like at the powwows. Only with so many more voices." It's entrancing. I can't figure out where it's coming from. It's like it's coming from people *beneath* the people.

I reach out to Beam. I've only just begun when I see her light staggeringly bright. She is shining up from where the crowd is gathering below—but through the very wall. No. Through a gate.

17

BLOOD FOR BODY. LIGHT FOR SOUL.

BEAM

The voices of all of the ancestors join in the song. A communal prayer. A somber beseeching. As their voices rise, the light from me shines out brighter. It occurs to me that part of fulfilling whatever calling has been placed upon me is simply listening to this song.

My people, my Tribe, come to me, one by one. They bless me with words that my heart accepts. And they enter through me because I have become the gate.

"Beam!" Grant says. "They're walking down that tunnel. They're passing through you into the tunnel, and there's light in the distance. They're laughing and skipping into that light. You're freeing them!" Grant turns to me, covered in joy.

It takes a long time, but as more of my people travel through me, the balance of the song tilts. More volume comes from the tunnel than from here in the hall. When only a few voices remain, Grant's joy fades. "You go too," I tell him. "While there are others to guide you."

"But we're not done here," Grant says. "I'm not—done here." For the first time, he reveals how much he regrets his death, and I ache for him.

The last to leave is the grandmother. She is seated beside Chenoa, a lone voice singing, tears running down her wizened face. Unlike the rest of those whom we've encountered today, Chenoa hasn't stirred.

"Oonchi?" I say to her and hold out my hands. Her song ends. She kisses Chenoa's hair and sets her own face like flint. Gripping both my shoulders, she kisses my cheek, and then from somewhere in the folds of her smock, she produces a wicked-looking blade. It's one I've seen before. One I've held. One I've even threatened to use upon myself.

The grandmother motions for my hand. She means to give the knife. Why does she mean to give me the knife? "No, Oonchi, please." I cross my hands to reject it. "Why would you offer me that?"

The grandmother gently insists.

"What does she want?" Grant asks. "Do you need me to do something?"

"I think that maybe she wants me to try to revive Chenoa."

Grandmother nods and continues to motion until I present my hand. She lifts the blade to my palm, but instead of placing it there, she slices through the skin at the base of my thumb. "No!" I draw back with a cry.

"Why did you do that?!" Grant raises his voice at her and then asks me, "Is it bad?" I must look shocked. "Is it deep?"

My blood runs down my elbow, but before it can drip to the floor, Grandmother catches it in her own shirt, and what falls as drops of red, lands as drops of light.

"Blood for body. Light for soul," she says in heavily accented English. It's from my oonchi's song.

I ask her, with my eyes, if she wants me to go to Chenoa. I could *try*, I guess. I move toward the bier, but Grandmother shakes her head emphatically and physically redirects me to Grant.

"Blood for body," she says again.

"Really, Oonchi?" I survey Grant.

"What does she want?" he asks.

"I think she means for me to try to heal *you*." *What if?* "Grant, drink it! What if it can save you?" When I hold out my hands to him, one binding the other, he shifts uncomfortably.

"You want me to..."

"Please, Grant," I beg him and circle my hands in front of his face. "I want you to live. Do it for Chausie."

"No, Beam." He cringes. "I'm not going to drink your blood."

"Dude, it can't be that off-putting. You're a lion." I continue to urge him until he takes my wounded hand, his face full of conflict.

"Are you sure?"

"Yes. Do it," I implore him, so he brings my hand to his mouth and places his lips over the cut, soft as a kiss—and draws on it.

As soon as he tastes me, the gentleness goes. He makes a sound of such raw yearning, I'm embarrassed to admit how it affects me. He sucks harder after that and swallows in gulps, wrapping his arm around mine to secure a better hold. My heart pumps to slake his thirst. My chest rises and falls with force.

"Grant," I gasp. "It's enough."

He doesn't hear me. Or he doesn't want to. He's insatiable now, crushing my arm against his ribs, tightening on my wrist when I try to pull away. All the while, he keeps pulling with his tongue, and now I can feel his teeth pricking the skin.

My knees are going to fold.

"Grant, it's too much. You have to stop." I can't hold my weight. I would slump to the ground if not for his vice-like grip holding me in place.

In a panic, I thrash to get free, and that's what gets through to him. He goes motionless. He's still latched on to me, but he's not swallowing. His tongue staunches the flow. And now he works to catch his breath through his nose, his nostrils flaring. So much for not needing to breathe.

"You have to let go."

Finally, he releases his hold, easing me to the ground where I steal my hand back and cradle it to myself. Afraid.

The haunted way he regards me is full of remorse. "Beam—"

"It's OK," I pant.

"No, it's not. I got carried away." He wipes his mouth with the back of his hand.

"It's OK, Grant."

"I wasn't listening to you. I was—" He shudders.

"Chausie was the same. He was desperate to—" I'd offer more of an explanation, but something hateful flashes through Grant's eyes at the mention of Chausie, and I drop the rest of the thought.

For a moment, an uncomfortable silence stands between us. But then he gives a cat-like shake of his head and sits back on his heels. "I got carried away," he says again.

"I'll be fine."

"I'm sorry," he says, but as he drops his head, he fixates on my hand and swallows reflexively. He licks his lips. I'm not sure we're out of the woods yet.

"It's quite...intimate, isn't it?" I ask.

And now I can see the beginning of his mischievous smile. "It's, um—it's *something*," he says.

I look him over. "You're not quite alive, though, are you? How do you feel?"

"Truthfully? Like I want to off Chausie."

"No, you don't," I say with alarm. "You love Chausie. *I* love Chausie."

His only response is an upward nod.

"I really, really do," I say.

A brittle bark of laughter reverberates through the room, but then fear comes into his eyes. "I know you do. I don't know what's gotten into me. Chausie's my best friend."

Another weird pause. And then before I can ask about how Grant feels again, he completely disappears.

"Grant?!" I turn full circle. He's gone. He's *gone* gone. My eyes land on the grandmother, who has been waiting for this wild episode to play out. She's doing one of those motherly expressions, the kind that says everything's going to work out.

I wish I had her confidence.

The grandmother wraps a cloth around my hand—where it came from I have no idea—and she knots it tight. Then she sits down beside Chenoa. I'm not sure what she's waiting for. But I sit down too. What a strange picture we must make.

Before too long, I hear the galloping of padded feet, and a lion tromps into the hall. Grant emerges from its form.

"Grant! Are you alive?!"

He crashes into me and twirls me around before he plants a hard kiss on my mouth. I won't say it's only friendly, but it's not a demand for anything more.

"Thank you," he says with weight.

"You are *welcome*, my friend." I'm so pleased. Won't Chausie be...pleased. A little bit of worry creeps in.

"Thank you, Oonchi," Grant says. He's using the word for *Grandmother* that I've been using. His smile is large. He blinks at the place where Oonchi sits. "Where'd she go? She was just there. Did you send her through?"

"She *is* there."

"She's not."

I begin to comprehend. "Oh, I bet you don't get to keep your sight now that you're corporeal."

"Chausie did."

"Yeah, that's a whole different thing. Chausie's—"

"Spare me the details," Grant cuts me off. "Wow. I am so sorry. It is really hard not to feel territorial over you right now."

"It'll wear off," I assure him and hope that I'm correct.

I hold out my hands for Grandmother. "Now?" I ask.

After a mournful glance at Chenoa—she doesn't want to leave her behind—she lays hands upon my shoulders and blesses me with words I feel, even if I don't understand, and says in English, "You must remember."

"Remember what, Oonchi?"

"The song of your people. The song of your lion's blood."

Then she straightens her back and walks through me.

At the same moment, a young woman cries out to us from within the tunnel. She's laughing and waving and running away. "I see her now!" Grant rushes to the gate to watch her go, and when I join him, he surrounds my injured hand with his own. It rings internal alarm bells. I mean, what am I going to do if he decides to eat me up? So, when he starts to bring it to his mouth, I jerk away and stage myself defensively.

His sad smile tells me I'm wrong. I offer it to him and, with his eyes fixed upon mine, he kisses my knuckles. "Just, thank you," he says and gives my hand back to me as if relinquishing a treasure.

When Oonchi is out of view, Grant recovers his bravado. "Where do you think these other tunnels lead?" He studies each in turn. "This one reeks." Grant pinches his nose and turns to get my reaction when something streaks toward him from within.

"Grant!" I warn him. The thing slams against that gate and grabs at him with a guttural snarl. It misses him by inches.

"Whoa!" Grant shouts and clambers out of the way. After he knows he's safe, he says, "Let's don't open that one."

"I think that might be exactly the one Chenoa opened. Hey, how did I call you out of your body? You said that you were trapped until I called for you. What did I say?"

"I don't know. You just told me to come out. It was all darkness before that. And silent as the...well, you know. Beam, come look through this one. It's the room with the symbols. There are more of your peeps in smocks. I think they have real bodies, though."

I'm only half-tending to Grant. If I could find a way to draw Chenoa out of her body—if she's even in there—couldn't she go home too? And then maybe Laurel could follow the others. The thought makes me a little sad, actually. It's selfish. I'd miss her.

"They're lining up around the room," Grant continues. "With their backs to the—*Waaah!* Beam, I think you're gonna want to come see this."

"What is it?"

"Just come."

So, I'm wondering about Chenoa as I amble over to Grant and see long fingers reaching through the frostwork gate from the other side. Long fingers I've grown to know and love.

"It's like I can't let you out of my sight for a *second,*" Chausie teases. That man has never looked so good.

"You found us," I gush. He tries to push through the gate to no avail.

"How do I get to you?"

"I don't know. But you're OK? It looked like you got hit."

He rubs his cheekbone. "Yeah. Fortunately, your juju blood's still healing me up." He nods toward Grant. "He doesn't look dead."

"Oh, he's not dead anymore! He wouldn't, you know, cross over. And then an old Lakota woman—you know what? Never mind."

"What happens in Darkness stays in Darkness," Grant volunteers.

"Shut up," I laugh.

From the outside, somebody bumps into Chausie but doesn't spare more than a quick, "Excuse me," before moving along with the rest of the crowd.

"The gate's not visible, huh?" I infer. That's disappointing. "I guess it was too much to hope that it was simply a gate."

"Looks like any other part of the cave wall, I'm afraid," Chaus says. "Until it doesn't. How do we get you out?"

Blue pops between Chausie and the gate. "I found them!" he screams.

You know the way a cat shoots straight upwards from all fours when it's startled? Chausie does that. But as a person. Grant and I find it intensely amusing.

"Dammit, Blue," Chausie curses. "You are not driving my bike. You didn't find them. I did."

Grant's clutching his ribs, howling.

"Can you see Blue?" I ask.

"No, but the way Chausie—" He can't finish. "Like a Chaus-in-the-box!" He wipes his eyes. "Oh, I needed that."

"Hey! Blue!" I have a stroke of genius. "Go get Laurel. Can you do that? Can you just be at her house, and—you know—be back with her?"

"Maaaaybe," Blue answers shrewdly and regards Chausie.

"You're not driving my bike," Chaus says again. Blue shrugs and turns his back on both of us.

Chausie and I commence a wordless conversation. My face says, *Come on, Chaus. I need Laurel.*

Chausie only talks with his eyebrows. *Why do you need her?*

My whole head says, *Just help me out.*

"*Ugh.* OK, you can drive it," Chausie says through clenched teeth, and Blue vanishes.

"Thank you, Chausie."

"You owe me more than *thank you.*" He sounds grumpy, but he twines his fingers through mine. "What does he mean, 'What happens in Darkness stays in Darkness?'"

CHAUSIE

"*Gah,* it's good to see you," Beam says, ignoring my inquiry into the Vegas allusion. "What's going on out there? Has that little group of ancestors been huddled the whole time? They're the ones who got locked out, aren't they?"

"I don't know. They search the faces of everyone who enters. Maybe it's good that you're stuck in there for now. No one can harm you."

"Chausie! This is *hell!* Get us out of here."

"I don't think it *is* hell," Grant says. "It's more like purgatory. A crossroads. Who do you think designed the gates? They're gorgeous."

I shake my head to let Grant know I have no idea and direct Beam's gaze to the others who are watching from the overhang where her dad clocked me. "I know something that will cheer you up," I tell her. "Your dad's up there."

"Daddy?" Beam squeals. A tiny view of him can be seen. She is frantic to find out what he's endured. She shakes the gate in frustration.

"He's fine. He's got a fantastic swing."

"He's not the one who—" she begins, horrified.

"Don't worry about it," I laugh. "He's on high alert."

"Is there news about Mom?" she asks. "Is she up there?" Her voice is so full of hope that I already feel the distress of her impending disappointment.

In the lapse of my answer, the blood drains from her face. She even swoons. I push toward her, but obviously, I can't get through the gate. It's Grant who steadies her—with an arm around her hip, cinching her close to his side.

"There's no news," I rush to say. "Are you OK?" She looks pale. Weak. I try to say something helpful. "Your uncle's up there too, with your dad."

She nods to show me that she understands. "How's *that* going?"

It's hard to answer because I'm preoccupied with the way Grant is wrapped around the woman I've been kissing, up close like he belongs there. They both look down at themselves to where I'm frowning and take a step apart. Grant's got blood smeared across his cheek, like a greedy cub after his first kill.

"You need to wash your face," I say curtly. I think it's obvious that my mood just took a dive. He rubs a sleeve across his mouth and stares at the ground.

"Chausie, is that you?" I turn to the very un-catlike purring of my name. Kimimela. "Your father didn't tell me you'd be here. It's nice to see you when there's no one around I have to mop up."

My jaw feels unhinged.

"Madame Omnituens," Grant says too loudly.

"Is that really a thing?" Beam mutters.

"MmmHmm. But she's the one who instituted it."

"Who are you talking to over here?" Kimimela says to me. I don't think she can hear through the gate.

I present it with a sweep of my hands. "Do you think this part of the cave was formed naturally?" I ask.

She follows my hands, but if she recognizes the gate for what it is, her reaction is ambiguous at best. "Chausie, I spend my whole life wondering how things came to be. The stars in the sky and the stars beneath the earth."

"The stars beneath?" Beam asks.

"Where spears of frost-like flowers grow," Kimimela intimates. "Where's your friend? You haven't lost her have you?"

"You're not really an omnituens," I say.

"I see things," Kimimela retorts. "I hear things. Not with the clarity of some, but enough to be...promoted. I wasn't born to it if that's what you're asking."

I struck a nerve.

"Ask her about the shoes!" Grant says. I have to school myself to keep from smiling. I clear my throat.

"Why do you wear shoes with the pattern of a big cat's fur?" I ask.

Kimimela grimaces in annoyance. "It's called fashion."

"Alright. Where are you hiding Maggie Redfeather?"

"Honestly, Chausie. Where's your father?"

"I haven't seen him since he and a dead man—who was supposed to be Beam's father, but was, instead, a dragon-like, prowler ex-con—delivered my bike to me."

She acts like she doesn't know what I'm talking about, blaming my attitude on our uncomfortable new familial bond. "Look. I know my presence may make you uncomfortable. I begged your father to bring you to town before the wedding so that we could get to know each other. He thought it would make things harder for you. Especially since your wreck." Her eyes go on a recognizance mission to my leg.

"Kimimela, I don't care about that right now. I'm trying to figure out how deeply demented you are. I've seen inside The Vigilance. I know Beam's mom was held there. Where is she now?"

"I don't know anything about her whereabouts."

"Then what about that lioness? All I saw of her was her *head*."

"That was not my idea, Chausie," she hisses but smiles politely at some people beyond us. "Keep your voice down."

"OK, we'll skip the part where I tell you you're still culpable and get onto whose idea it *was*. The fake crow shifter? How did you two pull off that kind of magic? You're not a shift—"

I interrupt myself as the truth sets in, and for the first time, Kimimela is visibly shaken. "Chausie, if you love your father, you will drop it."

"He didn't help you," I stammer. "He wouldn't." My blood runs cold. My dad's a good man. He didn't kill anybody. "What have you done?"

"It can be *un*done," Kimimela sings through her teeth. She opens her bag and directs my attention to the dead mountain lion's paw. "I just need the girl."

I am genuinely aghast. "No, you—that's—no."

"When things calm down some,"—Kimimela raises her voice like we've just been chatting it up at a party—"let's connect." She strolls off on her ridiculous heels.

"Chausie, are you OK?" Beam asks.

"Don't know," I answer coldly. The memory of her blood on Grant's cheek is still fresh in my mind. Is there *anybody* I can trust? I stuff my hands in my pockets. She's studying me. I can't hold her gaze.

"Chaus, your dad wouldn't have—" Grant begins but breaks off when I glare at him.

"G, can you give us a minute?" Beam asks. He doesn't like it, but he stalks off—me staring a hole through his back.

"G?" I question her.

"Chausie," she says. It sounds like a warning. It's quiet, for my ears only, but it's no less exacting. "Your friend was *dead*. And now he's alive."

"My *friend* is very comfortable with you all the sudden."

Her face takes on the hardness that it does when we disagree, and the fact that she's at her most beautiful that way is infuriating. For some bizarre reason, that makes me smile. Which confounds her.

"I'm sorry," I tell her. "I'm feeling very jealous."

"It's not like it was with you," she says. "It doesn't call to him. It didn't give him anything other than healing. I don't *love* him, Chaus. I love you." It's good to hear, but I'm not finished feeling pissy.

"Does *he* know it?"

"Don't."

I don't say, *Don't what?* but it's implied.

"Your friend was dead," she says again. "And now he's alive because of blood he sucked from my veins. If we have to deal with some awkward feelings of attachment from him, it's a small price."

I nod my acceptance. "You're right," I say. "You can bring people back to life now?"

"I don't think so. A ghost woman surprised me, surprised us both, by slicing my thumb."

Beam traces an imaginary line over her bandage. It needs to be changed. It's bleeding through. "She directed me to—you know—give some to Grant."

She means to allow him to *feed* on her. I bite my lip as the visual comes to mind. Beam glares a warning.

"Keep going," I say.

"I think something about the song of the people and the nature of this odd place made it work. Chausie, Chenoa is in here." Beam glances around. "She's mummified. I'd like to try to call her spirit out so that I can send her on. And then Laurel may be able to get free too."

Beam sets both her hands on the gate, and then snatches them up with, "That is not the best place for a cut." Before she can finish babying her wound, there's a loud click and a cracking sound, like ice breaking.

The gate swings inward.

CHAUSIE

Before she can put together what's happened, I've shoved through the gate and I'm squeezing Beam so tightly she can hardly move, but she's laughing and she's burying her face into my neck.

"I'm going to tie you to my side somehow," I tell her. "Literally." Lifting her face with both my hands, I kiss her hard, and she kisses me too, but over her shoulder, I catch sight of a sulking Grant.

"Hey, I'll be right back," I whisper and rush to my friend who flinches to find me upon him. I don't care. I grab him up and hug him too, tell him I thought I'd lost him, tell him I love him. By the time I release him, he thumps me on the back, and just like that, all is mended.

"Let's get out of here," I say and find Beam sitting beside a creepy pile of what can only be called human remains because it's wearing a dress and has hair. "What the hell is that?"

"Oh, that's Beam's *other* dead friend," Grant says.

"Seems way deader than you."

"Are you still in there, Chenoa?" Beam asks. "I want to send you to your family."

"Hang on, Beam," I caution. "Is that a good idea?"

She shrugs at me. But something seems to be happening. There's a stirring, not in the body itself, but *around* the body, like the reverberation of a basketball dribbled down the court.

Nothing materializes. Beam tries several more times to call Chenoa forth, but with even less result. Her shoulders fall. "I identify with her," she says. "I want her to be free. I want Laurel to be free."

"Let's go see your dad, Sweetheart." Before I help her up, I bend to kiss her head and try to ignore the way Grant intentionally turns his face away. "Come on G," I say, mimicking Beam's nickname for him. "Eden's gonna freak with joy that you're alive." That pleases him.

He says, "She may even forgive *you* for my earlier demise."

"Hang on," says Beam. She digs through the sling bag and produces a water bottle with which she soaks a tissue. Then she wipes the blood from Grant's face, while he suffers the bath with his eyes pointed upward. "You act like a four-year-old," she teases, and he cuts his eyes to her with a grin, but then catches her hand. "Woman, you have to take care of this."

Beam frowns. "It's not that bad. It looks worse than it is."

"Oh good. Because it *looks* like you're bleeding out."

Beam protests as I untie the bandage and wince. "That's quite a slice." In my haste, I'm not careful about where I discard that bloody thing. That's a mistake. I dig in Beam's bag for something else to tie around her hand. Finally, I rip a piece of the shirt Laurel gave to me.

"Can you use your thumb?" I ask.

Beam makes a face when she tries. She says she can, but I doubt it.

"Ooo, can you drink your own blood?" Grant asks.

"Guys. Can I just go see my dad now? Please?"

"Try it," Grant says. "It's tasty."

I admonish him with a scowl.

"Oh please," he says. "Don't act like it's not."

It's not...*just* tasty. It's intoxicating. It's incredible.

I shrug. *Maybe?* So, Beam tentatively tests it. She doesn't find it delicious as we do. And anyway, it doesn't help. Plus, Grant's licking his lips. "OK, that's enough, Grant." I shove him aside to wrap Beam's hand. I don't understand why it's still bleeding.

We are careful to close the gate behind us when we exit, and nobody seems to notice that three teenagers have just stepped out of a rock wall. Grant jabbers on about rare cave formations, and we meander across the torch-lit cavern, headed for the nook where we can observe the room from above. "There are rocks that act as a staircase. This way."

But before we can access them, we're surrounded by young Lakota warriors. They're posturing and pointing, and speaking excitedly in a language I don't understand. Grant doesn't stop to listen. In fact, he's now bragging about what a hero he is, and he steps right through the warriors, unaware of their presence. Beam consults me with a sidelong glance. Through her teeth, she says, "If only I'd been taught the language..."

The leader among the warrior ghosts thrusts a finger at Beam. He's yelling, and I react by becoming a lion and gnashing my teeth at him. He doesn't balk, but he does eye me with suspicion and disbelief. I pace back and forth between him and Beam, and the rest of the warriors. We have every right to be defensive. What they did to Chenoa was unconscionable. If he comes any nearer I'll tear him apart. No qualms at all. He's shaken. I assume he's surprised I can see him.

Beam draws herself to height and adorns herself with confidence like a crown. "My brothers," she says. "You have sorrowed and raged and tried to set things right. But your rage has misguided you. You became susceptible to forces that fed upon your hate, and you are responsible for the evil that befell you. Worse, you are responsible for the deaths of the innocent. If not for Chenoa, you'd be responsible for the devastation of our entire world."

The warriors somehow understand what Beam is saying, and they're listening. She's radiant. She's the woman she was when she addressed my dad for the first time. I don't know how she strings together words to form such well-formed thoughts. She'll make an outstanding lawyer.

The warriors mumble among themselves, nervously. They know it's true. I get the feeling that they're looking to Beam for absolution. They're seeking her forgiveness for their part in what happened that night. Finally, the leader raises a hand, and all of them bow their heads.

"What is the will of Wakan Tanka?" the leader asks. "Find out from the Great One if we are damned or if there is still hope for us."

"I do not know the will of Wakan Tanka," Beam says. "But inasmuch as it has to do with me, I will make a gate for you into the afterlife, *if* you will see the rest of this story well-written. It should give you courage to know that your part is not yet finished."

A change comes over the warriors. The leader covers his heart in some kind of salute. I think he could cry, though I'm sure, because of his steely resolve, he will not. Either way, I need to get Beam somewhere safer than out here in the open. People are staring at us.

The warriors take to their new assignment, and Beam asks them to let us know the moment they locate her redheaded mother. She produces a picture so that they'll recognize her. The warriors give us passage to the stairs as a sweep of movement catches my eye. A black feather, flirting with the ground in small arcs before landing. I scan the ceiling above us for the crow who is as troublesome as a hangnail.

When Beam tops the stairs and sees her dad, she rushes to him and buries herself into his chest.

"I'm fine, Sweet Beam," Hawk assures her, gently and strokes her hair. He's a different man with his daughter in his arms. I know the feeling. "I can't tell you how happy I am to be holding you right now," he says. "Are you alright?" Hawk pulls back to look her over and sees that her hand is bandaged. "You're hurt."

"No, I'm OK. What about you?"

"Fine. Other than being anxious for you and your mother. The

Council asked a lot of questions about you and...what they should *do* with you."

I can feel my lion nose reacting to that, and I want to hiss, but I'm not part of the conversation, so I settle down on the ledge beside Eden and Grant—who have yet to stop rolling around in a catty embrace even though they're in human forms—and peruse the gathering crowd.

About a hundred people are present now, alongside the spirits of the warriors and the leftover ancestors who got locked on this side of the gate. Those ancestors search each live face in turn. The living are none the wiser. Kimimela works the crowd. I see why folks are drawn to her. She's like the hostess at a party. I watch her talk to a pair of other women, and the ancestors walk through her. She straightens up and puts her arms around herself. She felt that. I'm sure of it.

"Have you heard anything about Mom?" Beam asks her dad. She's watching the activity below too, but from behind us.

"You know as much as I do," her dad answers. Hawk lowers his voice. "I'm not sure whom I can trust, Beam. And, I mean, of *anyone*. Do you understand what I'm saying?"

"But not me," Beam says. It's not a question. It's the kind of relationship they have.

"No, not you. You are my star."

"If you ever ignore my calls again, I'm going to be your worst nightmare."

Her dad chuckles.

"I'm not joking," she says. "In fact, I have several new rules for our relationship, but we'll go over that later. Do you think Mom is in danger?"

"I do." He doesn't baby her. He respects her enough to talk straight. "And I'm not certain it really has to do with you being what you are. She'd been working on a case that could ruffle a lot of feathers." He turns the conversation to me. "What's the cougar kid like?"

He must not know about my exceptional hearing. Or maybe he does.

"His name is *Chausie*," Beam admonishes. "But you know that."

"What else do I know?"

Beam regards him. I think this must be a game they play. Her dad's an attorney. He can manipulate conversations to produce answers. "More than you knew about Cody," she says. Her dad laughs.

"You told on your own self that night. I wasn't even trying to find out if you had someone in your room."

I guess Grant's eavesdropping too. He mutters, "Cody's a prick."

Of course, neither of us knows the slightest thing about Cody, but apparently, he was in Beam's bedroom. "Yeah, I hate that guy," I agree.

Eden's not listening. She's actually doing her job. She did her best to get me to wait before I leapt into Hawk's head swing. She'll probably take over for my dad someday, and she'll be my boss.

"What?" she grumps when I keep staring at her.

"You're really good at all this."

"Oh...thanks."

From below, there comes a clatter. A swell of shocked voices. A cry repeated through the din. A few of the people are prostrating themselves before the remains of a woman who has walked in on her own long-dead legs from the room we just left, by the gate we just used. She's holding what appears to be Beam's bloody bandage in one shriveled hand and with the other, she secures the gate. It's as if she's moving against her own will. As if one side of her body is fighting the other. But maybe that's how you move when you've been dead for a hundred fifty years.

BEAM

Everybody can see the mummified corpse stroll into the room. Some bow to it in fear. Or worship. Others remain on their feet. But most just make for the exits.

The three lion friends, in human form, sit side by side overlooking the peculiar party, and I creep up behind them on my knees. Chausie's biting his bottom lip and he's a shade of green when he turns to say, "I think I did a bad thing."

The leftover ancestors huddle together in a knot like timid girls at a dance and stare into the unseeing eyes of Chenoa. Maybe not unseeing. She moves her head like she's searching for somebody.

"Who do you think she's trying to find?" I whisper. Nobody answers me. But everybody stares at me with less than admiration for my skills of deduction. I guess they all assume that it's obvious enough that Chenoa wants to find me.

"*You're* dumb," I tell all three of them (because I'm mature). "I need to go to them."

"To whom?" Grant asks.

"To the leftover ancestors."

"Oh, I'll get us tickets. Their new album is amazing."

"Shut up, Grant," Eden says. "There are ghosts down there?"

I nod my head yes. "They need to go home."

"The dead people?" Eden asks.

Chausie's being conspicuously quiet for a Chaus. He's craning his neck to take in everything about the place.

"You stay here with us," Grant says. "Chausie, you usher them up here, since you can see them."

"No," Chausie says. He doesn't elaborate, but I know it's because he's not going to leave me again, not willingly. Something new has him on alert. He crawls behind me and practically drags me to the wall beside my father.

"What is it—" Before I can finish asking, a sinister voice rises from below, but we can't see who's speaking.

"The Elixir," it demands. "Produce the Elixir."

Everything goes eerily quiet. The voice is human. And yet it's not. Grant's a lion as soon as he hears it. He vanishes down the stairs, followed by Eden and Uncle Joel. Chausie remains with me up top, padding back and forth from stair to overlook. With his big cat head, he directs me and my dad to stay put, but Daddy has other plans.

"Don't leave her," he instructs. "Do you understand?"

Chausie nods one time, his brow knitted, his whiskers twitching.

And now Daddy's gone too.

So, turns out, among the things that rank as torturous for me is sitting still and waiting for something horrible to happen to the people I love. I risk a glance into the room and inadvertently catch Kimimela's eye, but she doesn't acknowledge me or betray my hiding place.

Beside Kimimela, Blue appears with Laurel on his arm. Or rather, he's on Laurel's arm. Like a parrot. Upon seeing her undead friend, Laurel goes ashen. "Chenoa?" she wails, and her hand flies to her mouth. Her voice is hoarse with emotion.

Chenoa reacts to her name, twisting her head with unnatural stiffness in the direction of the sound, and she moves toward Laurel, who shrinks back, whimpering.

Chausie drops his lion to confess, "I think I'm the one who woke her up by tossing your bloody bandage. Beam, I am very concerned about who is—"

"Blue!" I scream, and Chausie instantly lions back up to rebuke me for the noise I've made. Blue vanishes from the ground level and reappears at my side.

"What is *that?!*" he demands. "What have you *done?!*"

"Go get Laurel and bring her *here!* She's in danger!"

"*Laurel's* in danger?! What about Chenoa?!"

I'm at a loss. "Blue, you have to help."

At that moment, Chausie begins to growl in earnest as he blocks the stairway. It's a warning, a threat to whoever is ascending to us. Over his shoulder, I see the crow in mid-air. Chausie bats it down with his big paw, and the crow lands beside me, as Kanji Brings Justice.

"It's a good place to watch the show," Kanji says. "Birdseye view?"

Chausie pounces and Kanji jumps from the ledge with a ripple of human laughter that morphs into a crow's cackle as he shifts above the crowd. "I think we're about to establish for everyone just who the real Elixir is," the bird squawks.

Chausie dives right after him, down from the height without missing a beat. He clamps down onto Kanji's whole crow body and slings him downward. He would have landed on top of him too, but somehow Kanji is able to change course before he hits the ground. He soars onto a high, narrow ledge where he flaps his wings, first this one, then that, and he hops from foot to foot. Is he making fun of us? Or did Chausie injure him? Or some other reason altogether. At any rate, he's preoccupied with this weirdo bird dance, and now I'm all alone, except for Blue—whom I'm not counting because he's ignoring me in one of his ridiculous tantrums.

"Chausie gave me his motorcycle," I gloat loudly to no one in particular.

Oh, interesting. Now, I'm the most important thing in Blue's whole world.

He narrows his eyes at me and says, "He loves that bike."

"He loves me more," I counter. "And *you*. Can. For. Get. About riding it. You are very unhelpful this afternoon."

"I got *Goliath* for you!"

"*Huh*. How did that help *me* at all? *I* fell into Darkness. And Chenoa wouldn't even be walking around down there if I *hadn't*. Don't you dare get all pissy with me."

"Chenoa has changed in that gross, old body," Blue sulks. "She's acting like the Shadow Man now. Or maybe the Shadow *Woman*." Blue shivers at the unpleasantness of the thought. I'm not sure if it's because Chenoa is acting like an Umbra, or if it's because of the gender of the Umbra. But a sickening thought occurs to me, and I now realize why Chausie turned green before. Chenoa wrestled the Umbra inside herself until she died. Her corpse became its prison. Did reanimating her body just allow it to walk out that gate?

You know how I get snarky when I'm angry and scared? I'm afraid the very cleverest thing I can come up with right now is: "Blue, do you know that I have never used the f-word? Not once in my whole life. But I am about to drop it right now. And I am about to drop it hard. Can you *imagine* the impact that will make, coming from my mouth? You think my *light* burns hot? You have not even—"

A terrible voice hisses into our ears. I said that the voice before sounded a bit inhuman. No. It does not compare with the inorganic texture of this new one. This new one is without tone, like the speaker's vocal cords are dried and cracked. "Hintooo," it hisses from Chenoa's mouth.

Blue clasps his hands to himself and stares at me in horror before he disappears.

19

THE MAGPIE

CHAUSIE

This time I will not spare the crow. It is clear to me that he will stop at nothing to confirm who the Elixir is and destroy her. I bet those notecards belonged to him, and President Tumbling Rock interrupted his research. I chomp down hard and sling him to the ground, but the moment I think I have him, he changes tack and flies up into the cavern's roof.

Landing on all fours, I find Beam's dad standing against the wall, flanked by two lions. One of them is Grant. The other, I am beyond thrilled to see, is my dad—doing what he's supposed to do.

Chenoa has abandoned her attempt to molest Laurel and is instead fixed upon a lovely blue-eyed woman who has long red hair. Beam's mother, Maggie. Her dad makes a break for her but is immediately checked by my dad with two paws on his chest.

Everything seems to pause as if the whole cave has to inhale to prepare for the coming event.

"Reveal yourself, Elixir!" The voice reverberates through the cavern with the low timbre of a man's, but it is spoken from the mouth of Beam's mom. And just as I couldn't tell what manner of being Baalesh was while he inhabited the dead man's body, I can't see what kind of thing is inside of Maggie, but I *can* see that she is very much alive, all the more so compared to the grotesque body of Chenoa.

"I'm here!" I whirl around when a confident, bold, female voice answers. "I am the Elixir. Let her go."

It's not Beam. It's Eden—using herself as bait. Grant rushes to her side, and I bolt back up the stairs to Beam, grateful beyond words for my two faithful friends.

When I get to Beam, though there's no way she can see her mother from this vantage point, she's trying to come down the stairs. Her face is stricken, and soon I know why. "No, she's not dead," I assure her. "Beam, she's not dead." The leftover ancestors have rallied around Laurel as if to protect her, and there's another ghost in their grouping as well. Beam's mom.

That gives me an idea. I search around for the ghost warriors and wave them up.

I don't have time to explain, because at that moment her mother —I mean her mother's actual body—comes into view, stalking toward Eden, the would-be Elixir. She sniffs at Eden and narrows her eyes.

"Chausie," Beam squeaks.

And now Chenoa, through words that are stammered and slurred, instructs Blue to, "Deliver the knife." It's like her mouth won't fully obey her mind's order to speak. But the words come out, and Blue, much like Chenoa's mouth, haltingly obeys them. His eyes are full of regret as he glances up to where we are and then appears before Maggie's body to hand over the knife with trembling hands. I have to physically cover Beam's mouth when she begins to scream.

"Hang on! Let the lions do their job. You'll ruin everything if you expose yourself now."

But Beam's mom has raised the blade to her own neck.

"Don't do that," Eden calls out. "I'm here. What do you want from me?"

"Are you the Elixir?" Maggie's mouth moves, but its deep male voice makes my stomach cramp. I've got my arms locked around Beam's shoulders, less like a boyfriend and more like a bouncer.

"I *am*," Eden answers. "I am the Elixir."

"Prove it." She's going to tempt Eden to demonstrate she's the Elixir by saving Maggie's life.

"Wait!" Eden says. "I'm listed in the Visions of Blood." She's done her homework. Of course, she has.

"The Elixir pumps through a lion's heart." I whisper it at the same time she says it aloud.

At that moment, Kanji crow caws repeatedly. I catch sight of the frenetic tips of black feathers way up high. "Prove it!" he squawks. "Prove it!"

Maggie says it again too and begins the awful motion that will slit her own throat, but Grant is fixed upon her. As soon as his lion eyes see the first twitch of muscle, he leaps, forcing Maggie's elbow in the opposite direction. Her arm swings to maintain balance, and the blade slashes the inside of Grant's arm instead. He falls to the ground as a man, clutching the inside of his elbow, blood pouring from between his fingers. It must have hit an artery. Already, there is so much red blood, it's astonishing. The knife clatters to the ground.

From beside me Beam exhales a horrified breath and thrusts herself toward the stairs, but I shove her down. "Stop it," I chide her. "Let me handle it."

"I have to get down there!" Her eyes are ferocious, like a rabid animal.

"That's exactly what they want." I consult the leader of the warriors and thrust a finger toward Beam. "*She* is your way through the gate." Then I shove his shoulders and glare into his eyes. "She *alone* can make right what you made wrong. But not if she is dead."

"Don't you dare, Chausie!"

I ignore her. "Do *not* allow her to leave this rock!"

"I can *save* him!"

I round on Beam and say through gritted teeth, "This is the

moment Laurel told you would come. In this moment, you have to trust me. Stay. Here." The warriors bar her way to the stairs.

I do actually have a plan. Not much of one, but—well, really it's more of a hunch. I jump from the ledge, becoming lion along the way. I bound to Eden and tear lines across the top of her hand with my claws. When I become man again, I say, "Give it to him! You have to save him!"

Eden's kneeling beside Grant, wide-eyed with fear, applying pressure to the wound on top of the hand Grant's already using. She hardly spares a glance for me, but it's clear she has no clue what I'm asking of her. I don't think she even registers that I scratched her. I push her hand to Grant's lips, hoping that I'm right in thinking his arm's going to heal itself the way my face did.

Grant's trying to say something, but it's garbled because I'm mashing Eden's hand into his mouth. He's still clinging to his arm, but not as much blood is leaking through. I should probably take a closer look, because if the power of the Elixir isn't still working upon him, he's going to need real help, real soon.

"Stop!" he manages to spit out. "You're gonna smother me to death!" He slowly releases the pressure from the cut, and it's hardly a cut at all. I exhale in relief, fighting the urge to glance up at Beam's hiding place.

Eden's studying the back of her own hand in amazement, which makes me want to laugh, but now I'm worried about what kind of danger I've just put her in.

BEAM

If there weren't so much to tend to, I'd be fuming. I'm sequestered up here under armed guard—I mean, they're *ghost* guards, but they're solid enough to keep *me* from going anywhere—and Chausie is forcing Eden's hand into Grant's mouth. I catch sight of the other spectator, who is higher than I. Kanji again.

He's stationed in an outcropping of boxwork formations (yeah, I know about boxwork. I just hiked with a speleologist through the weirdest cave ever). Where the rock has crumbled away, these boxy compartments have been formed, and the crow has stuffed himself inside one of them.

As soon as it's apparent that Grant's going to be OK, the crow begins to vibrate his wings, fanning them up and down. Maybe it's a form of ornithological applause, but I think not.

The thing that controls my mom's body simply rolls out of her, and I swear it is in response to what the crow is doing. It's a dense dark vapor, and it crosses over the crowd the way the shadow of a cloud might cross the earth. I study the crow to make sure I'm not just making this up, but I'm becoming increasingly confident that the Umbra is taking its cues from Kanji Brings Justice.

The one inside of Chenoa is not. Chenoa lurches as *that* Umbra makes a bid for freedom—and for its mate. Chenoa grasps her body and jerks from side to side. Has she been wrestling this damn thing all these years?

When Kanji is satisfied with all his flapping, he distinctly nods at me. A truce. He no longer has any need to hunt me. He no longer believes me to be the Elixir. Taking flight from his den, he exits through a large hole toward the top of the limestone wall.

The warrior standing to my left is tracking Kanji the same way I am.

"That crow is up to no good," I tell him, and I let my eyes wander over my company. "None of you are bound by gravity," I point out. "Follow that guy and see what he's up to." They stare at me blankly. "Please," I add. One of them throws a look of concern down at Chausie.

"Why do you listen to him over me?" I ask. "Because he's a lion? I'm your ticket home. Go."

They see the sense in this, I guess, because they jog through the air and disappear through the wall. Meanwhile, my mother's body, unoccupied by any spirit, including her own, falls to the ground, and Daddy rushes to cradle her. I don't think he knows that her ghost rests its head upon his shoulder. It's sort of sweet, really. In a sad way.

Now that I'm no longer impeded by Chausie's order of containment, I bolt down the stairs.

Kimimela has instructed the people who remain to begin the ritual ceremony, so I have to weave through the melee of dancers. Drummers beat their instruments in turn with three or four people to each large drum. Voices take up a song. It's noisy, but with a compelling structure of answering rhythms.

Kimimela's not much of a participant. She walks around the dancers following my progress with her eyes.

CHAUSIE

"You're supposed to be with Beam!" her father says. He's holding his wife's pretty head in his lap. She's unconscious.

"Don't worry. I left her in good hands." I turn my attention to his wife's ghost, who is appraising me while resting her chin on his shoulder. "Mrs. Redfeather?"

She quickly locks eyes with me. "You can see me?"

I nod.

"Well, then you can call me Maggie."

"Maggie, can't you just..." I gesture to ask if she can re-enter her body. "Now that the thing is out of you?"

She tries it. She sort of assumes the position that her body is in, and she occupies the same space, but she can't make her body contain her ghost.

"Hey, how'd you get back into your body?" I ask Grant. I'm sure Hawk thinks I'm insane. Probably not the man he was hoping his daughter would end up with.

Grant thinks about it, his eyes darting around like he's trying to find a way to explain it. "One minute I was joking with your girlfriend about offing you, and the next I was in my body, running to get back to her. Oh, and before that, the old Indian woman kept saying 'Blood for body. Light for soul.' Or something like that."

"I think I can help," I tell Maggie. "Or, I think Beam can. I bet she can make a bridge for you." I don't love the idea of bringing Beam into the open yet. Maybe she could do it from up there.

Instead of responding to my suggestion, Maggie says, "So, you're a *lion?*"

I smile broadly. Definitely Beam's mom. "My two friends are too, and my dad." Over my shoulder, I say, "Eden, your acting skills need work." But when I turn to congratulate her on a job well done, Eden is nowhere to be found, and it occurs to all of us, I think, that that is a very bad thing.

"On it," Grant says and takes off at a trot with my dad on his heels.

It's no wonder, with all the chaotic movement and noise around... Now that the ritual has begun, the leftover ancestors seem less afraid, and many of them even participate. Chenoa is staring up at a hole in the wall. No idea what that's about. I wave Laurel over. "Will you keep Beam's mom company for a minute?" The way Hawk is glaring at me...

"Certainly," Laurel says and sits down next to Maggie's ghost. "Does anyone ever call you Magpie?" she asks.

I'm convinced that that devious woman is always plotting, so I wonder why she's asking that seemingly innocuous question, and I file it away for future reference. Somehow, they begin to discuss the connection her daughter and I share. That same daughter who's probably sitting above us right now pissed as hell. I have to go face her fury. But Maggie is scrutinizing me, so I suffer it the way Grant suffered Beam's cheek bath.

"Do you really care about her, or are you just infatuated with...all this?" Maggie waves a hand to indicate *all this*. I know what she means. And I do love it. The action. The call of duty. The adrenaline bang.

"Oh my gosh, I see where your daughter gets her knack for forward questioning."

She smiles softly. "Hazard of the job."

"Well, it's better than the first conversation I had with your husband." I grin at Hawk, but...he's not really ready to joke about things yet—as he strokes his unconscious wife's hair. Also, I think he's becoming annoyed with the one-sided banter since he can't hear Maggie respond to anything I say.

"It's not just *all this*," I assure her. "But you'll see."

At the same moment, Beam arrives. I glower up at her failed captors, but I can't catch sight of them. Beam only has eyes for her mom(s). Since only her ghost mom is awake, that's the one she addresses but ends up hugging air. It's like she absorbs her mom's spirit. But then her mom's body begins to move, rolling her hands and feet, and blinking like she's been asleep. I guess Beam became a bridge for her without even meaning to.

"Maggie?" Hawk says and fawns over his wife, the muscles around his eyes relaxing for the first time since I've known him— excepting the short moments he was reunited with Beam.

When Beam is convinced her mom hasn't been permanently damaged, she rounds on me. *Uh-oh.* "There was no time to come up with a better plan," I spit. "And since the warriors—"

"What?"

"You're mad at me for benching you."

"Oh. Yeah, I am. But you're gonna have to wait your turn."

"Who's ahead of me?"

"That. Stupid. Crow. He's *controlling* the thing that came out of my mom."

"How do you know?"

"I saw him do it! From up there." She points to the basket-like formations up high.

"Where are the warriors?" I ask. "You haven't sent them *on* have you?"

"I had them trail the crow. He flew through that hole up there."

Beam points the way. "After he did some weird flappy thing that the Umbra *obeyed*."

"I think he sent it into Eden. We have to find them."

"The only thing *we're* going to find," interjects Beam's dad, "is a place to get your mom checked out, and then we're going home."

"No, we're not," Beam says. Her dad looks like he's been slapped. Beam must realize what she's done by overtly refusing to obey. With a gentler tone, she says, "*You* are. But I'm not. Dad, I have to finish this for—gah, for *everyone*. Take Mom and go. I have to do this."

"I'll watch her like a—hawk," I finish lamely. He ignores the unintentional play on his name. It pales in comparison to what's on his mind. "I'll bring her back to you," I swear. "If you don't trust me, trust the visions. She does own a lion's heart."

I don't know whether or not I'm helping. I get distracted when Beam removes her catcher and places it on her mom. "No way." I pull it right back over her mother's head. "Excuse me, Maggie, but your daughter needs this far more than you do."

"Chausie, I am not going to allow my mom to be a target again!"

"Non-negotiable."

Beam scratches for the necklace, but I deny her, holding it against my chest. "Beam! Use that beautiful, big brain of yours. They are *life-light eaters*. You are the brightest damn life-light around."

One side of Beam's mouth bunches to tell me how much she hates to concede, but then a scratchy noise cuts through the din of the dance, and all goes silent to make room for it. It's a screeching pick-slide of a sound that I assume is being wrested from Chenoa's throat as she fights to maintain control of the Umbra inside of her. Beam yanks the catcher back at the same time I cram it over her head. So...team effort.

The music becomes louder and wilder than before.

"Get Mom out of here," Beam commands her dad. She takes my hand and we jog to the wall where she last saw Kanji. It's the same as where I last saw Chenoa.

BEAM

The dancers are really ramping things up, bouncing on one foot while spinning around with the other knee lifted. The drums bang out hypnotic rhythms. The voices chant to one another in calls and responses that bounce around the cave.

Though we jog the length of the wall, we can't find any place for beings without wings to cross through. And to convolute things further, we're interrupted by Kimimela.

"What are you looking for?" she asks hopefully. "Are you looking for the gate?"

"No," Chausie spouts. "We're looking for your crow of a partner."

"He's not my partner. We don't want the same things."

Chausie disregards her statement with an eye roll and continues to scan the area for an outlet.

"Where has he gone, Kimimela?" I ask her.

"Answer me this," she says. "And I'll tell you."

"We don't have time!" Chausie says. He's worried about Eden. Kanji was all too ready to be convinced that she was the Elixir.

"Why are you bleeding?" Kimimela asks.

I hide my hurt hand behind my back. "I was cut."

"By what?" There's a ring of intrigue to Kimimela's tone that disturbs me.

Chausie glances at my hand with concern. It's another drop of concern in a bucket that's already too full. "I'm fine," I tell them both.

"You got cut in the In-Between," Kimimela says. "Didn't you? I've been searching for the gate for a *decade*. And you just what? Fell into it?"

Pretty much.

Chausie straightens to regard his stepmother. "Please don't tell me that's why there's a massive drill at The Vigilance," he says.

Kimimela doesn't mean to, but she does tell him, by saying nothing at all.

"You can't get there with a *drill*," Chausie whines. "Why would you even want to?"

There's a moment when Kimimela looks so small and desperate, I want to comfort her. She must sense it. She bustles to me and takes my hands, but Chausie forcibly shoves her away.

"Are you kidding me right now?" he bellows. "You caused this whole mess. We should have been able to seek *help* from The Vigilance."

"You're not a parent," Kimimela sobs. "You don't know what it's like to have your heart live on the outside of you, only to have the life crushed out of it."

Chausie puffs his derision, so Kimimela addresses me. "Please. I've waited all this time. I've given *everything* to find you. And now you're right here. You have to save my babies."

The demented longing in her mother's heart twists my guts. She speaks of her children as if they're only sick, as if they haven't been dead for years. "Oh, Kimimela—" I start to tell her why it won't work, why it shouldn't even be asked, but she cuts me off.

"Please, just come meet them. Please. They're such beautiful children. They're my world."

"What do you mean...meet them?" I ask, but it's drowned out by the rest of Kimimela's offer. "After that, I'll tell you whatever you need to know to help your dad." She's speaking to Chausie again. "He's in a real bind, Chausie."

The conflict is palpable. "Your dad is tracking Eden," I remind him. "And that's where we have to go. We have to set *those* things right."

"Yes!" Kimimela says. "I know exactly where Kanji has taken them. I'll take you there after you heal my babies! It's on the way!"

"Take us now," Chausie says. "And then we'll see."

"No, you'll be deaaaad. You'll be deaaaaad." Kimimela might as well have curled up in a fetal position on the floor.

"I appreciate the vote of confidence," Chausie says.

"I won't take you!" she screams. "And you'll never find it! Your lion friend is full of Umbra by now. Just how long do you think Chenoa will be able to keep its mate enslaved? Once they're mated she'll die! You'll *never* find her without me! You'll *never*—"

"Shut up!" Chausie yells. "Move quickly. No promises about your kids."

Kimimela brightens. She dances ahead of us. "Don't say that. Don't say that," she sings.

Chausie and I exchange a look. I'm not afraid of Kimimela. I don't trust her, but I do feel sorry for her. Grief has driven her mad, and I worry that she has indebted herself to some kind of merciless dark magic. This is not good. It's not right to rip those kids back into the world of the living. I think of how Laurel and President Tumbling Rock refused my blood on the basis of its sacrament. There are probably repercussions for the misuse of special elements.

Kimimela leads us back through the dancers and outside for the first time since we began our journey this morning. It's evening now and the fresh air is enlivening.

I've never stopped to think much about the equinox. Yeah, I know that there are two days in the year when the light and dark share equal time. The sun over the equator and all that. And I'm vaguely aware that people in China balance eggs on end, and that the coming of Spring is celebrated in one hemisphere while the coming of Fall is celebrated in the other.

But as we step out for the first time, after roaming in the dark bowels of the earth, I get it. The balance between light and dark, visible and invisible. The bridge the soul walks into its eternal home. It's an evening in which everybody sees more than usual. Or they could. If they would only look.

We are of no small interest to prowlers and other invisible creatures as we follow Kimimela across the sparse dirt pathway and up to an SUV that's parked in what has now become an unpaved parking lot for several off-road vehicles. I don't guess the space gets used much, except for these rare festivities.

Chausie surreptitiously ties another piece of cloth around my hand as we walk. It is definitely not clotting. I don't try to assure him that I'm alright. I think maybe I'm not.

Meanwhile, Kimimela is coming unhinged. She's as bubbly as a bottle of soda like we're headed for a sorority party. She can't quit talking about how long she's been waiting for this, and how this is going to fix everything.

"Kimimela," I begin. I sound as if I'm wooing a stray animal. "If you and Kanji want different things, then why does he have access to all the information at The Vigilance?"

"Oh." She waves dismissively. "Wellll the ritual got a little out of hand last October. Many of my followers were, umm, disenfranchised. They come from generations of hardship, and some are quite angry. The ritual grew turbulent. And, I suppose the dancers got whipped into such a frenzy that the Council felt the need to involve themselves. Kanji came to deliver a reprimand, but then snooped around—which he was not allowed to do—and found my—experiments, shall we say—and in the end, I had to work with him or risk—" Kimimela stops abruptly, then says, "Ooooh my. Ooooh my. Don't worry. It's all going to get fixed now. Why he even demanded to be a shifter is beyond me."

Chausie and I are in the back seat. Kimimela takes turns playing the steering wheel like a drum and worrying her bottom lip with her fingers. She rocks in her seat to urge the vehicle up the steep road. I've never seen Chausie's face so devoid of emotion. It's all trapped behind his eyes as he stares ahead. He's probably ruminating on the fact that his father is *married* to this lunatic. I squeeze his leg with the hand that is *not* oozing, and he looks down at me without any change of face.

Finally, he says to Kimimela, "You and my dad happened how?" I can tell it behooves him to ask.

"Oh, your father's so sweet. I went to The Outpost because I'd narrowed down dates from the Visions of Blood, and I wanted to ascertain whether or not there was a lion alive who might be the Elixir. He was very helpful. We hit it off. I hate that he's in so deep. I really do. But our Elixir can fix it! Kanji would have ruined every-thing if your dad hadn't helped me."

"Kimimela, just what can I do to fix things for Chausie's dad?" I ask.

"Well, we killed someone to activate the shifter magic, but you can raise her up. Everything will be fine!"

I think Chausie surmised as much. He remains blank and still. How can anyone fix that?

Kimimela takes off-roading past limits with which I am comfort-able. There's a drop on this side of the narrow path, and the wheels slip on loose rocks more than once. Up. Up. Up until we arrive.

20

THE BLADE FROM WHICH NO WOUND CAN HEAL

CHAUSIE

"Welcome to The Vigilance!" Kimimela croons. She throws the vehicle into park and hops out. "Come along!" Before she can fit the key into the lock, the big, white front doors to the public entrance swing open from within, and someone says, "Well, you've finally got your fingers on her." It's Uncle Joel.

"You're one to talk," Kimimela snaps. "Everyone knows you've been working her for years, trying to get a little sip for yourself." Something passes between Uncle Joel and Beam. The knowledge that he *has* had a sip. *Well, I know about that too, buddy, and it still rankles.* As if he can hear my thoughts, Uncle Joel's eyes slide to me.

I don't realize I'm glaring at him until I realize he's glaring at me, and the longer I wait for him to look away, the more I feel it as a challenge. Is he judging me? I was about to die! He did it for no good reason at all. I'm about to bow up when he—quite purposefully—shifts his focus to the ground. He's not thinking about that at all. He's trying to tell me something.

I follow his pointed gaze to a drop of blood that has dripped from Beam's fingers into a small puddle of others.

Unaware, Kimimela trills, "Come along. Joel can come too. I don't mind an audience." She hurries across the museum floor to the inconspicuous door in the back, the one that leads to the hallway where I chased the crow.

Joel lowers his voice. "How bad is it?"

"It's bad," I answer. "It's getting worse."

"Beam?" Joel says because Beam hasn't responded. "How do you feel?" The gentle worry in her uncle's voice magnifies my own. Now that I look at her, I see that she is actually losing ground, and just like that, I change my mind about everything.

"To hell with this. Let's get you out of here. Let the lions take care of things."

"*You're* a lion," Beam reminds me.

"I'm *your* lion. You need a doctor."

She sets her face with quiet resignation and says, "A doctor won't help. And the lions can't do it on their own. This is our job. Remember? Our destiny?"

"Not if it means—"

"Come alooooong," Kimimela sings, and as Beam proceeds past the pipes and the hanging Ghost Shirts, she smiles at them mournfully.

"There's a lot I wanted to learn."

"Whoa." I turn to brace her with both arms. "Why do you sound so hopeless all of a sudden?"

"I'm sorry, Chausie." She barely whispers it, and she regards me through sad, solemn eyes. "I don't know why the grandmother used that blade. Maybe she didn't know."

"Didn't know *what*? You are freaking me out." While she waits for me to sort it out, I shake my head to ward off the growing mixture of fear and anger.

"It's the same knife Chenoa used back then," she prompts. "The blade from which no wound can heal."

"No, it's not," I spit and draw back from her like she's being hateful. "No, it's not."

"I'm so sorry."

"Stop *saying* that! It's not true." I reach for a reason it's not true, and I find one! "*Grant's* OK! *Grant* was cut by that blade."

"But he had just drunk from me. I don't know."

Uncle Joel says, "Could you...drink from yourself?"

"We tried it," we both say. I tug Beam's sleeve back to inspect her bandage and blow out like I've been punched. The skin around her wrist is turning grey.

Kimimela stamps her foot. "Come now!" she demands.

"Shut up, Kimimela," I growl. "I've had enough of your—" It was her. She did something to Beam to make it worse. I'm across the room clutching that woman by the throat before I mean to take a step. "What did you do to her?!"

When she only splutters, I roar, "You touched her hands back in the cavern. What did you do?"

"Nothing," she chokes out.

"Stop it, Chausie!" Beam says. "It wasn't her. It was the blade."

"Come and let her *fix* it!" Kimimela says.

I thrust her away from me, and I do not mind that she bangs into the wall. "There's no *fixing* it, Kimimela! There are consequences to the things you do! Beam is not *God!*"

"Well, she's the closest thing we've got." Kimimela fairly snarls it and with that, she disappears down the hall.

"We have to follow her, Chaus," Beam says. "We have to follow her to end this thing. Come on, partner."

I'm running a hand through my hair in frustration.

"We *have* to. This is the ending we have to write—the larger story. Isn't that what you believe? Believe it for us now."

BEAM

It's Uncle Joel who convinces Chausie to move. "If Kimimela did do something to keep it from clotting," he says, "we need to find out what."

It wasn't Kimimela. I know it wasn't. But Chausie composes himself. "I know the way."

Even though Chausie has described the space for me in detail, I am not at all prepared for what I encounter. The eerie blue lights. The subterranean river. The couches. But, yeah, mainly the bodies. Kimimela is reclining on one of the couches beside two smaller corpses, caressing them lovingly.

I'm not sure what I thought would happen at this point. I guess I was in denial about how absolutely out of sync with reality she is. I assumed that we would all come to a mutual decision that reanimating people long dead is not a good thing.

"Kimimela?" My voice again betrays my opinion about the fragility of her mental state. "You saw Chenoa tonight. You must know that this is a terrible idea."

"She is still in there, Love. Still fighting to fix things. Now it's your turn."

Please don't let that be my fate. I force the thought aside and say, "She was only in there because she couldn't both imprison the Umbra *and* go into the afterlife. I don't think it would have been her preference. I see the bodies of your precious children, Kimimela. But I do not see *them*. They have passed out of reach."

Kimimela's eyes shine with unnatural light, the way Mars shines when you can almost see that it's red. And in a low, chilling reply, she says, "I have recovered them."

I've been through some morbid and disturbing things now. But *this* is truly unnerving. Has she really detained the souls of her own children? Who gave her the power to do such a thing? "You're lying," I say.

"She's not," Chausie interrupts. "When I was here before, I wasn't alone. There were other living things. Scared things."

"I want to speak to them," I demand.

"No," Kimimela says. "You just bring their bodies to life."

"It doesn't work that way. Without their souls, they're beyond my ability to revive."

I'm not positive that that is true, but I think I'm right. Anyway, it's not something I want to try. "If you have them here, then call them forth. I need to know what *they* want."

Kimimela wags her head defiantly.

"I'll call them myself," I tell her.

At first, concern flickers across her face, but then she laughs. "Even a Soul Gate has to know their names to do that."

"Sammy," Uncle Joel volunteers. "Isn't that right, Kimimela? And Violet."

"Not their names," she snickers like we're playing a round of *Guess What's In My Hand.*

"Why don't you want me to speak to them?" I ask.

I'm beginning to suspect that Kimimela only has the slightest grip on her children's souls. Or that the way she acquired them was so perverse, they've been damaged. Or maybe she's simply afraid they won't cooperate.

What she doesn't know is that it doesn't matter she won't tell me their names. My mother did. Mom is meticulous in her fact-finding, and though Kimimela had her children's given names legally changed, my mom discovered them—and recorded them in her notebook.

"Mato, come out," I call. "Macha?"

"No!" Kimimela screeches. "I forbid it!" She leaps from the couch and cranes her head wildly to see if her children will appear. "I have them locked away."

"How does that seem like a good idea?" Chausie asks. "To imprison your own children."

"Come out, Mato," I call. "I need to talk to you."

Kimimela begins to chant. The words don't sound like the language my dad speaks, and they're not full of the comfort and ease with which President Tumbling Rock sang his smudging song. They're guttural, jammed with retching sounds.

The children appear before me. A sandy-haired boy around nine and a girl with long, black braids. They're not solid, though, as the ancestors were. They're more like projections, lacking color and form.

The boy bites his lip as he tries to ascertain his whereabouts. "What is this place?" he asks and hugs his younger sister to himself. They view their mother, who is still invested in her heinous antics, with horror.

"Mommy?!" Macha cries and then buries her face into her brother's side.

"Don't be afraid." I kneel before them. "Your mommy made this place because she misses you." When Kimimela notices what I'm doing, she stops her own ungodly communications to gape at me. She can't see them. How has she kept them if she can't even see them?

"Would you like to speak to them?" I ask.

In response, Kimimela simply nods and comes to kneel beside me, huffing from all her efforts.

"Chausie, will you help me the way you did when you could hear Grant through me?" Chausie's not listening. Rather, he's not listening to me. He bolts past us to where an enormous shaft is dug into the earth, and then he clambers back to us frantically.

"What have you summoned?" he asks sharply. "Kimimela, what have you summoned?" To me and to Uncle Joel, he says, "Things are climbing up the drill shaft."

Uncle Joel hurries to look. "Chausie, get her out of here."

"No!" Kimimela grabs hold of me, but Chausie shoves her to the ground.

The children go stiff with fear, and Chausie backs off. "If you touch her again..." he says and allows the rumbly threat to finish itself.

"Please," Kimimela begs.

"Joel?" Chausie calls. My uncle is leaning over, trying to keep tabs on our impending doom.

"I don't have your keen ears, Chausie. I don't hear any—wait. Yeah. Faintly. Things are clawing their way up."

Chausie searches the room. I think he's trying to conceive of a way to defend it. "Call them off, Kimimela!"

"Please!" she begs. "I can't. My children."

"What else do you have in here?" he asks and stomps to a row of what I now recognize to be metal cages made into the ground. "Release them," he demands.

"Yes," Kimimela agrees.

"Every one of them. No prisoners."

"Yes," she says again, but she doesn't move.

"Now!"

At his insistence, Kimimela rushes around unlocking the cages. Strange beings stare up at us, too frightened to come out. Prowlers whom Kimimela has been catching and trapping to use in her experiments.

For Chausie's next demand: "What did you do to Beam's hand?"

"Nothing. I swear. The blade is wicked. I don't know more than that."

"What's coming up that shaft?"

"I don't knooooow." Kimimela is about to lose it. Her children are visibly quaking.

"Chaus," I whisper. "This is the most urgent thing at the moment. Help me."

He swallows his come-back and submits to my request. "You stay right where you are," he warns Kimimela and pins her with his eyes, but he can't reach for my light that way, so he turns his back to her with a less-than-happy look for me. Meanwhile, the prowlers have begun to exit their confines. I think curiosity gets the better of them. They circle around with great interest.

It's no good. Chausie's too on edge to concentrate.

"Look at me," I say.

"Just hang on." He exhales tension and tugs my forehead to his.

The children are murmuring to one another. "I don't think it *is* mommy," the little girl is saying. When the prowlers begin to *ooo* and *ahh,* I notice the little boy is staring at me, his face open in wonder.

"You're the *angel*," he says. "We prayed you'd come back."

"Have you seen an angel before?" I ask.

"After the car crashed, the angel made a big door. We wanted Mommy to come with us, but Daddy said she would come later, so we kissed her goodbye."

I stretch a hand beyond Chausie, to try to physically connect Kimimela to her children, but when she touches me, she shrieks in pain. At the same time, her children begin to scream. I almost scream too, because, for that brief moment, Kimimela appears as a monster to us.

"They're coming!" Uncle Joel calls. "I can't tell how many—fifty? Maybe more. The first line of them is about twenty feet below."

"The *first* line?" Chausie says. "You summoned an army?!"

"Mato? Macha?" I say with new energy. "Let's go see Daddy."

Kimimela's shouting something over Chausie's shoulder, but he won't let her come near me. I lift the children together at the same time, one in each arm, which is not that easy. They're kids, but they're not small kids anymore. But, anyway, as soon as I'm hugging them to myself, they're through the gate, and my light dims.

Now I hear what Kimimela is trying to tell them, that she loves them, that she'll force them to stay, that she'll kill herself if they leave. These are not good momming techniques, but it doesn't matter anymore. The children are free of her. I press into the tunnel, in my mind, and I can see their father greet them. He scoops them up at the same time and, unlike me, he has no trouble with that at all.

"We've gotta get outta here," Joel says. Chausie joins him at the shaft.

But his distraction gives Kimimela an advantage. She makes a desperate lunge for me, ripping the bandage from my hand and dragging me to the couch where the bodies of her children lie.

When I scream, Chausie dives for us, becoming lion along the way. He claws lines into Kimimela's face, batting her against the wall of rock, but she has covered her hands in as much of my blood as she can, and she slithers forward fast as a snake to smear it over each child's face and into their small mouths—which don't open well at this point, since they've been dead for so long.

We all wait for something to happen, but nothing does.

Nothing except dead men and women breaching the top of the drill shaft. Their eyes are lit like there is fire burning inside of them, and they make sounds like fire too. Hissing and snapping.

Chausie knocks a few of them back, but there are dozens. Uncle Joel goes down underneath them while Chausie fights to fling them off. I expected these strange enemies to be slow, lumbering corpses, but they're more like prize fighters. No matter how Chausie tears into them, they're not incapacitated for long.

More and more of the beings pour in through the shaft.

I call for Blue. Blue doesn't come. I call for Goliath.

Uncle Joel doesn't have the ability to defend himself. He's getting pummeled. He'll be torn apart. "Get her out of here!" Chausie yells at him. "Take Beam and go!"

"You can't do it on your own!"

Chausie glances around and yells, "You have to help me. You have to help Chenoa."

At first, I think he's yelling at Kimimela, but he's not. He's ordering the prowlers to engage. "This is your time to repay Chenoa!" he says.

The prowlers gawk at one another. "For Chenoa?" one asks.

"For Chenoa!" one bellows.

And now all those sweet, strange beings enter the fray.

Some of them pay for it. Several of them disintegrate into puddles under the force of Kimimela's army. But this enlivens the rest of them, and they take up a name, like a battle cry that they all repeat in unison. "Drake! Drake! Drake! Drake!" It's the name of their champion. They're calling him to action. When they erupt into uproarious applause, I follow their gaze, but I can't figure out what there is to celebrate. Maybe their hero is invisible, even to me. The Prowlers widen out to give this mysterious Drake ample room.

Drake...is a butterfly. A beautiful, large—but only large as butterflies go—orange butterfly with black spots. He flutters and floats through the crowd as if the pathway they've made is a flower garden. He flits and flirts with prowlers upon which to land. Everyone in the room pauses to monitor Drake's progress. Men and monsters, uncles and lions.

It is upon my lion's nose that Drake chooses to alight. Chausie stands stock still, eyes crossed to focus on his visitor.

In the next moment, two things happen. Prowlers drag Uncle Joel out of the way and, from Chausie's nose, the butterfly puffs out his chest and then spews a river of black liquid, far out of proportion to what his small size should be able to conjure. The liquid coats the undead men and melts them down to asphalt before our eyes.

A roar of triumph erupts from the prowlers all around, and a victory song emerges like their team just won a football match. They cheerfully hoist Kimimela, jog with her over their heads, and toss her down the drill shaft. As soon as we realize what's happening, it's done.

Chausie hasn't moved. Drake still occupies his nose, and he seems concerned.

"Chaus?"

Only his eyes slide in my direction. Meanwhile, Drake turns to walk up Chausie's nose. He pauses to stroke the fur between Chausie's eyes with one of his six graceful legs. Then, he simply flutters off and out of sight, followed his the hoard of raving prowler fans. Chausie collapses to the ground as a man.

"Where's your uncle?" he says.

I call for him until a groan issues from where his crumpled form lies on the floor. "Are you OK, Uncle?" I ask.

"He'll be fine," Chausie says with surprising coolness. "Won't you?"

Uncle Joel pushes to a seated position and, sure enough, his scrapes are visibly receding.

"*Someone* had to test the theory," he says.

"*Hmm.*"

As I observe my uncle, I'm not so sure everything *is* healing the way it should. His eyes are unfocused, and he pinches his nose, closes his eyes tight. "I feel you worrying, Sunbeam," he says. "Go do what—"

Chausie breaks in. "There's smoke. The smell is wafting down the shaft. There are lions up there too."

"The stairway," Uncle Joel says and points toward the hallway without opening his eyes. "There's a door with stairs up to the tower."

Chausie picks up the bloody cloths that Kimimela dragged off my hand and stuffs them into his pocket without meeting my eyes. I guess he's still upset with himself that Chenoa is on the loose.

"Uncle Joel?" I ask when he doesn't rise.

"Give me another few minutes," he says breathlessly. "I'll catch up."

21

A SECRET NEVER TO BE TOLD

CHAUSIE

I slam into the metal bar to release the door's hammer and burst onto a helipad that tops the eight-story tower of The Vigilance. There is no helicopter. Instead, in the painted circle where a helicopter would land, there is an enormous teepee of wood and a roaring fire sending vapid plumes of smoke into the air.

I'm greeted by the warriors who have obeyed Beam's directive to follow the crow, and they are now appraising me defensively. They must think I'm going to scold them. No. I am extremely pleased to see them. Though I'm not really sure how they can help.

Eden is seated on the ground at the edge of the circle. She hasn't been tied. She doesn't look harmed or frightened. She looks vacant, the same way Beam's mother had when the Umbra filled her body. Beam now makes her way outside and asks Eden how she's doing.

"Not great," Eden responds curtly. But her mouth doesn't move. I turn to find Eden's ghost, slightly confounded and wholly pissed off. She says, "Can you believe this guy? He sent that thing into me, and out I popped like a cooked piece of corn. Out of my own body!"

"We're gonna fix it," I say.

"How?"

"Working on it. Where's Grant?"

"Lying behind that wooden barrier over there." Eden points to a section of utility fence. He and your dad were both shot with a tranquilizer while they were lions, and they were both dragged over there. Nothing I could do about it. I don't think they're in any real danger though. The man kept apologizing—like he has this rigid code of ethics—and saying he didn't mean any disrespect, that he would never harm anyone. Except me, apparently, whom he wants to burn at the stake."

"Why burn?" I ask.

Eden is testy in her bodiless state. "Because he thinks I'm a witch, Chausie! I don't know."

"I think it's so that he can destroy her without spilling her blood," Beam says.

"Right," I say. "Wow."

"I think the real question," Eden spits, "is why does he want to kill me at all?!"

"He believes you're an abomination," I answer. *Like you believed Beam to be,* I don't add. She has more than made up for that.

"Here he comes, Chaus," Beam says.

Kanji Brings Justice emerges from behind the wooden divider, out of breath. It's no small task to lug the inanimate weight of two fully grown lions. He takes note of us and slows his gait.

"This is over," I call over the noise of the fire. "You have to release her. You have to stand before the Council."

He disagrees. "The Council should be *thanking* me. I now control the two most devastating beings on our planet. An Umbra and an Elixir. I don't think a boy like you is in any position to lecture me."

The Umbra is grimacing at Kanji through Eden's face. It's making hostile sounds that I don't think Eden's body could manufacture on her own. The warriors cast wary glances from Eden to Beam.

Like me, they'd rather fight a battle than stand around not knowing what to do.

Beam's catcher is riding on the outside of her shirt. Seeing it calls to mind the trinket that got away. "Just how much of his power do you think is tied up in this choker?" I mutter.

"The ability to shift," Beam says. "Right? That's what President Tumbling Rock intimated."

"But how does he control the Umbra?"

I think of the drawings in the workspace and see that last horrific page in a new light. The spirit that was clawing to get inside of the woman. The person holding the bracelet like a talisman. The billowing dark stormcloud of a beast.

"I think the shifter magic was just an add-on," I decide, and before I think it through, I'm a lion aiming for Kanji's neck. One swift swipe severs the choker before he can react, and now I'm sprinting toward the fire. Kanji must have used rocket fuel for propellant. The heat scorches my face as I sling the choker into the hottest part and retreat.

I glance from face to face, but nothing happens. Well? That was melodramatic.

But then Eden's body begins to convulse like I've tossed *her* into the fire. I'm not sure what to do for her. She rises to her knees, throws her arms out to the side, and screams with joy through a voice that doesn't belong to her. Out of her gaping mouth exits the Umbra, a vacuum of light, a black hole.

It's clear to me now that this Shadow demon was completely subdued before. In its newfound freedom, its malevolence can be felt as a sort of physical despair that grates on my nerves. Kanji's face goes white. Will it seek its revenge on him?

Eden's body, which slumped forward after the Umbra left it, now lies dangerously close to the fire, so I pull her to safety by her sneakers, but the flesh on one arm is blistering.

"Ow, that's going to hurt," her ghost says. "Somebody get me some ice."

"Let's put you back together before anything else can happen," Beam says. She engulfs Eden in a hug, and Eden reappears inside her own body.

Kanji cuts his eyes from the Umbra to where Beam is speaking to and hugging nobody he can see. "It *is* you!" he hisses. "Why doesn't it sense you?"

Beam's catcher, on the outside of her shirt, appears to me like a target now. I silently will her to put it away without daring to voice it aloud. I think Kanji sees it for what it is. He makes a sound of acknowledgment and hell if he doesn't try to do the same thing to her that I did to him. Before he can yank the catcher from her neck, I cat-tackle him. We roll to the ground in tandem somersaults across the helipad's painted circle. The teepee of firewood collapses. My fur catches, and I rebound instantly, out of the scorching flames, but in the time it takes to stop, drop, and roll, Kanji is upon Beam and has her up against the side of the building.

Eden's watching on like it's a movie. I don't think she has fully recovered yet. Likewise, the Umbra hovers as if it's confused. I pounce right through it, screaming, landing lightly enough to pounce again. But I'm too late. Kanji has his arms wrapped around Beam's, rendering them useless, and, though she's giving it all she's got, kicking and struggling, Kanji manages to steal the catcher away from her.

I define the Umbra by what I see, the shadow-side of the moon, the darkness like a mass. But there is sound as well, and when the crow man steals Beam's catcher from her, the Umbra's garbled language vibrates in my inner ears. Kanji forces the catcher around his own neck and pushes Beam away from him. Now the Umbra is no longer confused. It clearly wants Beam, whether to inhabit her or to devour her light, I don't know. We can't let it do either. And we can't let it find Chenoa.

The leader of the warriors, finally finding a clear job to do, commands his people to jostle Beam to the far corner of the tower where they set a guard around her. When the Umbra advances, a few of the warriors attack it and are gobbled up. Whatever light or life made their souls visible to me simply ceases to exist.

"Run!" I yell to Beam. The crow man is running too, not for the building, but for the end of the helipad. I catch up to him and we struggle over the catcher, which, in my mind, is Beam's only hope. I have to get it back to her. Have to—but with a sudden flash of inspiration, Kanji purposefully hurls the catcher over the side of the tower.

It's one of those moments when every detail is crisp like a slow-motion film. The web-like hoop, the ivory dove, the starry beads, falling end over end over end. Kanji leaps onto the wall with a brief pause to gloat and then swan-dives after it. He twists in mid-air, but no crow emerges. He twists again and now he is thrashing wildly—while his body simply plummets. The look of smug triumph morphs into realization, and he screams. No longer able to shift into an animal with wings, his body bounces when it hits the ground and then lands at unnatural angles.

When I turn back to the crisis at hand, Beam is gone. The warriors are gone. The Umbra wafts in one direction and another. Finally, it opts to sink down to where Kanji's body lies below. Kanji's ghost watches, aghast, turns to flee, and is swallowed up in Shadow.

Eden. I start for her when, from the fire, a lioness rises. She stretches, first forelegs, then back, and becomes a woman. I don't know her, but she smiles at me. She walks to me, walks through me. It's odd but strangely comforting. And then, she's gone. She didn't stop being. She just stopped being *here*. From the fire, seven spirit crows take flight.

BEAM

Before I can heed Chausie's command to run, the warriors have become for me some kind of spiritual chariot, flying me away from the top of the tower, past The Vigilance, and up into a ridge of rock, where they then direct me into what I think is a hiding place. I don't know how I can actually hide from an Umbra who can now sense me keenly and is bent upon swallowing me whole, but I'm willing to try.

It turns out, this nook is not for hiding. Some of the warriors enter the dark place. And jump. Before I can figure out where the tunnel leads, the leader bumps me from behind, and now I'm falling too, down a long—and not-so-smooth—slide. I know what this must be. They've thrown me down Kimimela's drill shaft. The same one she must surely be lying at the bottom of. Is that my fate as well? Will it all come to a tragic end with a misguided rescue attempt?

I'm not sure how long I fall—eight seconds?—before the warriors shove me sideways through an opening in the wall of the shaft. The drill itself is several more feet below where they've forced my exit, and I try not to consider Kimimela's remains down there.

But I am still alive. And now I am being led through another corridor of the sacred cavern. I know because I can hear the drums, so the ritual must still be in process. Soon, I see torchlight. We're back in the room where we started. Kimimela's search for the In-Between was so close. But on an entirely different plane.

The warriors are all business. They huff impatiently every time I have to actually step around a live dancer instead of passing through them, as they do. But finally, they place me on the ledge where we were secretly surveying the crowd earlier—feels like an eternity ago—and station themselves around me.

I'm dizzy. I'm just gonna lie down for a second.

22

THE HEART OF A LION

CHAUSIE

I snap in front of Eden's face, and she comes to her senses. "Your dad," she barks. "Grant." And we jog around the dividing wall to find them.

Grant's lying on his back, groggily peering around. When Eden leans over to check his pulse, he cups her cheek. "Oh, Eden. Now's not the time."

"Shut up, Grant. We have to save Chausie's woman."

Dad's still asleep. "Dad?" I push his side causing his supple lion body to move, but not to tense. One eye slightly opens, but it closes again.

I address Eden. "I have to—"

"Go," she says. "I'll take care of them. We'll find you."

"Here," Grant says. "Take this." He holds out the knife that sliced him—the blade from which no wound can heal—and I just stare at it. I abhor that thing. Finally, I say, "That was good thinking, Bro." And I toss it into the fire.

My dad manages to give his feline head a shake, but he's befuddled. From his prone position, he sees Eden and then me.

"Dad, I have to go," I tell him. "I have to find Beam. Kanji Brings Justice is dead. Dad? Kimimela is dead." I stop to let that sink in. I know that he understands what I'm saying, but I'd like to hear him say so. I don't know how this will affect him. "Dad, will you man up for a second? I have to go. I need to hear you speak."

His eyes grow large, and he calls to me in short cat growls. Something's wrong. He gets to his feet and bends his head and shoulders. I think he's going to shift. But he doesn't. Or he can't.

"Dad?" I'm getting scared.

He paces a few feet away to try again. I recognize the usual process, but it's like he aborts the change at the last second. When he whips around to us, his catty expression is full of shock, not unlike the face he wore in the vision in the spring when he was stuck halfway in lion form and dying.

I'm gonna throw up.

"Dad, how much of your own power did you invest in Kanji's necklace?!"

I cover my mouth as the truth sets in. In destroying the choker, I've inadvertently destroyed my dad's ability to shift.

Blue materializes in front of my face and I bat him away from me. "Can you not be taught personal boundaries?!"

In the next moment, I am physically doubled over as if sucker punched, and the terror that courses through me is not my own.

"Come!" Blue yells.

BEAM

The terror I feel reminds me of the look on my grandfather's face when he woke up from heart surgery while he was still intubated. A machine was breathing for him, so he couldn't take any breaths of his own. He was receiving all the oxygen he needed, but he felt like he was suffocating.

I resist the presence pushing to penetrate me. *No,* I tell it. *You're not allowed.* But it keeps pressing.

The warriors attack it. Every single one of those brave souls. And every single one of them vanishes into nothingness.

It's inside me now, filling my mind with its own dark thoughts. It talks back to me. Tells *me* to get out. Berates me with images of loss and despair. There are children, shining like stars, and screaming as they run from me. They dart this way and that, begging me to leave them alone. Begging me not to eat them.

But I do eat them. I devour them. I can't stop myself.

It's not real. It's not real. Or at least, it's not me.

I reach for Chausie with all my might. I pray to him. I beg him to find me.

"Blue?" I whine. He pops into view, but then he's gone again.

The thing grips my heart and squeezes until my whole body bucks against pain so sharp, I'm afraid it will burst. It keeps straining for room to pump oxygen to me. I can't see through the jumble of black and white dots that have clouded my vision.

At some point, I become aware that Chausie is peering down at me from above, so I think I must be lying down. He shakes me by the shoulders. I can't make my tongue form words. I can't command any part of my body at all.

Chausie braces himself with his forearms on either side of me and places his head to mine. "What *is* that thing?" he says. "It's not the Umbra, is it? It's something...even worse."

"It's the Umbra *Woman*," Blue says. "Chenoa couldn't contain her anymore."

"What can she do?"

"She can obscure Beam's light. Can lie to her. Make her think she's dying. Make her want to. That's all for now."

"What happens after *now*?" Chausie prompts.

"Well, her mate will seek her, won't he?"

"And then what?"

Blue only shakes his head, so Chausie urges him for the answer. "Blue, what happens when he finds her?"

That prowler makes me so mad. *Chausie, remind that little, blue prick that I will drop the f-bomb hard.* I only think it, but Chausie hears me.

"Blue?" Chausie says, "I need you to speak quickly and plainly. Beam is about to drop the bomb on you. I think you know the one I mean. None of us can survive that." Chausie sounds so convincing, so deathly serious that, despite the Umbra inside my head, I laugh. For real. From my mouth. And I can move my eyes again, and my—nope. Not my head. That kills. *Augh.* I stop trying to move my head.

"Once rejoined, they will devour Beam's life light," Blue says. "And probably half the stars—certainly the sun. Life on Earth will cease to exist."

"How do I get it out?!" Chausie's fury strikes my brain like a bolt of electricity, and while he's yelling, I seize.

Another voice comes to my rescue, Laurel's. "Stop. You're going to kill her. She's already withstanding all she can take."

"Then what do I do?!" Chausie demands.

Chaus, you have to lower your voice, I plead without speaking.

"I'm sorry," he whispers. "I'm sorry."

Laurel kneels beside us. "Why is she bleeding?"

Through gritted teeth, Chausie seethes as quietly as he can. "Because one of your damn ancestors cut her."

That grandmother said to remember something. What am I supposed to remember?

CHAUSIE

"Chausie, don't let go," Laurel says.

"I can't *hold* it. Beam, I need you to shine out as you've done before." She's so pale. So cold.

The effort to do as I've asked tortures her. The more she tries, the more she groans. It's like I'm playing tug-of-war with her against the Umbra inside of her. When Beam shines brighter, the Umbra becomes more excited. It pulls her light into its own darkness and Beam cries out in pain.

"The Umbra *wants* her to shine out," I tell Laurel.

As if I can possibly tend to anything else, who should pull herself over into our hideout, other than Chenoa? Now, Chenoa is a zombie. I mean, she is. There's no point pussyfooting around it. How she was able to negotiate the vertical rocks we've been calling stairs, I have no idea. She crawls—literally—like a tortoise, over to where we are fighting for Beam's life—and also, I guess, the existence of the world. Chenoa, who has been working to just stay alive, or undead, or whatever she is, opens her dull, dusty eyes as Beam's light brightens, and she focuses upon that light—she even smiles—until the beautiful soul of a young Lakota woman rises from her corpse, and rolls toward Beam with a sigh.

But just as she tries to enter the gate that Beam has become, a shadowy hand unfurls like a whip out from Beam's chest, grabs her by the throat, and jerks her inside.

"Laurel?!" In an effort not to hurt Beam, my voice sounds like it's tethered to the roof of my mouth.

I look up, but Laurel's head is bowed in concentration. Or prayer. Or...I don't know what. She holds Beam's corporeal hand. I think she must be reaching for Chenoa. So, I reach for Beam.

I find the brightest point of Beam's light, the anti-Umbra, and I just hold it in my mind. She's being fed visions that would unfaith a priest. "I love you, Sweetheart," I speak to her. "Please stay with me." I hold her. I surround her. "Right here, close," I say. And I catch a glimpse of Chenoa wandering further away. She's lost. She's fumbling around. She can't find Laurel, no matter how much Laurel calls and pleads. She's...shrinking. The Umbra is growing. It's minimizing her somehow, consuming her.

Chausie, we have to go get her, Beam says to my mind.

"Are you strong enough?" There's no way I'm risking her. I can barely hold on as is.

We have to, she says, but she sounds exhausted. *Keep surrounding me like that. Keep talking to me.*

Beam and I wade through the mire of her imagination that has been talked into existence by the Umbra, and I counter that by telling her about my plans for us. How I want her to go to prom with me. How I want our families to sit together at graduation. But then I worry about my dad, stuck as a lion. Will he even be—

Chausie?!

"I'm here! I'm here, Sweetheart. I'm sorry."

The Umbra bends her ear to me. She's too interested. She's sussing out my weaknesses. It doesn't matter. *Compartmentalize, Chausie,* I tell myself. *Eden is with Dad.*

We come to Chenoa, who trusts us not at all. I don't know if she's afraid or feeling guilty or what.

"I'm the same as you," Beam cajoles. "Don't give up now. We're so close."

After she seems convinced, Chenoa turns to search *my* face.

"He's one of us?" she asks Beam.

"My blood calls to him," she answers.

"He's very bright."

We grip her by both arms, gently but firmly, and trudge back through Beam's mind, following Laurel's voice.

"I'm not going to give you up," Laurel says. "I'm going to keep calling, keep looking for you, my dove."

Dove. Something about that sticks. It's important. Because of the catcher. It holds a dove. And because of the song. *The dove takes flight.*

"Laurel?" I call.

"I see you! Keep coming."

The Umbra starts shrieking in some god-awful language that pierces Beam, and she whimpers. But this time, there is also an answer. A chill works its way down the length of my spine as I whip my head toward the cavern's entryway.

The very torchlight floats toward that opening as if it's a vapor, and the body of Kanji Brings Justice lumbers through it. When he falls to the ground, the Umbra Man exits him, grown to four times the size it was when it was up on the tower. God knows what it's been feasting on.

This is it. The last chapter. The whole reason I was blessed with this beautiful girl.

A calm overtakes me, the same kind I got at the end of that championship game. Time was out. The score was tied. The crowd noise faded away. The whole game was decided in the quiet of my own head while I stood on the free-throw line bouncing the ball. I knew I could knock 'em down. I've shot about five billion of them in my lifetime. I saw in those moments how the whole thing would play out.

I see in these moments how this is going to play out too.

"Beam, you have to light up." She's all but gone out, but she opens her eyes. Has she been sleeping?

"Sing the line of the song," I demand. "Laurel keeps calling Chenoa her dove. *The dove flies*—what is it?"

She can't think straight. She can't understand what I'm asking. "What song?" she whispers.

It's Laurel who answers. "The dove takes flight on the magpie's light."

I knew that witch had a reason for asking Maggie if they ever call her Magpie.

BEAM

"We're gonna do this right now," Chausie says. He keeps his focus on me, but he says to Laurel, "When it's time, you've got to tackle Chenoa through that gate. Get yourselves through. Let me take care of Beam. Beam? *You* are the magpie's light. You gotta dig in, Sweetheart."

No sooner do I try, than I feel a different force pushing to get in, and the thing inside is clawing to tug it into me.

I'm no match for them, Chausie. I can hear my inward voice, but as if it belongs to somebody else. I'm trembling. It's like I'm exerting enormous pressure, though I can't feel my body at all. I'm so tired. *I can't do it Chausie. Let me go.*

"Not an option. You *can* do it. You look at me." How is he so strong right now? "Laurel?" he warns. "Hold on to her." Laurel reaches for Chenoa, and Chausie concentrates solely on me. He's absolutely focused and whatever he sees inside my head, he refuses to cower.

Instead of directing me to brighten up, or hold on, or—I don't know—whatever I expect him to do, he kisses me. Soft and sweet. And into my mind, he speaks. *We've already won.*

Everything else stops. No one pushing their way inside. No one shrieking inside my head. The whole world is bright, brilliant, silent, sparkling light. Chausie's hands on my face. Chausie's lips on mine. I'm not even sure I kiss him back, I'm so wholly absorbed by it. I let go. It's a perfect way to die.

The Umbrae burn up—like a developing image on a photograph that was overexposed in the darkroom. They cease to exist. And I am ready to cease to exist.

At that same moment, Chausie swallows down hard.

And I don't cease to exist. I relax into the relief. Chausie is kissing me still. And my oonchi is cradling me—I do hear how weird that sounds for both to be happening at once—but she is smiling down at me. Singing over me. That song, as softly as she is singing it, *pounds* through my mind like the bass end of the music in a dance club. Just one line, actually, over and over.

Oonchi, you didn't use to sing it that way, I tell her.

The Elixir pumps through a lion's heart.

And now it's no longer the line of the song that's pounding in my mind. It's the steady boom of Chausie's heart pumping. The sound of strength. The sound of life. It sharpens my mind like a shot of adrenaline. It swells my desire until my only driving force is to take for myself what that heart is pumping.

I bite down on Chausie's lip so hard, it pops open, and his blood bursts into my mouth. I gulp it down and go back for more, as greedy as can be. After his initial shock, he lets me do it.

It doesn't occur to me how strange it is to be sucking his lip like it's a bottle. I would take it how ever I could get it. The Elixir of life.

The echo of my oonchi's song decays like a hallelujah, and I draw a deep breath, finding that I have control of my body again. The world outside my head goes silent, except for Chaus. He hums a pleased, little, satisfied tone and pulls his bleeding lip out of my teeth —then puts his forehead to mine, his expression so full of love, I just want to hold onto this moment forever. I don't know how long we stay like that.

"We did it," he whispers.

I touch his mouth. "Your lip's not bleeding anymore," I tell him.

"Neither is your hand."

He's right. I rip off the bandage to be sure. "Chaus, *you're* the El—"

He shushes me with another kiss and then sucks on his own lip, where I bit him. "You're more of a lioness than you let on."

I allow him to help me to my feet. "I feel so *good!*" I tell him.

"Let *me* see." Chausie makes a show of running his hands over me, and I smack him away laughing. It's only now, around his shoulder, that I notice several silent spectators gaping at us. Including my mom and dad. I clear my throat.

Chausie senses my new and rising horror.

"What's wrong?"

"Did we just"—I cover my mouth to conceal my words—"do all that in the real world outside of our heads? In front of my parents?"

He laughs outright. "Even I'm not that reckless." And yet...his lip...

Chausie takes my hand and positions himself beside me like an escort. Now, I find another reason why everyone's gone silent. They can all see the light that is emanating from us right now.

Blue comes to stand behind us, hugging one of each of our legs and peeping between.

"Laurel got through?" I ask and Chausie nods.

"Chenoa too. There are a few folks, though, who still need a ticket to ride." Chaus gestures with our combined hands to the left-over ancestors, and I wave them up.

Each one of them comes around to the stairs to ascend to me like it's a throne room and I'm the queen. "If they bow to me," I mutter, "I'm gonna call BS."

They sort of do bow—to both of us—and they walk through.

Everyone has the eyes to see tonight, whether it's because of the equinox, or the ritual, or something else. No one speaks while the procession continues. Except for Blue. He climbs onto Chausie's hip, and Chausie holds him like he's a child. At first, I think Blue's just feeling affectionate, but then he says, "Did you really give your motorcycle to Beam after you promised I could drive it?"

CHAUSIE

When the ancestors have gone to their rest, Beam's mom and dad rush her, hug her, search her, and separate her from me.

I get it. They've been worried sick. When I have kids, I'm gonna do all the same things.

Beam is radiant. I wonder what she'll wear to prom. She did agree to go with me, right? On the back of my motorcycle? I feel myself grinning as I survey the rest of the gathering. You know who's missing? Uncle Joel.

Down at the entrance, staring at Kanji's vacated and broken body, are three mountain lions. Thank God. I lion up and leap from our hiding place to the delighted *oohs* of spectators, and land in front of my dad, who is hanging his head.

"Dad?"

"Chausie, he needs to be seen," Eden says. "Let's get him to The Outpost."

I don't think there's anything to be done, even by a doctor who's familiar with shifters, but I don't say it. I glance up at Beam, safe with her parents. "Yeah, one second."

BEAM

While I'm reassuring Mom and Dad, Chausie reappears and kisses my cheek. "I have to go with the lions," he says. "I'll find you later, OK? Or—can you come to The Outpost?"

"We'll bring her by," my dad says. He clutches Chausie's shoulder briefly. They seem to have come to terms. Chaus goes bounding back to his friends, and it's only now I wonder if something is amiss.

Kimimela steps into view. Death suits her. It's the first time she's seemed halfway normal and undistracted. She gazes after the lions as they leave the cavern.

"Leo lost his ability to shift," she tells me.

I wave her off. "What are you talking about? He's a lion right now."

The sympathetic frown she offers is irritating. "Stop patronizing me with your eyebrows," I tell her. "What do you mean?"

"Shifting goes both ways. He can't shift back into a man."

"What? Chausie's dad is stuck as an animal? How is that possible?"

She doesn't have a ready answer. She considers Kanji's body lying in the entryway. At length, she surmises, "Kanji's choker was destroyed."

"Yeah? So?"

"Leo transferred his power to it."

"What are you telling me? He's stuck like that for good? *Chausie* destroyed the choker."

"I lied to you," she says. "Leo didn't kill that shifter. But we convinced him he did. She wasn't even supposed to die. We only needed her teeth."

"She was decapitated," I remind Kimimela. "You carried one of her paws in your purse."

Kimimela shrugs. "Things went south. Kanji got a little over-zealous."

"And Chausie's dad was involved how? The truth this time." Although, I'm fairly certain I'd rather not know.

"At first he was only supposed to point us to the Elixir if, in fact, that person was a lion. But the more Kanji found out what else was possible, the more he was seduced by it, and the more he required of Leo. Kanji decided it was his birthright to become a shifter. Kanji means—"

"Crow. Uncle Joel told me."

"Yes." Kimimela smiles an unsettling sort of smile. Where *is* Uncle Joel?

"So, then we needed to find a shifter willing to sacrifice their power. And Leo delivered her to us. But it didn't take."

"You just kept pulling him deeper and deeper into your maniacal schemes. Were you going to kill him too?"

"Turns out that killing the shifter kills the magic," Kimimela says. "In order to transfer one's power, other things have to be sacrificed. Allegiances. Affections. Or the power isn't the givers to give. It belongs to those to whom he is bound."

"To his family," I infer. "You wrecked his marriage on purpose."

"I didn't wreck anything he wasn't willing to part with."

"You wrecked his relationship with Chausie—at a time when Chausie desperately needed him. I don't understand what you got out of it."

"Well, nothing, in the end," she says, and in an abrupt change of conversation, she adds, "You have to send me through now."

I stare at Kimimela like she's gone mad. "You would not want to go where I would send you right now. Are you not one bit sorry? All that talk about fixing things? This is something *you* have to fix."

CHAUSIE

"What is *she* doing here?" I snap.

I'm pacing the hall outside my dad's office, where he's being examined when Beam and her parents stroll in—along with Kimimela. Ghost or not, she is not my favorite person right now.

"Hush, Chausie," Beam says. "Hear her out. There may be something you can do to override your dad's condition."

Beam's folks take a seat in the lobby, and I show her to the end of the hall. Kimimela comes too. Her hair is no longer platinum blonde. It's thick, black, and long. She's younger than I thought. Or maybe she just looks so, now that she's dead.

"What is it?" I ask her.

"Your father loves you very much," Kimimela says. "He's so proud of you that it took everything I could think of to shame him into shunning you. I undermined your relationship and played on his sense of failure as a father and a husband and, in end, even as an officer of the law. We convinced him he was to blame for the death of the shifter woman he'd brought to us."

"Isn't he?"

"He didn't kill her."

"He led her to you, though? Knowing what you were doing? Why are you telling me this? What good can it do now?" I lift a palm to ask Beam why I have to endure this...*woman's*—not the word I want to use—quasi-confession.

"Your dad's ability to shift can only be transferred when there are no allegiances," Beam says. "No bonds that have a claim on him. Kimimela tried to make that happen."

"Well, she did," I say. "And I destroyed the only talisman. That's the gist of it, right?"

"Wrong," Kimimela says. "*You* are a talisman. Your father transferred his power to you naturally. A natural shifter doesn't need magic. Magic is cheap. It can be distributed. What you are—is a gift of Creation. From Wakan Tanka, whose power is limitless. You are not bound by magic. I think that if you own your father's heart, even the smallest piece, you can give him back his power."

Kimimela's words kindle hope in me that is quickly snuffed out. "I'm not sure that I do own even a piece anymore."

"Yes, you do," she and Beam both say, and Beam continues. "I saw the depth of feeling he has for you, Chaus. I saw the sorrow and the longing to have back what he traded."

Kimimela says, "You know how I said that my children were pieces of my heart outside of my body? That is so true. Your dad never forgave himself for what he did to you. He just felt he was in too deep." Kimimela swallows. "I'm sorry, Chausie, for my part in that. I really am."

After a moment, Kimimela looks at Beam expectantly, and now I can't tell if she is sincere or she just wants something, but I think about how much she went through to try to keep her own children.

"What do I need to do?" I ask.

"I'm not sure," Kimimela says. "But go to him and let him know he's still your dad. That you still need him. See what happens."

The door swings open and the doctor exits. I can see into Dad's office that he's still a lion before it swings shut again. The doctor shakes her head. "I'm sorry. I've never seen anything like it. I'm going to make some calls. There was a bear shifter in Germany who got locked out, but then recovered the ability."

Beam's mom rises to walk the doctor to the door and to tell her about selkies in Ireland, and how they get locked out when someone steals their skin—in reverse, though, since they are seals first and humans second. As their voices disappear, I stare at my dad's closed door.

"Will you wait for me?" I ask Beam without looking at her.

"Of course, I will."

But I don't make a move.

"You've got this," she says and squeezes my hand.

Then we both speak at the same time. I bemoan the fact that— "It's my fault." While she says, "It's not your fault."

"Chausie?" she continues. "It's not your fault. You weren't in on any of those schemes, and you wouldn't have condoned them. How could you have known that your dad's abilities were bound to that necklace?"

I couldn't have. And anyway, the necklace had to go. Eden's life was on the line.

Beam is speaking again.

"Remember that night I freaked out because I woke up beside you and you were in human form?"

"How could I forget?" I turn to face her with a smile. "What about it?"

"You said something that gave me peace even though we were uncertain about our future relationship. You said you'd take care of me, and I'd take care of you, and as long as we had that, the rest would work out."

I nod. It's a sweet memory. Brings back the feel of Beam's weight against my chest, her soft hair on my cheek.

"You love your dad and your dad loves you," she says. "You don't have to work through everything else right now tonight."

I wrap both arms around her and sigh into her hair.

"You *are* going to prom with me, right?" I ask.

She snickers into my chest where she answers with a muffled yes and then raises her bright blue eyes to get me to kiss her. That makes me bold.

I can do this.

When I enter my dad's office, he eyes me from where he is pacing behind his desk and comes to a halt. I wait until the door is fully closed.

"I need you to know something," I say and find it's easier to talk to him while he's a lion. "I've missed you. I thought that maybe I'd pushed you away by being too reckless, too angry. But now I think that you were dealing with your own stuff. Either way"—I feel a sting behind my eyes and clear my throat—"I love you. You're my dad."

I swipe a tear out of my eye and look away to regain my composure. "And I need you to know that we lions can come back from our mistakes. Can become reliable again."

He's watching me silently. Well, it's not like he can talk.

"So, why don't I take you back to your place? And we'll go from there."

Still nothing. I don't know what I'm looking for. Maybe a lion-ish hug? I decide he wants some space. "Well, I'll give you a minute to consider that. I could drive us in your car and—"

I crane my head back toward him when I hear him crying. Not as a lion, but as a man. He's sitting on the floor with his head in his hands, and I rush around the desk to get to him. "Dad?"

He throws an arm around my neck while he's still crying into his other hand. "I'm so sorry, Chaus," he says all high-pitched. "You're a better man than I ever was. I went off path."

"At least you *are* a man," I say and he gives me the reaction I hope for, laughing through his tears. He observes his hands and his body and sighs through his cheeks. "Thank God."

We stand up, and he pulls me into the hug I've been longing for—for months. I lose it, weeping against his shoulder.

"I never stopped being proud of you, Son. Never stopped loving you. I just couldn't face what I'd done to you. To your mom. I hope you can forgive me someday."

BEAM

Chausie and his dad walk out, arms around each other. Chausie's wearing his lopsided smile, but his eyes are a little swollen. Leo asks my folks if we'll stay with them at his home.

Kimimela *humphs*.

I'd forgotten about her. "Oh, yeah, you can go now," I tell her and open my arms to make a gate for her to the afterlife.

"No, I'm not going *any*where," she retorts. "I'm going to stick around."

"Well, you can't come with us," Chausie says.

"It's my home too," she argues.

"You're dead," he points out. He doesn't sound as irritated as one might expect. "You're dead to me." He laughs.

"Well, that was *rude*," she says and disappears.

"Now she's going to haunt us," I predict.

"Maybe we can catch her and *force* her through."

Chausie's dad volunteers to make dinner. Says he has plenty of bison meat in the freezer, which my mom finds interesting, and the whole time he prepares the meal, she asks questions about which hunting laws apply to lions.

We eat at the table where Chausie grew up, and we hear stories about his achievements. But everyone is exhausted. Everyone except for me. I feel amazing! After we all go to bed, I sneak out of my room and up onto the flat roof where there is a patio with a full view of the craggy buttes under the incredible expanse of nighttime sky. What. An. Adventure.

I've only just settled onto the futon when my lion falls in beside me.

"Took you long enough," I say.

"I fell asleep on the couch," he admits. "While pretending to fall asleep on the couch." He nuzzles into my neck. "But I got lonely."

This is great. We lie back and watch the sky. Chaus tugs a blanket up over us.

He's asleep long before I. I could live like this forever. His arm over me. His breath deep and steady. The stars shining down. "Why are you still trembling?" I ask them.

"*Hmm?*" Chausie hums.

I'm just drifting off when there is a flash of shiny, black flapping over the railing, and a huge crow settles onto a small, round table in the corner.

Caw.

I sit up.

Caw.

Chaus sits up.

"Kanji?" I ask.

Caw.

"Chaus, you don't think..."

A metal object drops to the ground with a clang, and Chausie looks like he's about to cough up a hairball. It's a knife. It's *the* knife.

"We cannot seem to get rid of you," he says to the blade. I rise to pick it up and hold it out for him to see.

"It's not even singed," he says.

"What should we do with it?"

I watch the crow watch us as Chausie scratches the back of his head in thought. "I'll store it in my dad's gun safe till we figure it out."

I'm wrapping the knife in a sweatshirt I have close by when the crow speaks up with a throaty bird voice. "Take the purse." It leaps into flight and is immediately met by several answering calls as it soars into the night.

What purse?

Another voice makes us jump. "Is this the afterparty?"

"Uncle Joel?" I say. "Where have you been? We were worried."

Uncle Joel frowns like he can't remember. Then he says, "It took me a little while to recover from the attack. But then I got to looking around The Vigilance. I never had unfettered access to the visions before. There are still things I don't understand."

Kimimela's ghost appears from out of nowhere. "There are things you are not *qualified* to understand," she spouts.

"Get her!" Chaus yells. He pounces on Kimimela and I try to shove her through the soul gate. But she's a slippery soul, and now she's mad at us.

"What is wrong with the two of you?" she scolds and smooths her hair, which has returned to its platinum-blonde bob cut. "This is not a game!"

Uncle Joel's face is stretched like he wants to laugh but also doesn't think he should. At first, I think that he can see Kimimela, can hear her, but then he asks, "It's Kimi, isn't it?" When we nod, he rolls his eyes. "I'm gonna go commandeer a couch. I'll see you at breakfast."

"Oh, no, you will *not* stay in this house!" Kimimela bellows. "You have your *own!*" But Uncle Joel keeps marching, so she follows him down the spiral staircase and when she smacks him, I hear it connect. I even see him react.

"He felt that," I say. "I'm sure of it."

Chausie shakes his head to show me that he doesn't know what to make of it, and I don't think he really cares. "Where did he even come from? Has he been here all along?"

I take a breath to answer, but then just blow it out. "Are we dreaming all this?"

Chausie chuckles. "Come back to bed."

I like the sound of that. I tell him so.

"Oh, you do?" He embraces me, kisses my neck, and slow-dances me to the futon.

Later, I'll realize that we should have taken more time to consider the many oddities posed in the last few minutes. But right now, this is so much more fun.

BEAM

It's been a few days since Chaus and I became a light bridge to the afterlife. He calls his mom every morning, just to check in. His dad *is* a man again, but he can no longer shift. It's a huge loss for him, like becoming paralyzed, and it's hard for Chaus to watch—harder to hear that his dad is resigning from The Outpost. Chausie spends most of the hours helping his dad figure out what's next.

In the meantime, President Tumbling Rock gives my family a personal tour of the government buildings. Again—really disappointed that he doesn't preside in some kind of powwow tent instead of a modern brick building, but oh well... In the Hall of Records, he hands me a letter, and before long I am accepting ownership of things that Laurel left to me long before she died. I doubt that back then her home came with solar power or a satellite telephone, but they're mine now, along with her photographs and all her Oglala Lakota treasures. So, now I own real estate, such as it is, smack dab in the middle of Badlands National Park.

My flight home is on a commercial airline out of Rapid City's regional airport. Daddy and Uncle Joel sit two rows ahead of me making up for lost time. Mom's asleep, holding my dad's hand. She's alive. I checked.

I'm alone and feeling sorry for myself even though I knew Chausie might have to stay here to do all the good things that reliable lions must do. Still, I kept hoping he'd show up. A bit of doubt creeps in. Will he come back at all? Finish up the school year? If so, will he still want to go to prom and do all the terrestrial things that high school seniors must do? They seem small in comparison to the adventures we had. Even to me.

After we're in the air, I try not to worry. I reach into Laurel's bag, which is at my feet, and find a stowaway. Blue. He's grinning up at me through large, aviator sunglasses—no idea where he got them—and he says, "Could you move over? I want the window seat."

I hug his little, blue self and comply. It's nice to have him with me. Makes me feel a little saner to know he'll be accompanying me into the otherwise mundane existence of life *before*. "All this really did happen, right?" I ask him.

"All what?" he says.

I re-read the letter Laurel left for me.

Sister Sunbeam,
Your grateful ancestors send their regards and as one of them, I leave to you my home up in the rock. May it be for you a respite and a firm connection to your Tribe.
Keep shining. Laurel

The flight attendant offers me a soft drink, and when I say no to a snack, she says, "Actually, I was asked to deliver this one to you." From somewhere in her cart, she produces a huge bag of wasabi almonds and hands it over before moving on to serve the next row. I stare at it.

Before too long, a voice from over my shoulder asks, "Do you think I could try some of those? My girlfriend raves about them." Then, the owner of that voice comes round to sit next to me so that I can look into the familiar, yellow eyes of my lion. "Sorry I was late," he says. "The airline wouldn't take my bike, but Dad figured out a way to have it shipped to the house."

"Chausie Louris," I say. But that's all I can come up with.

He nods at Laurel's letter. "I've been thinking about how Laurel left her place to you. Do you realize what it means?"

"It means she knew the whole time how this was going to play out."

"Yes, but more importantly, it means we can swim in our own private hot spring anytime we want." He flashes his eyebrows and reaches into the bag of almonds.

"Oh, that will be fun!" Blue asserts.

Chausie peers down his nose at him. "What are you doing here?"

To which Blue responds by rolling his fist forward a few times and saying, "*Vroom. Vroom.*"

"Chaus," I ask—before the ridiculous bike conversation can go any further. "Do you think you could deliver my almonds to Laurel's for a while? If I were to live there?"

"What? Really?"

"I'm considering a gap year after all."

"You? Delay college?"

"The Council offered me Kimimela's position at The Vigilance. The one she was hired to do, not the creepy parts she instituted on her own."

"And you're gonna take it?" Chausie asks.

"I'd get to immerse myself in everything I've missed. I mean, it would be my *job* to. And I'd get to live among the Tribe. Plus," I add sheepishly, "I wouldn't be six-hundred miles from you. What do you think?"

"I think yes! I think we should kiss on it. All the way back to Atlanta."

And that's pretty much what we do.

So, *that's* something that can happen in one week's time—if you're open to things like destiny and unlikely partnerships, and don't mind working without a manual or breaking a few rules.

I highly recommend it.

CHAUSIE

Because my bike remains in South Dakota, Uncle Joel volunteers to drive me home. I say goodbye to Beam's parents at the airport, but Beam insists on coming with us—much to her father's chagrin.

"I'll bring her home, Hawk," Joel says. "We should get to spend at least one ride together where nobody's in mortal peril."

Hawk doesn't look any happier about it. I get it. He wants to know she's safe and well cared for at all times. He acquiesces with a half-hearted nod.

Even though it's late, I insist that Beam meet my mom real quick, and Mom surprises the heck out of me by asking Beam to consider coming to the lake with us over spring break. Life is good.

After Mom goes back in, Beam and I loiter by the front door. She's acting uncharacteristically nervous.

"Feels strange to say goodbye, doesn't it?" I ask.

"Yeah. *See you at school* doesn't seem adequate."

"Let's get there early," I suggest. "Meet for breakfast."

"OK," she smiles. "Seven-thirty?"

"I'll be waiting." I kiss her. Uncle Joel honks the horn. I wonder if he and I are close enough at this point that I could flip him off and he'd think it was funny. Better not. I hold Beam's hand as she walks away, and then I still want to reach for her. But Mom's inside. I watch till they drive away.

Maybe I'll call her later to say goodnight.

When my phone rings, I smile that she was thinking the same thing. But it's not Beam. It's my dad. "Just checking to make sure you got in alright."

Feels good. "Yep, I'm home now. All's well." *Except that my girlfriend doesn't live here.*

"I forgot to tell you that I found a purse up on the roof that had fallen behind the table. Figured it belonged to Beam, so I stuck it in your pack."

"Oh, OK. Thanks." I dig around till I find what he's talking about.

"Get some sleep, Son."

"Will do."

"Love you."

There's so much to smile about. "I love you too, Dad. 'Night."

The small leather pouch is woven with red and black beads. I don't recognize it as Beam's, but I guess she could've picked it up while she was out. I text her a picture.

> Is this yours?

> It's beautiful, but nope, not mine.

I open it to search inside. She adds,

> If no one claims it, can I have it?

> Of course.

Huh.

> I think it just claimed you.

I send a picture of the contents. Seven coal-black feathers and Beam's catcher, the one that keeps Evil from finding her. The one Kanji dove after and died for.

> Remember that crow up on the roof? What was it he said?

Beam doesn't respond. I text,

> Let's video chat when you get home.

While I'm waiting for her answer, I open the pouch to see if it holds anything else. There's a small piece of paper rolled up tight as a toothpick at the bottom. I dig for it, unroll it, and go cold.

> *Beam, I am not the man I appear to be. Until I can find my way back, please keep this on you at all times, and for goodness' sake, don't ever be alone with me. The visions are not complete. Parts were stolen. Uncle Joel*

I. Should have stayed. With that girl.

THANK YOU!

Special thanks to the Oglala Lakota people who share their stories, language, history, and art. I don't pretend to be a scholar, and I certainly don't pretend to understand living as an Indigenous person just a few generations past such turbulent upheaval. It is with some trepidation that I offer this imaginative work to an angry and divided culture. But I trust that you, the reader, will feel I handled the story with respect for all people, and I even dare to hope that you are inspired to help with the humble, messy work of reconciliation.

Without encouragement and keen eyes, this book would be riddled with typos, confusion, and inconsistencies. My heartfelt thanks goes out to the following who took the time to give me feedback:

Susan Holland, you find typos I can't see even when you've told me what they are and I've read the sentence three times. Your kind attention helps me battle imposter syndrome and the usual artist despondency. I am so grateful to you and for you.

Jennifer Duran, you made me defend scenes in my own head so that I could make them clearer on paper. Thank you for your imaginative and thoughtful reading, for the texted snapshots of red circles drawn around whole pages, and for telling me which parts made you laugh.

Kelly Rhodes, for your long-time support and eager audience; Mandy Pickett and Jennifer Smith Blake because you made me think it was a good story; Carolyn Sunderland because it's not your favorite genre, but you fell in love with Chausie anyway, and forgot to question his ability to shift.

Colin and Kate Neal, for listening to the baby idea for this story and giving it a thumbs up. Colin even suggested the word "prowler" for Blue and all his friends.

Jeff Neal, thank you for the beautiful cover design and for reading the manuscript repeatedly. Mostly, thank you for coming installed with an automatic, factory setting to be on my side and have my back. You are the best best friend.

And, thank you, dear Reader. You are the reason we get to make songs and stories for a living, a gift you've given us for twenty-five years now.

I'm honestly gushing with gratitude as I write this.

May God bless you.
    Jennifer

ABOUT THE AUTHOR

Jennifer Daniels Neal is a performing songwriter, author, and teaching artist out of Lookout Mountain, Georgia who has released nine music albums, three novels, a picture book, and two humans into the world. Besides performing for kids  and adults, she and her husband Jeff Neal run a week-long school initiative called *Songwriting IS Writing! The write to record for literacy project.* For more information on performances, workshops, author visits, etc...check out https://linktr.ee/jenniferdanielsmusic

If you enjoyed this book, please do leave a review on the book's Amazon page and/or anywhere you're willing. It helps more than you may know. THANK YOU!

facebook.com/JenniferDanielsMusic

instagram.com/JennDanielsMusic

ALSO BY JENNIFER DANIELS NEAL

The Locke Box, 2021, a sensual but clean mystery/romance

The Bridge to Isla Sofia, 2022, a genre-bending mystery/romance with
Southern gothic flair

The Rucksack, 2020, a short and sweet, feel-good love story

The Soubrette, 2020, the follow-up novella to The Rucksack. Think
Breakfast at Tiffany's meets crime story drama

Cuckoo WooWoo, That Chick Can Rock and Roll!, a song turned picture
book

Music Albums by Jennifer Daniels include

Dive and Fly (2001), Summer Filled Sky (2004), Come Undone (2009),
Live at Red Clay Theater (2013), It's Gonna Be a Good Day! (2018, kids
music and movement), Songs from The Locke Box (2021)

Made in the USA
Columbia, SC
09 October 2023